Chronicles of Maradoum Volume 1

A Fantasy Anthology

By Ross C Hughes

First Printing 2019
ISBN 9781702601610
www.rosshughes.biz

Chronicles of Maradoum Volume 1

A Fantasy Anthology

By Ross C Hughes

Cover Design by Jamie Noble Frier

Published 2019

Dedicated to my beloved grandparents, all four of them, for all their weird and wacky stories, and the weird and wacky lessons they imparted. Thank you all.

Acknowledgements

I'd like to thank all my subscribers who read and enjoyed these short stories, especially those who reached out to let me know. Your kind words mean a lot. I'd also like to thank my cover designer, Jamie Noble Frier, for his sublime work on the cover art. Jamie, your efforts are much appreciated. Thanks once again to Jeff Brown Graphics for the design of the map of Maradoum.

Foreword

This anthology had many sources of inspiration – too many to list here – but the foremost was a photography book called Discovering China, published by Cypi Press.

Inside are 11 short stories set in the same world as the Convent Series, beginning with A Dead Wizard's Dream. That world is Maradoum.

I wanted to write this foreword primarily for one simple reason – to let you, my readers, know that these stories are entirely random. That is to say that they are not in any sort of chronological order. Most of them are set before the events in the Convent Series, some by only a few years and some by a century, with Arvid, Aslaug and the Undead being the exception.

That being explained, I hope you enjoy them!

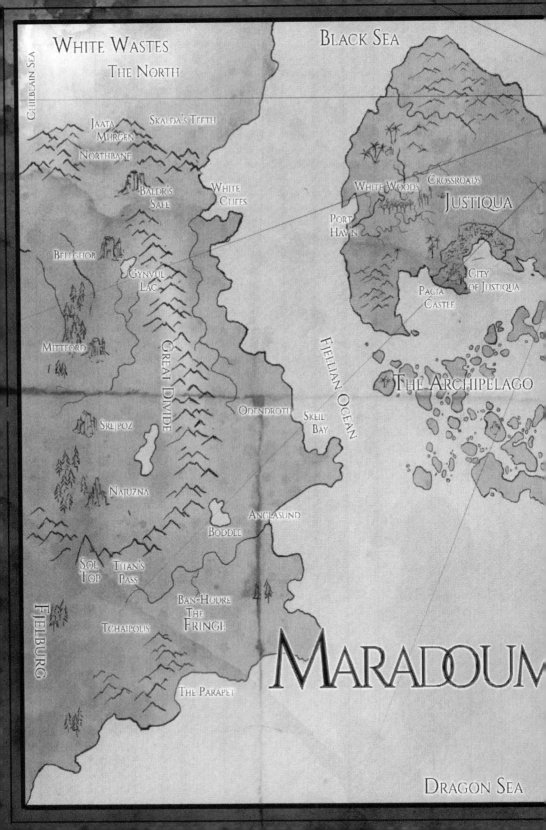

N
E
S

KIHARAZ

KLUNDUN

TEMPLE OF
CELESTE

HUMNUMSHBAL

o Bay

AEGIS
WATERS

LOMBONN

SIJAMBOT

QABDARA

JHANDO

AL KUTZ

HEVARRE

HANAVA

SHIMYAHEIN

VUUM

HARRUKATI

THE GOBLIN ISLES

ESHIMBRANIR

CRYSALI

THE TROPICS

BABESE
SULTANATE

SILENT STRAITS

LAMA KULUL
DESERT

CALYPRA

JUNGLESIDE

GREAT FISSURE

LOST ISLAND

SWASH ISLE

KAUAPUNKI MEREN

SHALA HYDDIN

OOA

THE ASHLANDS

QUING TZU

Li Mao and the Yaoguai

Li Mao had been fishing for hours beneath the strangely wan, misty sky, and would likely be fishing for a few more.

"I know, I know, my friend," he said.

He untied the string from around the cormorant's neck, and it squawked at him in gratitude, flexing its long black, feathery neck. The bird would fish for him no more until he fed it; it was on strike. So, though his catch was meagre, he smilingly took a fish from his wicker basket and tossed it to the bird. The cormorant caught it deftly, threw its head back, made a couple of perfunctory biting movements with its long beak, and then gulped it down.

The bird squawked again, letting the fisherman know it was ready, and he retied the string around its neck. The string only indented the supple neck slightly; just enough to prevent the bird from swallowing any fish bigger than a finger. The little ones it could have for itself. Once the string was tied, the fisherman started bouncing up and down on his little bamboo raft and singing discordantly but happily.

"Go, bird, go! Catch me my dinner!"

He was in the middle of the river the locals called Windsong, and so the raft splashed about in the water, sending ripples out in all directions. Finally, the cormorant took the hint and dove smoothly into the water like it had been born to do so.

Li Mao watched the water as it settled, studying the landscape in the mirror plane. It was like another, upside down, underwater world was looking back at him. A bamboo stand on the left shore was reflected in the slow-flowing water, phantom blue bamboos growing down into the depths of the river, swaying with the current rather than the breeze. On the right, a tangle of brush preceded a small fir forest, which when submerged became a black hill reaching down, a great shadow in the river like some hidden leviathan.

Back down the river the way he had come, the fisherman could faintly make out the green smog of a birch wood and in front of it his home, small in the distance. He thought he could even see a finger of smoke curling out of the chimney. Towering above his home were the distant karst formations; great limestone ridges, towers and, hidden from sight, sinkholes, moulded over the millennia by the elements.

There was something regal and indomitable about the green mountains.

Eventually, though, his smile wilted, and he rubbed his golden-skinned arm in concern. At fifty years of age, he was an expert on fishing and he knew when something was wrong. One of his other birds should have been back by now. He adjusted his wide, conical, straw hat and mopped his brow with the back of his hand. His hemp poncho and woollen tunic were making his skin itch as the heat rose. Noon must be approaching, Li Mao thought, throwing a glance skyward and frowning at the pervasive mistiness.

It was odd for it to be so foggy and so humid, almost like a great white cerement had been thrown over the land in preparation for its final rest. The mist seemed somehow oppressive, like it was bearing down on him, an inexplicable weight on his chest and shoulders. All the other fishermen had warned him not to come out today; they had said the fog was a bad omen. That was why he was all alone out on the river. It was normally peaceful out here, but not today. He began to shout and bang his long pole against the raft, splashing water on his sandaled feet.

"Birds!" he called, cupping a hand to his mouth. "Birds! Where are you? Come back up, I'm starting to worry!"

The water rippled some twenty feet away from his raft, and Li Mao's eyes widened. He was sure it had not been the ducks.

He stood very still for a while, feeling his pulse race. Then, something burst out of the water beside the raft, and Li Mao yelped in fright. He saw that it was one of the cormorants an instant later and would have felt chagrined, save that a large, toothy monster followed it up into the air a moment later, making the fisherman yelp again. He only saw the beast for a split second as its jaws snapped shut on the scared bird, and then blood and water spurted in Li Mao's eyes. He jerked back, cried out and wiped his eyes, but by the time he could see again both monster and cormorant had gone. The fisherman would not have been sure it had ever happened at all if not for the blood stains on his clothes and raft.

If he had thought his pulse was racing before, now it was truly sprinting flat-out, fleeing for its life. His hands were slick on his pole, and he slapped his lips together, trying to wet his dry throat.

A minute later, the beast was back. A moment after that, Li Mao felt a tug on his leg and then he was in the river, his straw hat in the wind. He had managed to suck in a breath, which was fortunate as he was dragged straight underwater with the claws of the beast digging cruelly into his calf. Li Mao had no idea how fast they moved, but it seemed inordinately, supernaturally fast. The water rushed around him, bubbles obscuring his vision, and all he could see was varying shades of blue.

His lungs started to burn before long, and he was just about to give in to the voice in his head screaming at him to take a breath when they surfaced once more. Li Mao cracked his back on the rocky floor and groaned and gasped as the beast vaulted out of the water. Then, without slowing, it continued to drag him onwards and it was all he could do to keep breathing and stay conscious. The fisherman's back was sore as it bumped over the ground, but it was not scraped raw thanks to the poncho. He could not lift his head to see the monster, though.

After only a moment, they were moving up and suddenly Li Mao was dangling upside down, hanging from the claws embedded in his leg. He felt warm blood dribble up his thigh toward his crotch. It occurred to him to scream then, but he just couldn't muster the energy somehow. He was exhausted, not to mention dizzy from the rush of blood to his head. The monster bounded up rapidly, and the fisherman realised he was in a narrow, rocky tunnel when his face started bouncing off the walls. He guessed the beast must be unnaturally strong to be able to carry him up such a chimney.

Concussed and only half-conscious, Li Mao was finally dragged out onto a level floor once more, and a moment later he was released. Tiredly, he lifted his head and looked around through bleary eyes. What he saw woke him in an instant, like a splash of ice-cold water, and made him want to vomit in fear.

He was in a mossy cave lit by a beam of sunlight coming in through a small hole in one wall. The cave itself was not what made him want to vomit, however; it was the group of bloodcurdling monsters that dwelled inside. There were eight of them in total, all half-hidden in shadow. They were ten-foot-tall beings straight out of nightmare with large fangs and claws. All were covered in fur of varying hues, and all were topped by two long, sharp, ribbed horns at each temple, like a gazelle's. All had the same six serpentine, yellow eyes with vertical black pupils – three in a row on either side of their face – and all regarded him in the same manner: hungrily.

Li Mao saw that the beast that had dragged him there had blue fur, through which poked numerous phosphorescent warts. The fisherman wasn't sure if they were warts or cysts or pustules, but they looked disgusting. They looked ripe, ready to pop. The creature had a pointed face tapering towards its long, wolf-like snout, and it had a long, furry flipper for a tail.

The fisherman thought he was going insane when the blue beast said in a high-pitched rasp, "See what I bring my pack!"

The others shuffled closer, at the same time revealing and hiding more of themselves as they shifted through shadow, looking like inchoate Demons emerging from the void. Li Mao's chin quivered, and he fought not to cry.

One of the monsters shoved past the others to get a better view of the man in their midst. The others gave way without dissent, for this one was larger than the rest, and blacker, too. It was covered in such dark fur that it looked like a hole in the world, like nothingness, rather than a colour. Its claws scraped the rock as it walked, upright, across the cave. As it passed through the sole beam of sunlight, Li Mao saw it more closely – and wished he had not. It, too, had glowing warts visible through its black fur, like bright blue stars in the darkest night. Its yellow fangs were huge, set into a wolf-like snout beneath its six hungry, hungry eyes. When it loomed over him, Li Mao thought he was going to faint.

"What this puny morsel?" the big black demanded in a bass rumble, pointing a claw at the trembling fisherman. "Pack need more! Need more!"

"Need more!" another echoed in a hiss; a green-furred creature with blue cysts and a scar running through one milky eye.

"This all I get," rasped the blue beast stubbornly.

"This good, this good!" snuffled one of the monsters, coming for a closer look on all fours. It had reddish fur, dark like blood, and it sniffed at the fisherman like a huge, curious fox.

"So hungry! Been at sea so long!" whined another beast, its six eyes blinking rapidly. This one was grey, which made it look old to Li Mao. Its blue pustules throbbed alarmingly.

An orange-and-purple striped monster licked its lips and drawled almost urbanely, "Has been long time since we taste man! Mm, tasty!"

A golden-furred creature, its breath reeking of rotten meat, thrust its face close to Li Mao and then drew back, purring, "A hundred years since we see lands of man."

"Is small, but can eat!" growled one of them, sounding youthful in its excitement. This one had stripy yellow and black fur, like a bumblebee. It prowled toward the fisherman, opened its maw wide for a bite, and Li Mao thought he could hear funerary bells tolling.

The big black smacked it back with a heavy paw, however, rumbling, "Wait! This puny. Me biggest. Biggest bit for me."

"*I* bring! *I* bring!" argued the blue-furred monster that had dragged the fisherman off his raft. "Biggest bit for me!"

"For me! For me! Biggest bit for me!" the others roared disharmoniously.

"No!" the big black bellowed, swiping a claw through the air and silencing the rest. It was so loud it hurt the fisherman's eardrums. "This small, too small! *Me* biggest. *Me* kill you. Biggest bit for *me*!"

The others growled quietly in the backs of their throats, their hackles rising, but none openly challenged the largest of them.

For some reason he could not explain, Li Mao chose that moment to squeak, "I'm not so small!"

All of the monsters' eyes turned on the fisherman, and he wished he didn't have a tongue. As it was, though, he did and he could never stop it from wagging when he was nervous.

"I mean," he said in a small voice, "there once was a man in my village, when I was growing up, who was only four and a half feet tall. A full grown man! So, I'm not as small as him, obviously. The Gods know I'm not the biggest man in Maradoum either, but I like to think I'm a decent size … I don't know what you're used to eating, so I don't know how I stack up. This one," he gestured at the warty monster, "seemed good at swimming, so maybe you're only used to fish and whatnot, in which case I bet I'm a pretty good catch by comparison. People tell stories about you, you know, about the Yaoguai. Only people think you're mythical – just a tale to frighten the little'uns if they don't eat their greens, ha! Anyway, they say you're seen off the coast sometimes, snacking on fish."

Why he was speaking of himself as food, he did not know. He hated himself while he did it.

"You speak! You know the Yaoguai!" several of the monsters, the Yaoguai, clamoured at once then, shuffling closer and making the fisherman flinch.

"Stories ..." the big black repeated the word, his voice almost reverential. "You are storyteller! Tell story now. Eat later."

Sitting on the floor and looking around at the beasts gathered around him, Li Mao suddenly felt like a schoolteacher surrounded by inquisitive children. He had their attention, and they were not going to eat him – not immediately anyway. So, he knew he had to entertain them somehow, to play for time while he came up with a plan. Surprisingly, a plan leapt into his mind full-formed as soon as he thought the word. He crossed his legs and cleared his throat.

He glanced around at the Yaoguai, forcing himself to make eye contact, to draw them in. Then, he began to tell his story in a slow, lilting, theatrical voice.

"Once upon a time, a greedy, greedy man became the governor, or Shenzhan, of our humble little province, Guifung. This man was so avaricious that he defied the Emperor's laws and used his own personal army to force his people to work for him as slaves, digging riches out of the earth in the mines, panning for gold in rivers and streams. He forced hundreds of people to tend to thousands of silkworms, so that he could sell the decadent material they fashioned to enrich his own pockets.

"People died on their feet for him, unable to ever take a rest, unable to keep up with his outrageous taxes. They brought him gold and gems, exotic food and drink, spices and herbs, ornaments and gaudy clothes ... But it was never enough. It is said the Shenzhan lived in a palace to rival the Emperor's, a palace made of gold and filled with paintings and tapestries and busts and statues, each worth a fortune. It is said he ate a different dish from a different plate every day, using only the finest and most expensive of china, that he owned every type of beast known in Quing Tzu, that he had the largest army in the Empire, that he had concubines enough to sleep with five a day and still never sleep with the same one twice before he died.

"Still, it was never enough ... and so he continued to work his people to death, never rewarding their toils. While the Shenzhan gorged on roasted pigeon and rabbit stew and plum duck, his people starved. The Emperor of Quing Tzu ordered him to change his ways, to protect his people rather than abuse them, but he ignored the warning, confident in the might of his army. Eventually realising the Shenzhan had gone rogue, the Emperor marched his armies on the province and on its governor.

"As it turned out, though, he needn't have bothered. Sick of the Shenzhan's selfishness and greed, the people of Guifung rose up against him in the biggest rebellion the province has ever seen. It was peasants against armoured warriors, peasants against the largest private army in Quing Tzu, pitchforks against katanas. And yet, the peasants had right on their side. They may have been half-starved and overworked, but they had passion and the will to make the world change. In a pitched battle, they would have lost for sure. As it was, though, they took the city streets as their own, hiding in shadows and lashing out at the Shenzhan's forces whenever they could with hit-and-run tactics.

"Through such guerrilla warfare, they were able to decimate the Shenzhan's army; he did not know what else to do but root them out in their homes, and so he kept sending in more and more men. The peasants knew the cities, however, knew the streets. They knew their homes better than the army, better than any palace-dweller. They killed the soldiers in the streets one by one, dropping rocks on their heads from rooftops, shooting arrows from high windows, slinging stones from the shadows, a knife in the back.

"Soon, the Shenzhan didn't have enough men to both protect himself and root out the traitors in the town. At that point, he stopped sending in soldiers, too afraid for his life and his riches to risk losing more men. By then, however, it was too late. The people had sensed his fear, had seen him hide in his golden hole. Like wild dogs, they sniffed out the fear and followed it to its source.

"It's said the Shenzhan wailed to see the populace of his province bearing down on his palace, torches, pitchforks and the swords of dead soldiers in hand. It's said he tried to flee with as much of his wealth as he could carry on his ceremonial barge, the largest but slowest vessel in his fleet. He did not get far before the barge was caught and sunk and the Shenzhan himself was hauled back to shore.

"The people of Guifung cheered to see their Shenzhan brought low before them, brought to his knees in the mud. They erected a gallows as fast as they could. For all the people he had enslaved, for all the lives he had ruined, for all the families he had destroyed, for all the people that had died under his rule, they strung him up and they hung him from the neck until his legs stopped kicking!

"Then, freed from his gluttony and enslavement, they took all the food he had hoarded for himself and distributed it among the starving masses. They tore down his palace and distributed his incredible wealth among themselves. Without the Shenzhan, the people of Guifung were finally able to lead the lives they had dreamed of, lives of prosperity and endless joy! All they had to do was take their fate into their own hands. All they had to do was remove the one obstacle in their way. All they had to do was kill their leader."

The moral of the story dawned on the big black too late. Snarling at the last words, the terrible beast rose to its full height, cysts throbbing. It cast itself at the man with a bestial roar that froze Li Mao's blood in his veins. The beast was too late, though. The rest of the Yaoguai had understood the parable as well and they were on the big black in a flash, all of them sinking teeth and claws into their leader's vast frame simultaneously.

The big black bellowed in pain and rage and beat at its attackers with its claws, but there were too many of them. Seven against one is poor odds even for a monstrous Yaoguai. The others tore at their leader's flesh, burst its pustules and gouged out chunks of it between their teeth while it screamed. As they did so, Li Mao was up and moving fast.

Sprinting over to where a chink of sunlight perforated the mossy cave, he kicked the wall as hard as he could. The stone crumpled beneath his foot, and he felt his heart leap with hope. Imbued with fresh vigour, he kicked again and again.

As the Yaoguai bore their leader down to the ground, covering it in their writhing bodies of varying hue, Li Mao kicked the wall a fourth time and the limestone gave way easily beneath the hard sole of his sandal. He was suddenly looking out over the anarchic, green-and-white tors and troughs of a karst landscape, and beneath him the Windsong river churned and frothed, white at the mouth, in the grip of rapids. It was a more southern stretch of the river than where he had been fishing, but he recognised it easily. Rocks clattered down the mountainside, setting off further rockslides along the way in a great rumble like thunder. The stones splashed into the river below.

The sound of the rockslides was enough to distract the Yaoguai, who had almost finished their grisly business, although Li Mao could still clearly hear the big black's plaintive roaring. Snarling and snapping their gory jaws, the Yaoguai tore across the cave toward the fisherman, unwilling to let their prey escape. Li Mao would never forget the sight of them in the increased light from the gaping hole in the wall. Chunks and ribbons of their fellow's sundered flesh hung from their great yellow fangs, and their many eyes were wild, aglow, with the need to feed.

He lost sight of them, however, as he tugged his poncho over his head. Then, he turned his back on them and leapt out of the gap in the cave wall into sunlight. Little did he know he jumped a scant second before claws clutched the air where he had been standing and teeth rent the place his head had occupied. With the dying howls of the big black and the furious growls of the other Yaoguai, who were too scared to follow, ringing in his ears, Li Mao fell.

He held the poncho above his head, each hand grabbing a corner, and the wind whipping up past his ears and making his eyes stream suddenly caught on the thick fabric. With a lurch, Li Mao levelled out and then he began to float down more slowly, buoyed by the air resistance on his poncho, which had puffed up like a taut sail. Drifting down slowly, like a feather on the breeze, the fisherman was able to direct his movement by tugging at one side or the other of his poncho. So, soon enough, gravity called him home and his beloved Windsong river swept him up in its rabid embrace.

He made his way straight home, and from there to the closest village. There was not a proper town or city around for leagues in the backwater province. When he got to the village, the people there were understandably, infuriatingly sceptical.

"Yaoguai?" the village elder, Sum Fi, repeated after Li Mao had told his story. He puffed on his pipe, and thick wreaths of pungent baui smoke filled the air. "You expect us to believe there are Yaoguai in the mountains?"

"I suppose there are Faeries in the streams and Spriggans in the trees, too, eh?" sneered a fat woman called Fan Wong.

Her husband, Huaxia Wong, spoke up beside her, "There hasn't been a Yaoguai sighting reported for a thousand years! We all told you not to go out into that cursed mist. You've let your imagination get the best of you!"

"It's been about two hundred years actually," Sum Fi corrected, looking troubled, blowing smoke through his nose. He was an old, bald, stick-thin man, whose golden skin hung in droops and folds off his bones. He was the records keeper in the village; if anyone knew when the Yaoguai had last been spotted, it was him. "We thought they were all gone ..."

Huaxia frowned and crossed his brawny arms. He was a big, strong man with a thinner, leaner face than Li Mao's, like a greyhound rather than a husky. His big bushy brows were heavy and low over his dark eyes like storm clouds.

"They *are* all gone!" he insisted.

"Of course they are!" Fan snapped. "They're just a legend, just a story!"

"You say one dragged you underwater and you came out on top of a mountain?" Sum Fi said, shaking his head. "I don't know how it can be, but you're not one for lies, Li Mao. I know this as well."

Li Mao bowed slightly to the old man in thanks. He was unsure how to convince them he was telling the truth, but then a thought occurred to him – Huaxia was fond of gambling.

"What will you lose if you come with me to check?" the fisherman asked. "You, Huaxia, and a few others could come without repercussion. Your sons can do your work and there are others to pick up the slack as well. If I am lying, you lose nothing. If I am telling the truth, however, the village could be in danger and we could save it by going up there now and killing those beasts before they get hungry again and come down here and kill us all! I'll even sweeten the pot. Like I said, if I am lying, you lose nothing. Add into the bargain this – if we get there and there is no evidence of the Yaoguai, I will withdraw from the fishing competition next week."

It was an annual fishing competition held in the village, and Li Mao was a shoo-in for the win. He was the finest fisherman around. Huaxia was a close second. So, Li Mao was offering to forgo the substantial prize money, allowing Huaxia to win and claim it. With Li Mao gone, Huaxia would be the sure thing.

"Ooh, do it, husband," said Fan, her fat face wobbling with excitement. "Prove him a liar and win the competition!"

Huaxia nodded and uncrossed his arms. "Very well. I accept your terms. If there are no Yaoguai, you withdraw from the fishing competition. And if there are Yaoguai, we slay them where we find them."

Li Mao sighed with relief. Huaxia was a prominent figure in the village. With his support, they were sure to find a few men to deal with the monsters.

Huaxia Wong and a few of his friends followed Li Mao back to the karst mountain where the fisherman had escaped the Yaoguai. After a long and arduous climb, they at last made it to the top, to the hole in the mountainside leading into a mossy cave. They could smell the beasts before they even entered.

The cave was a bloodbath. Gore streaked the rocky walls and puddled on the uneven floor. The drip-drop of blood droplets dropping from the ceiling was the only sound, a macabre chime. Li Mao and the villagers held their superfluous rusty weapons in front of them, wide-eyed and open-mouthed. Eight bodies were scattered around the cave, all bloody and holey, covered in bite marks. Huaxia Wong was struck speechless by the sight of the bizarre furry creatures with their wolf-like snouts, their six eyes apiece, their flipper-tails and their oozing pustules.

He turned to the fisherman. "I'm sorry I didn't believe you, Li Mao. I will never doubt your word again, I swear it on all the Gods!"

"It's understandable, Huaxia," Li Mao said, laying a hand on the other's shoulder. "It was a tall tale, after all. I'm just glad it's all over now."

"What do you think happened here?" Huaxia asked, pinching his nose.

Li Mao looked around. "I think somebody convinced them to tear one another apart. I think there was a power vacuum and they all tried to fill it. I think they fell victim to their own nature, just as do we all in the end."

Huaxia nodded, not understanding. Then, he flinched. "There's one still alive!" he said, pointing and backing away a step.

Li Mao followed his finger and saw the blue-furred creature, the one that had pulled him off his raft, twitch. The fisherman carefully advanced on the battered and bitten Yaoguai, hatchet at the ready. He had only ever used the blade to chop wood; he had never thought he would be facing down a mythical beast with it one day.

The blue beast wheezed and spat blood and Li Mao inched closer, certain now that it was on its deathbed.

"You!" it managed to rasp when it laid eyes on him. It looked scared and angry, not hungry anymore. *"You* do this to us! *You* kill us! A hundred years we live, and *you* kill us! *You* call us monster, but Yaoguai only kill for food. *You* kill us, but *you* not eat. *You* kill us

with stories!"

"You killed them with stories?" Huaxia repeated in awe, looking on Li Mao in a new light.

"I suppose I did." Li Mao's hatchet clove down and the Yaoguai never spoke again.

Back at the village, Li Mao, Huaxia Wong and the others were received as heroes, particularly once their exploits had been described. Li Mao was hailed as the finest of them all, the man who had killed the legendary Yaoguai with only his words.

When Sum Fi offered him the position of village elder along with a substantial monetary reward, however, he declined, saying, "I only wanted to catch some fish."

He took only enough for a few cormorants to replace those he had lost, and the following day found him fishing again.

The Boulders and the Buffalos

Ikriff Jal Vuum stared out over Saddle Lake, bored.

The huge, crystal blue lake was fringed on all sides by grey mountains marbled with snow, like white veins running through the landscape. It sat in the saddle between several peaks, high up in the northern mountains of Al Kutz. The lake was still frozen at the edges; winter was reluctant to let go, like an overbearing matron. Shards of ice, some as large as him and some only foot-sized, floated around in the water; a glassy empire shattered into tiny pieces. The clear, still waters were a mirror, replicating the blue sky and the few scudding white clouds.

"D'you wanna play dice again, Ikriff?"

Ikriff turned slowly to behold the man beside him, Matthias Strongspine. "I think I'd rather pluck out my eyeballs and feed them to the fishes. We must have played a thousand games of dice."

"I know." Matthias was unhurt by the reply; he well understood the tedium. "It's just there's nothing else to do around here."

"I know."

The two were sat in a lookout tower – if you could call it a lookout tower, Ikriff thought sourly. It was the smallest watchtower in history, he was sure. High amid the peaks here, it needed no extra elevation for vantage and so it had been built small. It craftily nestled and hid among the peaks, in the shadow of one particularly tall crag, almost invisible to anyone approaching. The tower was more a formality, a precaution, than anything else, Ikriff had always thought; nobody ever came through here. The two men stared out over the lake in silence for a while, sat on wooden chairs, peering through narrow windows in the stone walls. The dice sat on the table between them, unused.

Eventually, growing bored of the silence, Ikriff said, "You know your name?"

"I do," agreed Matthias, who had made a baui roll-up while they sat in silence and was now puffing on it contentedly, leaning back in his chair.

"Strongspine. Did you give yourself that name, or was it given to you? D'you have to earn it? How does it work in Shimyahein?"

Matthias grunted in amusement, blowing smoke. "I gave it to myself."

"Oh. Bit … arrogant, no?"

Matthias chuckled. "Yes, you could say that. My people have a saying; a name must be formidable, but not ridiculous."

"Sounds ridiculous to me."

"Well, you are only a Kutzian. How could you understand? In the Empire of Shimyahein, men are reared as warriors and when we are ready, we choose our own name. We choose a name we can take pride in. What is so strange about this?"

Ikriff shook his head. "Nothing, I suppose. It makes a lot of sense doing it that way around when you think about it. It's stupid letting your parents name you. I mean – Ikriff. What kind of a name is that?" He gave a bark of laughter. "It's equally stupid to name yourself after where you are born. I am Ikriff Jal Vuum – always will be – but I haven't lived in Vuum since I was a pup. So anyway, how did you pick the name Strongspine?"

"Well, when a warrior picks a name, he must pick a name that is well-suited to him, or else he will look foolish. It is no good for an ugly man to call himself Darren Prettyface. No, he must be Darren Boarface or Darren of the Grease. In this way, warriors are limited. Also, when they pick a name, they must announce it before the community. The community then has the right to reject the name if they think it foolish or ill-suited. This brings great shame on a warrior, so it is important to get the name right. I was at a loss for what to call myself for a long time, but then I was given a mission to escort a wagon of supplies to my people from southern traders. My group and I were attacked as we brought the wagon back. We managed to kill the raiders, for there were only a few of them – outcasts, I judged. But all of my men were wounded and died soon after. Even the horses were all wounded and had to be put down." He shook his head and looked at the roll-up, which had gone out while he spoke. "A sad deed for any warrior of the grasslands. So, I was left alone with the wagon. I pulled the wagon back to my clan myself, in place of the horses. When I got there, dead on my feet and drenched in sweat, a friend of mine said to me, 'By the Gods, you must have a spine of steel!' That was when I knew what my name would be."

Ikriff nodded, mildly impressed but sure the tale had been hyperbolised. He could not resist a barb at his companion's swollen ego.

"What kind of an Empire has clans, anyway?"

Matthias bristled, as he always did when Ikriff mocked the legitimacy of the Empire where he was born. Both men were Winter Wolverines, mercenaries working for the Warlord, Sciarv Jal Shambot, but they had differing heritages. The warriors of the grasslands – Matthias' people, horsemen by nature – maintained Shimyahein was an Empire, but all those outside its borders laughed at the small country with the grandiose name. It was a place of infighting, never at rest, never at peace with itself. Hundreds of clans made up its populace, and each had its own laws and believed itself above the rest.

Like many of his people, Matthias was big, broad and bronze with umber hair. He was wrapped in brown stoat fur to combat the cold. Ikriff, on the other hand, was small and wiry and had the olive complexion of a Kutzian. He was swaddled in black bear fur; he still had the scars on his ribs from slaying the beast. His hair, too, was black and curly, so it was difficult to tell where the high collar of the coat ended and his mane began. Unlike the clean-shaven Matthias, Ikriff had let a scraggly black beard grow out from his thin chin. Also unlike the young romantic, Matthias, Ikriff was old enough to be cynical.

"It's no different to all the Warlords in Al Kutz," Matthias pointed out. "This is hardly a unified nation, either. Every Warlord is at war with all the rest."

"I never said it was."

Ikriff was about to tease his friend further, for watching him squirm and seeing his hackles rise was the only fun he could find in the remote watchtower anymore. Something caught his eye, however, and he froze. He stared out over the water, the lake so vast that its far shores were lost to the mists of distance.

"Matthias, look! D'you see anything out there?"

One second, there was nothing; the next, a fleet of longships loomed out of the blue, sailing fast over the crystalline waters.

"Ah!" Matthias exclaimed, grabbing Ikriff unnecessarily. "Ikriff, look!"

"I see, I see!"

As the boats came closer, Ikriff saw that they were long and narrow with both oars and a sail. The prows were carved with

Dragon-head figureheads. The canvas was taut and those aboard were rowing, too. They were making quick headway over the lake and would be washing ashore by the watchtower in under an hour. He squinted to make out the emblem on the sail, and when he did, he muttered, "Galush-Kagen, you're in for a treat today."

It seemed there would be blood aplenty for the God of Gore.

"How did they even get boats up here?" Matthias asked.

"I don't know."

"Who are they?"

"I recognise the symbol they fly," Ikriff said grimly. "It's the sigil of the Golden Buffalos, the men who work for Imr Abdul Burai'abul Shamash, the Ishambrian Warlord who rules in Jerekleia."

"How in the Gods' name do you remember all that foreign nonsense?"

Ikriff shrugged absently. "I dunno. Just do."

"Well, what are they doing here?"

Ikriff gave his companion a withering glance. "Come for a picnic, of course. Why d'you think, numbskull? They're attacking us!"

"Attacking Shambot?"

"Yes!"

"By the Gods, we have to do something! We have to warn them!"

"Yes, we do," Ikriff agreed thoughtfully. "Let's get to the fire."

The warning fire was high among the peaks, set in the lee of a curving granite ridge that blocked the majority of the wind coming from the north. The city they were protecting to the south, Shambot, would easily be able to see the flames if they could get the wood lit.

Ikriff and Matthias hurried out of the watchtower and rushed up the mountainside, climbing around the ridge to get to the warning fire. The clouds thickened above them, warning of worse to come. The wind flayed their faces, cold enough to numb, and stung them with little flecks of rain and hail, or perhaps just whipped-up snow. They had both donned fur gloves for the short journey, but they still felt like their fingers were getting frostbitten. So high in the mountains, they were also short of breath remarkably quickly as they tried to move at speed.

When they reached the small plateau where wood for the fire

was stacked as high as they were tall under weighted canvas, the wind howled around them, around the ridge, but no longer buffeted them directly. A stash of oil and some strange green powder with which Ikriff was unfamiliar was secreted in a nook in the rock nearby; they removed the canvas and doused the wood as they had been ordered. Then, with flint and knife, they struck a spark. It took a few tries, but soon a spark caught on the oil and the wood went up in a blaze. Thanks to the oil and green powder, the flames roared to life quickly, growing high and turning a vivid and easily recognisable green colour. They stunk and threw up a huge black smoke signal, too, which Ikriff had not been prepared for.

He had never had to light a warning fire before, though he had been in many battles. It was hard to live in Al Kutz and not get into battles, and he had lived there all his life. It sometimes seemed like the whole country was just one big battle.

Ikriff knew the invaders would likely see the flames, and if not would definitely see the smoke. "Alright," he said, "the city is warned. Now, let's get out of here before those bastards in the boats come looking to see what's going on."

"Where are we going?" Matthias asked. "Back to the city?"

Ikriff gave his companion a disparaging look. "You know what we have to do."

Matthias' broad shoulders sank. "I thought you were going to say that. I hoped not, but I thought so."

Climbing back out of the lee of the ridge, they made their way to a new position, high in the crags, looking south. The sky was white with cloud cover now. The lake was lost to sight and Ikriff found he missed its placidness now, missed the boredom. Climbing frozen, slick rock faces in the biting winds was no way to pass a day. His nose was sore after a while, then numb by the time they reached their next destination. He could not feel his fingers and toes, either, but kept using them regardless to drag himself onward.

When they reached their new vantage point, Ikriff and Matthias slumped to the ground, trying to shelter behind small crags that provided little in the way of windbreak.

"What do we do now?" Matthias asked.

"We wait."

They shivered and clung together and waited. It began to snow, and still they sat motionless, under a thickening white veil.

"There they are!"

After what seemed an age, when both were hidden under a layer of snow, saturated and shaking, the Golden Buffalos finally came into sight once again. It was a large raiding force, as such forces went in Al Kutz. A thousand men, Ikriff reckoned, swarmed the level rock floor a hundred feet below the two lookouts, looking like miniatures in the distance, like toys. Most of them had dark skin and wore colourful turbans, yellow and scarlet and white, likely signifying them as Ishambrian natives who had followed Imr Abdul when he had migrated to Al Kutz. Some did not; mercenary groups in Al Kutz were always diverse. Regardless of ethnicity, any man could achieve greatness in Al Kutz with a strong enough sword arm.

As well as the turbans, a lot of the warriors wore Ishambrian-style robes beneath mismatched armour. There was little chainmail, but a lot of rusty cuirasses, greaves and gauntlets. The thousand warriors converged on the clifftop on foot at speed, little knowing they were being observed. Once arrayed along the clifftop, they began anchoring lines by tying them around crags and then letting the spools spill out over the cliff edge.

They had come prepared, Ikriff acknowledged. They had known they would need long ropes to abseil down the cliff face to get to Shambot, which lay a league distant to the south, in the lee of the great escarpments. This was a well-planned raid, and any attack from this direction was likely to take the city relatively by surprise. Normally, no one came over Saddle Lake.

There were, however, precautions for just such an emergency, and the two Wolverines had been well drilled on how to put them into place.

"When do we do it?" Matthias asked, teeth chattering.

"Wait until they are on the ropes," Ikriff replied, rubbing his arms. "Then, we move."

They did not have to wait long. Soon, the ropes were ready and Buffalos were swinging out over the cliff edge, dangling over a drop of at least a hundred feet.

"Let's go," said Ikriff, levering himself up with a creak and a groan. Middle age was doing him no good, he decided.

"If we have to," Matthias muttered glumly.

The two of them moved swiftly down the mountainside, hidden by crags and ridges from those below for the most part and well-camouflaged besides in their snow-choked gear. When they reached another plateau, less than fifty feet above the raiders, they stopped and stared at the long row of boulders laid out on the edge of the platform, above a slope leading down toward the cliff edge where the invaders were abseiling. The score of boulders were perched precariously, with only manmade wooden supports holding them in place, stopping them from rolling down the slope. In fact, the whole arrangement was manmade. Teams of big, strong men had pushed and hauled those boulders to the top of the slope, or else brought them down from above, and had placed them carefully in their positions before building the supports to hold them in place.

"Are we really going to do this?" Matthias asked. "As soon as we do, they'll know we're up here. We'll never get off this mountain alive."

"They're already taking the easiest route down," Ikriff pointed out. "There's no way out for us as it is, unless we risk a sheer face. We have to do this. It's what we signed up for. It's our duty. And I, for one, have a wife and kid back home to protect."

Matthias sighed. "You're right. I just wish I could have lived long enough to find a woman, too … maybe have a kid of my own … Ah well, at least Galush-Kagen will welcome me with open arms in the Bloody Pagodas when I die, eh?"

"That he will, my friend, that he will," said Ikriff, patting the man from Shimyahein on the shoulder. "He will receive you with highest honour when he hears of what you have done, how you met your end."

Matthias clasped Ikriff's shoulder in return, looking down at the littler man. "He will welcome us both like brothers, my friend, and I, for one, am glad to meet my fate by your side, Ikriff Jal Vuum."

Ikriff nodded. "I am glad, too, Matthias Strongspine. I would have it no other way. Ahem. Alright, let's do this. Time to put those big muscles of yours to use. Grab the rope."

Matthias did as he was bidden, rooting around in the snow for the rope. When he found it and wrenched it clear of the white powder, he began to pull on it. Nothing happened. He pulled harder and harder, his tendons standing out like iron rods under his skin, his muscles bunching, his veins bulging. Still, nothing happened. He pulled even harder, until he thought he was going to pull his own arms out of their sockets. Still, nothing happened.

Panting, he said, "Give us a hand, Ikriff."

Together, they both tugged on the rope, straining and grunting and spitting with effort. Finally, red in the face, they achieved the desired effect. Strongspine earned his name.

The rope was actually several ropes woven together. Further along, the ropes separated and each attached to a separate wooden support stand beneath a boulder. When yanked hard enough, the supports snapped and gave way beneath the pressure of both rope and boulder. Released from their imprisonment atop the plateau, the score of boulders suddenly ran free, rolling off the edge and down the slope. They barrelled down the mountainside, picking up speed and clattering and booming like thunder.

Imr Abdul's men's faces were a sight as they turned and saw the boulders coming for them, unstoppable as the passing of seasons. A thousand faces twisted in fear and surprise in an instant. Ikriff could almost have laughed at the picture. Then, the boulders were upon the invaders, and the Kutzian did not feel like laughing anymore.

He watched the men below shoving one another, shouting and screaming, trying to get clear of the boulders' paths. There was a mad, mass jostling, and he was sure some Buffalos were knocked down and trampled in the ruckus as the rumbling stones bore down on them. There were too many men, though, and nowhere to run. They were suddenly pent up like pigs in a pen, caught between crags on either side, the cliff edge behind them and the boulders in front. The enormous stones ploughed into the swathe of Buffalos, rolling over those that had not moved fast enough. The boulders crushed men, flattened them, and left a gooey red paste on the rock and in the snow in their wake.

A second later, the boulders had rolled through the soldiers, decimating them in a great clatter, and were tipping off the cliff edge where some of the invaders had already started to descend on ropes. Ikriff could not see what happened to the boulders after that, but he hoped they took out some of the abseiling men.

One thing he did see astounded him and forced him to rub his eyes and look again lest they be deceiving him. The enormous boulders had killed hundreds of men in less than a minute, but one stone had not done its job. Before Ikriff's eyes, one of the boulders was blown to smithereens by what looked like an indecipherable, spinning, crimson sigil shooting through the air, leaving a glowing red trail in its wake.

The Kutzian replayed the scene in his mind, flabbergasted. The boulder had been barrelling toward the enemy, but then the Buffalos had parted, revealing a dark-skinned, richly clad figure in their midst. Ikriff had known who it was as soon as he laid eyes on him; it was the Ishambrian Warlord, the ruler of Jerekleia himself, Imr Abdul Burai'abul Shamash. Even at a distance, Ikriff had been able to make out the Warlord's bushy black beard, his golden turban, and his crimson-and-gold raiment over which he wore a bronze cuirass, as well as greaves and gauntlets which glittered like gold. Ikriff was sure Imr Abdul hoped everyone thought it was gold.

The Warlord had traced odd patterns in the air with his arms for a moment, swaying this way and that as if he might be dancing, and then he had shouted and pointed one hand at the oncoming stone. His shout had been a boom, a thunderous clap, and from his hand had appeared the phosphorescent sigil which had flashed across the plateau and pulverised the boulder in a heartbeat. The great rock had rained down on the remnants of the army as small shards, stone rain, but had killed no one.

Ikriff and Matthias just stared at Imr Abdul, aware that they had just witnessed sorcery in use against them, but scarcely able to believe it. Magic was just a children's tale after all, a Faery tale, like the legendary, unbreakable lazarinthian swords supposedly made on a sunken island populated by non-humans. Yet, they had seen it with their own eyes, and they knew it had been real in the pits of their stomachs. They had seen magic.

Ikriff felt excitement budding in his gut at the thought; magic was real! Then, however, Imr Abdul stared up at the mountain, right up at the two lookouts, and their bellies clenched as if in the grip of a convulsion, terror scratching at their insides. Ikriff thought for a moment he was dying from the inside out, that he was under assault from some unseen, unknown magical force beyond his comprehension.

Then, when he managed to suck in a breath, he realised he had crippled himself. Nothing but fear was convulsing him. He forced himself to let out the breath slowly, and then suck in another even more slowly, trying to ease his drumming heart. Fear was the greatest enemy, he reminded himself. There was nothing to fear but death after all, and death was but the doorway to Galush-Kagen's realm, to the

Bloody Pagodas, where all the vaunted warriors who ever lived would be honoured until the end of time.

He stared back down at Imr Abdul, and he watched as the Warlord gave orders. Moments later, bowmen were taking aim and half a dozen swordsmen were beginning the climb up the mountain toward the two lookouts' position. Then, arrows were clattering down all around the two Wolverines, pinging off rocks on either side of them, above and below, shafts splintering on impact.

"Come on," said Ikriff grimly, hidden behind a crag. "They know we're here now. Let's get down there and meet our fate."

Matthias Strongspine stared at the Kutzian, wide-eyed for a moment. Ikriff was afraid he was going to bolt like a spooked horse, but then the big man unslung the large battleaxe with its bearded blade and counterweighing spike from his back, let loose a wild, inarticulate roar and threw himself out from behind cover, still bellowing like a wounded bear.

Snarling like a great cat, Ikriff joined him, tugging out his twin katanas from their sheaths at his belt and springing out from behind cover. He and Matthias ran across the uneven plateau and then took the boulders' route down the slope toward the enemy army, of whom perhaps four hundred remained. Ikriff was gratified to think that he and Matthias had killed more than half of the invading force by themselves.

They were running flat out by the time they got close, which was perhaps the only reason they had not been made into pincushions by Golden Buffalo archers. Ikriff also thanked the Gods as he ran for the thickening snow, which may have helped throw off their aim. Whatever the reason, once the two got close enough, the archers could not fire for fear of hitting the swordsmen in front of them. So, free of arrows, the lookouts sprinted the last short distance, brandishing their weapons and howling like wolves.

A row of turbaned, robed, Ishambrian swordsmen wielding crescent-bladed scimitars awaited them. As they closed in on the enemy, Matthias hefted his mighty battleaxe high with a defiant shout and Ikriff hung back a pace to give him room to swing it. Matthias hit the Ishambrians like a rampaging bull with Ikriff a step behind. The big man's axe arced out in timely fashion and, with greater reach than the scimitars he faced, carved a bloody path through two swordsmen, clawing open the face of one to the skull and smashing the second's shoulder to bits. Then, he was among them, lashing out left and right with manic speed, hewing down foes like a farmer does so much wheat.

As always, Ikriff was impressed; Matthias may have been short on brains, but what he lacked in intelligence he made up for in sheer unbridled ferocity and raw power in a fight. His huge muscles bunched like he had hidden rocks under his skin, his umber hair whipping this way and that with his movement. Behind him, Ikriff fought with less bearlike savagery, more catlike grace. The twin katanas – weapons he had picked up off a dead Tzunese man he didn't know how many years ago – were like a steel symphony in his hands, singing of death to all around in a high-pitched whine. They wove a bloody melody of grunts, cracks, screams and squelches wherever they roamed, humming and hissing like silver serpents whose bites are deadly.

Just as fast as Matthias, but less powerful, Ikriff had been forced to grow his skills over the years in order to survive in Al Kutz. There was a saying among the warriors – a poor swordsman is a dead swordsman. Not a very funny saying, he thought, but apt. So, he had spent hours honing his swordsmanship against dummies and opponents in training, and though he occasionally wondered why he bothered, every time he got into a fight like this one he well remembered why. All the welts and bruises, the aches and pains, the late nights and early mornings; all of it was suddenly worth it. There was no substitute for practice, be it in swordplay or playing a musical instrument.

Ikriff felt like a master composer among amateur musicians. He was old enough now to be considered a veteran, and many of those he faced hadn't a whisker on their soft cheeks. So, by dint of practice, trial and error, repetition and dedication, he cut the youths down in a stroke or two. Occasionally, he came across a foe who was faster or stronger than him, but rarely were they as well-practised. Ikriff always had a trick up his sleeve for those particular enemies.

One, a skinny youth, jabbed at him with his scimitar lightning-fast, and Ikriff knew a pang of worry as he dodged. This kid was quick, he thought, but was he sure on his feet? The lookout barged the boy, and instead of backing away or swinging around to gain room, the youth stumbled back, lost his balance and fell with his arms cartwheeling. Ikriff put his left-hand sword in the boy's gut even as he blocked an overhead chop with his right-hand blade. Then, he stamped on the boy's face, pivoted out from under the high attack and sliced his new attacker's guts open with his left-hand blade.

Another – a dreadlocked Chilpaean brute with twin cutlasses and gold in his teeth, ears, nose and eyebrows – gave Ikriff butterflies in his stomach when he saw the large, dark-skinned man coming for him. The Chilpaean sought him out with savage, wide arcs of his cutlasses, and Ikriff was forced to bob and weave for a moment to evade the blows. He knew he needed to end the confrontation quickly, though; to get bogged down fighting one opponent for too long amid the masses was to die.

So, the Kutzian threw caution to the wind, and – when he saw an opening, when the Chilpaean chopped and then thrust – he sidestepped and then leapt forward beside the man's lunge. The tip of his blade plunged an inch deep into the bigger man's throat as he tried to back away. It was deep enough, and the Chilpaean's eyes went wide as blood gushed out of his severed jugular. A moment later, his legs buckled, his eyes lost focus, and he collapsed, boneless. Ikriff spun, parried a stab from behind just in time and slashed at his attacker with his other blade, cutting through the man's nose and making him squeal like a stuck pig.

That was when he saw Matthias Strongspine die. The man whose face he had mangled fell, and as he did so Ikriff saw beyond him a spear impale Matthias through the shoulder, catapulting him back through the air to land roughly on the ground. Ikriff followed the spear's trajectory back the way it had come and saw Imr Abdul again, resplendent in crimson and bronze, with his hand outstretched, pointing towards Matthias. The Kutzian understood in a flash that the Warlord had once again used his magic against them, this time somehow launching a loose spear at his friend with the power of his mind.

"Yargh!"

Ikriff's heart crumpled in his chest like a rotten log caving in on itself. Blood covered his vision, and all that remained of his once-civilised mind was the primordial, bestial urge to kill, to slay, to wreak bloody vengeance among his enemies, among those who had taken his friend. Letting loose a wild war cry, Ikriff hurled himself at the Buffalos, all concern for his own life, his own safety, gone along with Matthias.

He fought to get to his friend, knowing it was likely too late to do anything to save him – and besides, what could he do? Regardless, his thoughts were consumed by vengeance and by reaching his friend. He clobbered men down as fast as he could with no defence, and though soldiers fell before his flashing katanas like rain in a monsoon, he accrued several slash wounds and a stab wound through the side. All those that had slashed him, however, lay dead in his wake, opened from groin to throat or from ear to ear. The soldier that had stabbed him lay screaming, his guts hanging out while he still lived, disembowelled.

As he made his way to his friend, though, Ikriff saw Matthias stabbed several more times before he could rise. When Ikriff did finally reach his fellow lookout, bleeding and wobbly, he pounced like a great cat on the soldiers gathered around Matthias. He bore several of them to the ground and stabbed at them viciously in the heap that ensued, not caring where his blades bit for he was surrounded by foes. After a few moments of screaming and wild, savage stabbing, he realised to his surprise that he was still alive. He wrenched himself up out of the pile of dead and dying men and crouched by Matthias' side, uncaring of all the hundreds of blades at his back.

Nobody stabbed him in the back, however, and he wondered why until he heard a thunderclap of a voice boom out, "Leave him! Leave him alone! He is mine! The first man to touch him dies by my hand!"

He could not see the speaker, but he knew it was Imr Abdul Burai'abul Shamash. It seemed the Warlord wanted to kill the lookout himself.

Ikriff did not care. He took Matthias' head in his lap and stroked the man's umber hair like he was a pet. "You did well, Matthias Strongspine," he murmured huskily, a catch in his voice. "You more than earned your name. Go now to the Bloody Pagodas, my friend, and know that Galush-Kagen will honour you for your valour forever. He will be proud to sit alongside such as you … as will I, when I get there."

Matthias smiled slightly, and then his final breath rattled out of his throat and he went limp in the Kutzian's hands. Ikriff realised he was sat in a pool of blood from all his and his friend's injuries; the hot liquid sank into the snow, kicking up steam like spirits, like departing souls.

Ikriff laid his friend's head down gently and then stood and turned to face Imr Abdul. The Warlord was ten feet away, watching him patiently. Up close, he looked older than he had from afar; like he had no right to be able to run around in that armour, nor even stand in it at his age. Nevertheless, he appeared spry. He cocked his turbaned head and stroked his bushy black beard as he regarded the lone surviving lookout. Snow and blood speckled his armour, but it still shone like gold beneath.

When he spoke, Imr Abdul's voice was far quieter than before, though recognisable in its bass cadence. Ikriff wondered whether his voice had been magically augmented before.

"Who are you," he asked slowly, speaking Traveller's Tongue carefully for his accent was thick, "to kill so many of my men? Who are you to throw yourself at death so fearlessly?"

"I am Ikriff Jal Vuum," said Ikriff venomously, "and I am going to kill you for what you have done!"

He knew he sounded like a fool – one man against an army – but he was beyond caring.

Imr Abdul just laughed. "Kill me? I don't think so, my brave friend. I tell you what – I am impressed by your fighting skill and I am feeling magnanimous, so I am going to make you this one-time only offer. I am the Warlord of Jerekleia, leader of the Golden Buffalos, Imr Abdul Burai'abul Shamash. Join me and help me take Shambot, and I will let you live and serve as one of my mercenaries. How does that sound?"

Ikriff considered it. A part of him wanted to live, to see his family again, but another part of him knew his duty, knew right from wrong.

"I am a Wolverine. I have sworn an oath," he said, "and I intend to keep it. I will not join you, Imr Abdul, this day or any other."

Imr Abdul frowned. "What makes you so loyal to your Warlord? What has Sciarv done for you that I could not?"

Ikriff bared his teeth. "Sciarv Jal Shambot is the best man I know, aside from Matthias there, and I would follow him into the Nether itself if he asked it of me. I will not betray him, so let us put aside the niceties!"

Imr Abdul shook his head. "What kind of a man can inspire

such loyalty, I wonder? Never mind. Very well, we shall dispense with the pleasantries. If you will not join me, then it is time for you to join your friend in death."

Ikriff was bleeding from half a dozen wounds, but he tried to charge the Warlord regardless, his swords held high. His side where he had been stabbed throbbed and burned, and his slash marks stung, and his heart was a crippled thing. He only made it a few paces before Imr Abdul waved his hands in familiar eldritch gestures and pointed at him.

"Senza bumbada!" the sorcerous Ishambrian cried.

A red rune, indecipherable, spinning and glowing, shot from the Warlord's fingertips. Ikriff was ready for it, however, and spun around it. He felt the heat of it on his skin as it whooshed past him, sizzling in his ears.

He sprinted on toward the Warlord, sure he was going to die but glad to think he was going to take the bastard who had killed his friend with him. Imr Abdul's eyes widened marginally when the magic rune did not destroy the Kutzian, but rather exploded among his own men, scattering and charring them.

Then, however, he regained his composure and pushed a palm toward the lookout, shouting, *"Pa'ptheon!"*

Ikriff was hit by some invisible force that felt like a horse's kick all over his body. He was lifted into the air and somersaulted back to land sorely on the jagged rock. He landed on his back and heard a crack. He cursed inwardly, thinking he had busted a rib.

Then, he tried to move and realised to his horror that the sound had been his spine snapping. He was completely immobilised, bent over backwards at an unnatural angle over a small crag. He wondered why it did not hurt, and then an excruciating fire started in his back and quickly spread up and down his body, an inferno ravaging him mercilessly. He found he could not even scream; he could barely draw breath the way he lay.

He lay there, looking up at the snowy sky, so white it looked like nothingness stretching away into eternity, until a face blocked out the clouds. Imr Abdul Burai'abul Shamash loomed over Ikriff Jal Vuum and smiled down at him sadly, like a father regarding a wayward son.

"I am sorry it had to end this way, Ikriff. Truly. I am sorry for a lot of what has gone on today." He sighed and rubbed a hand over his dark-skinned face, over his beard. "With men like you and Matthias defending Shambot, I don't know if I can take it with the men I have left. I don't know if it's worth taking if this is the cost of defeating only two of you. This whole thing may have been a mistake. There are hundreds of you bastards, you Wolverines, down there ... Anyway, it is no longer your concern, I suppose. Rest easy, Ikriff Jal Vuum. May Galush-Kagen receive you in honour, for it is no less than you deserve."

Ikriff let out his final breath with a small smile on his face, pleased to think he and Matthias might have averted the entire invasion, saved Shambot by their actions, saved his family. He thought he saw the Ankou, those who guided souls to the afterlife, coming for him before his eyes closed.

Conn and the Faun

Connalin Svarligson, called Conn by his friends, wound his way among the black-trunked pines of Myrkvior Woods, trudging through thick snow. The trees were closely-packed, so the green needles tickled his face frequently. He was a twelve-year-old boy, so he felt the need to go adventuring from time to time, even if he was supposed to be cleaning his room. He could picture his ma's face easily; it would be all screwed up in irritation when he got home, albeit with a bit of relief that he was home safe.

The cloudbank overhead was as dense as the snow underfoot. The wind howled above him, above the treetops, making them sway and rustle, but he barely felt it in the dense forest. He had wrapped up warm in his fur-wrapped boots, woollen trousers and tunic and the little beaver-fur coat and hat that his pa had fashioned for him. Snow drifted down lazily, lightly, speckling him as he went. He had to take big steps to clear the high-piled snow, and he used the trees' crisscrossing branches to help pull himself along.

He did not have any destination in mind as he moseyed along, desirous of nothing more than a jaunt. He considered himself an explorer, mapping new terrain. In fact, as he walked along, he imagined himself a great many things – a warrior, a Wizard, a beast-slayer, a king, a pauper, a man. In winter in the Highlands of Fjelburg, there was often little else to do but use his imagination. Though the snow was thick on the ground, it normally came down even heavier and snowed everybody in, sometimes for days. Some froze or starved to death the winter before, he recalled. So, he considered this a mild winter. Doubtless his ma would be furious at him regardless.

Myrkvior Wood was full of strange, black-trunked pines that grew almost nowhere else in Fjelburg. It grew up the side of a small mountain in the middle of the Highlands. Snow-capped as they were, the dark trees were oddly beautiful to Conn; a strange juxtaposition of black and white that evoked a feeling of cosiness, as if the trees were sleeping or hibernating. People in Conn's village at the base of the mountain called it accursed sometimes, however, and said they heard eerie music coming from the Wood at night. Few adults ventured there, and any that went for firewood did not venture deep into the shadowy forest, chills up their spines sending them running. As is often the way, the young boy felt no such chills – unless they were chills of excitement.

He felt those chills now as he passed a lightning-struck tree he recognised. The enormous trunk had been blackened and split in twain; a grand old giant resigned to beauteous death. He had never been past that particular tree before, having stopped to study it in the past, and so he felt a thrill course through him like he was the one who had been struck by lightning at the thought of exploring yet further. Though he could not see the sun, he knew it was still early afternoon, because it had not gotten dark yet. It always got dark so early in winter. He figured he had plenty of time.

He ploughed on up the mountainside. The snow started to come down more heavily.

Just when he was considering turning back, starting to worry about the snowfall, Conn was hurled from his feet by a sudden impact. He felt pain, hot and sticky, in his thigh and cried out. He felt sick as he locked eyes with the boar that had charged him. It was a big fat brute covered in brown bristles, with black eyes, a pig-like snout and two vicious-looking tusks on either side of its mouth. It snuffled at him angrily, pawed the ground like a horse and then charged at him again, snorting as it came.

Conn tried to leap up, but the agony in his leg would not let him move faster than a snail's pace. He watched the boar coming out of the corner of his eye, wishing he had stayed home, sure he was about to die. He felt cold and alone in that moment with a scary emptiness opening up before him like a doorway into nothingness, a pit from which he would never emerge. He wondered if the Valkyries would come for him and take him to Valhalla. He didn't think so; he didn't think dying at the tusks of a boar counted as dying in battle.

Then, a little red fireball roared through the trees and struck the boar in the flank with a fiery flash. The creature was abruptly catapulted to one side to smack into a big pine and then lay still. Snow knocked off the leaves and branches of the tree half-buried the dead boar a second later. Conn stared in amazement at the blackened and smoking body.

He heard footsteps in the snow and turned his head so fast he cricked his neck painfully. He blinked in surprise at what he saw and rubbed his eyes, sure they were deceiving him, the tricksters. Before him, padding through the snow was a myth come to life, a Faun.

The creature was half-man, half-goat, with the pale, muscular body of a man above the brown, furry legs, tail and hooves of a goat. It had ivory horns sprouting from its temples and curving back over its wavy, shoulder-length, earth-brown hair, as well as smaller horns either side of its delicate, clean-shaven chin. Its face was an alien rounded arrow pointing down with strange cheekbones that seemed to run vertical rather than horizontal, as in humans. It was twice as tall as the boy. The Faun strutted over to the boar with a pigeon-like gait and inspected the body, kicking it with a hoof. It then regarded Conn with the yellow eyes and odd, double-lobed pupils of a goat and spoke to him with the lips of a man.

"Hallo, boy," said the Faun in Traveller's Tongue, his voice deep, lilting and melodic. "What are you doing all the way up here in this blizzard?"

"I – I was exploring," Conn stammered, frozen in place.

His wound was throbbing hotly now, and his thoughts were growing sluggish. He couldn't remember if Fauns were scary or not, so he wasn't sure how to react. He was trembling with excitement, but his hands were clammy with fear. He felt like he had forgotten how to breathe in the face of the revelation of his discovery, like the new knowledge had ousted the old.

He tried to remember what his pa had told him of Fauns; that they were solitary creatures to be left alone, he thought he recalled. He felt like he was forgetting something that was dancing around his mind's periphery, taunting him, but he could not remember anything else.

"So I see," said the Faun, "and a long way up the mountain you have come. You were lucky I heard you cry out. A brave boy you must be to have come so far through Myrkvior. Or foolish. What is your name, brave boy?"

"M-my name is Connalin, Conn for short. What's yours?"

The Faun smiled, looking strangely sad as it did so. "My name is difficult for your kind to pronounce. You may call me Driff." He rolled the *r* in a way that Conn knew he could not.

When the boy said it, the name came out flatter, less musical. "Driff."

Driff nodded. "Now, let me see to that wound of yours."

Conn's leg was on fire. He watched the Faun approach and then passed out.

He awoke in the middle of a round cave beside a fire over which the dead boar was spitted. The smell of it made his mouth water. His leg had been bandaged and now only ached dully. There was no visible way out of the cave except for a narrow crevasse that looked too small for Driff. Conn wondered how he had got in. Then, he remembered what the Faun had done to the boar. He turned to Driff, who was squatting beside him, puffing on a pipe and staring into the flames.

Wafting away the stinky baui smoke, Conn levelled a finger at the Faun. "You did magic!" he croaked, his throat dry.

Driff passed him a water skin and said, "Here. Drink."

Conn guzzled a couple of mouthfuls, wiped his lips and said again, "You did magic back there! To that boar! You killed it with magic!"

"I did," the Faun said flatly, not boasting or ashamed. "It was that or let it kill you."

"Yeah … I guess it was. Thank you for saving my life, Driff."

The Faun smiled at him sadly. "It was my pleasure. You have been feverish all night, but I think you're on the mend now."

"All night?" Conn exploded, feeling suddenly nauseous with guilt. He tried to push himself to his feet, but his injured leg was numb. "My ma will be losing her mind with worry!"

Driff nodded. "It can't be helped. You need time to heal, my boy. Then, you can return to your ma."

Conn slumped back down miserably. He would be in for it if he ever did get home, he reflected. He was silent awhile then, thinking of his ma and pa, of his home, which had once seemed so boring but now seemed like the greatest adventure of them all.

Driff cut some strips of meat off the spitted boar and handed them to Conn, saying, "Eat."

The boy did so in silence.

Eventually, Driff commented, "Sounds like the snowstorm is worsening out there."

Conn didn't know how the Faun knew what was going on outside; he could barely hear the whine of the wind now that he was inside. He finished the strips of meat; they were gamey and delicious.

"I've just realised, I never did ask what you are. Are you a Faun?"

"I am indeed."

"Wow! We all thought Fauns were just a legend, a story! Are there many of you up here in the Woods?"

"No. Just me."

The sorrowful answer brought Conn up short. "Oh. I'm sorry to hear that," he said awkwardly.

"As am I, child. As am I. Once, we Fauns thrived here in the Woods of Myrkvior, but now I fear I may be the last and when I am gone …"

"What happened to you?" Conn asked when Driff trailed off.

"Your people happened to us, my boy," the Faun said evenly. "Not all reacted to the sight of us as you did today. Some took up bows and axes and hunted us with dogs and killed us for our fur, for our ivory, for the prize of our corpses. You Highlanders are a simple folk, you know. You see something, you kill something. Now, there are almost no Fauns left."

Conn didn't know what to say; he was on the verge of tears, feeling like he was being accused, verbally attacked. He hated his own people in that moment and felt sorry for the Faun.

"But let us speak of more pleasant topics, shall we?" Driff said more brightly. "Do you live in the village at the bottom of the mountain, Conn?"

Conn nodded and wiped his eyes. "Yes. Tamblin-Doon it's called. They're good people there … At least, I thought they were."

"I'm sure they are," said the Faun gently, nodding, "in their own way. They merely follow their nature; I hold no grudge or ill feeling towards them or you. It would be like getting angry at a dog for barking or at the sun for rising or at the sky for being blue. They cannot help what they are. Neither can I. And neither can you."

"Still, I'm sorry for what my people have done to yours," said Conn, feeling wretched.

"All is forgiven," said Driff with that sad smile.

"How can it be?"

"We Fauns have had to put up with a lot of antagonism over the years, my boy." Seeing Conn's nonplussed look, he added, "A lot of people trying to kill us or enslave us. We learned long ago that forgiveness is the way forward, the only way to peace. We learned long ago not to try to change what cannot be changed."

"But you can do anything with magic," Conn protested. "You can change anything. Didn't you defend yourselves?"

"We did," Driff replied, "but not to the extent that we were willing to kill you to save ourselves. We are peaceful creatures, we Fauns. Bloodshed does us ill."

Conn shook his head in disbelief; that was not the way he had been raised. His people were far more warlike than the Fauns. He began to wonder, though – what was so wrong with a peaceful life?

He had been taught that war was a way of life, that it would be his way of life. He had been taught that the Gods respected only the strong, that Baldr blessed only the brave and that the Valkyries would only take to Valhalla those who died in battle with a sword or axe or spear in their hand. Was there another way? he wondered – and if there was, which was the right way? He knew what his pa would say, and he knew what Driff would say, but he suddenly found he didn't know who was right anymore. Could a man get to Valhalla without bloodshed? Was there another place besides Valhalla where his soul might go after death?

"Then, how do you get to Valhalla?" he asked slowly with furrowed brow.

Driff gave a bark of laughter. "Ha! Valhalla! Not everyone worships war like you people! We Fauns revere peace and we believe that we will be rewarded for doing so in the life after this one by way of reincarnation. If we are violent, we will be reborn as slugs or snails or worms in the dirt. If we are beneficent, we will be reborn as eagles or lions or clouds in the sky."

Conn was puzzled. "But eagles and lions kill things," he pointed out.

"It is in their nature," Driff replied. "And one cannot fault a creature for its nature as I have said."

"But you killed that boar?"

"To save you, yes."

"But you still killed it. That wasn't very peaceful."

"I did it to save *you*, a man, a higher level of being than a mere boar. Sentient life is to be treasured above all else."

"So … if you can kill as easy as swatting a fly," Conn asked, his brows low in concentration, "isn't it *against* your nature *not* to kill? I mean, isn't it in your nature to kill? So, you can't be faulted for that, surely."

Driff cocked his head as if he had never thought of that. "We Faun are peaceful creatures," he said again more uncertainly. "*That* is our nature."

Conn puffed out his cheeks in bemusement. "Tell me about your people," he said.

Driff did. He told the boy stories of the Fauns on and off all day while Conn drifted in and out of sleep, and the next day, and the next day, too. He wove tales of mighty warriors, ancient castles, mysterious Wizards, bizarre creatures from faraway lands, noble Kings and Queens, brave serfs and farmers; tales of war and peace, of famine and plenty, of natural devastation and the struggle to rebuild. The way he told it the Fauns had once been a plentiful and powerful people many centuries ago, but had been decimated since.

Conn recovered enough to travel on the fourth day of storytelling, but Driff said the blizzard was vicious outside and the young boy insisted he needed another day. So, on the morning of the fifth day, Conn awoke ready to depart. They had survived on roots and winter flowers for the most part after the boar had putrefied. Driff hadn't eaten any of the boar at all; he said he ate only of the land, not its animals. Conn had shaken his head at that, too.

That morning, he ate a few mushrooms Driff had picked and then stood by the crevasse, ready to leave. He knew Driff would not come with him for fear of what the people of his village might do if they discovered him. So, he hugged the Faun and said, "Thank you for everything, Driff. You saved my life and I'll never forget you."

"Nor I you, my boy."

Conn beamed. "I hope we meet again someday."

"Under better circumstances, I hope so too," Driff replied wryly.

Then, Conn squeezed through the fissure and left the cave and the Faun behind. Leaning on the black trunks of the pines when he grew tired and his leg ached, he made his way carefully back downhill through Myrkvior Wood. The snowfall was as light as it ever was in winter; it was a good day for travelling.

His heart sprang about and sang for joy when he finally came in sight of a deciduous tree hours later, a frozen larch. It was leafless and skeletal, and its thin branches all glistened white as pearls, coated in a thick layer of rime. The sight spoke to Conn of home; it was like a pure white beacon of hope amid the black pines. At the sight, he knew he was close to Tamblin-Doon, close to home.

Near sobbing with relief, he laid eyes on the village not long later. He hopped the low fence around the village and trudged through the snow towards his home. When he reached the little thatched lodge where he lived with his ma and pa, he found his parents bag-eyed and sleepless with worry.

"Conn!" his ma squealed when he strode in the door, lurching over to him and hugging him so tight he couldn't breathe.

His pa echoed the gesture a moment later, ruffling his hair and then coughing and saying gruffly, "Where have you been, boy? We've been worried sick!"

Conn told them the whole story, about his walk through Myrkvior, about his encounter with the boar and the Faun that had rescued him and nursed him back to health. His parents didn't believe him and when he stuck to his story, his pa beat him with his belt. The blows were gentler than usual, however. So, Conn swore never to tell another living soul about the Faun and he got on with his life, much as it had been before his foray up the mountain.

Two weeks later, however, when icicles still hung from eaves like frozen tears and snow still blanketed the ground, the trees, the roofs and everything else in sight, the village was attacked. At the break of dawn, beside the cockerel's crow, the sleepy villagers heard a loud, grinding roaring like a rockslide, and the earth shook under their feet like an earthquake had come to visit. The men and women of Tamblin-Doon rushed outside in their night attire and gasped in shock at what they saw by the grey pre-dawn light as the first fingers of gold uncurled over the eastern horizon.

They saw half a dozen Rock Trolls charging toward the village from the south, the opposite direction from Myrkvior Wood. The ten-foot-tall stone monsters had the rough shape of men, with two arms, two legs, a torso and a head, but they were barely recognisable as such. Their bodies were blocky and craggy, like weathered rock peaks high up on a mountain, and their slab-faces were featureless save for wide cracks that proved to be mouths when they yawned open and trumpeted. There was no intelligence in their noises or their movements; all knew they were beasts at heart, even if they were vaguely man-shaped.

They smashed the little fence and rampaged through the village like bulls in a china shop. Flailing their massive arms, they destroyed houses in a few swipes. One big, bearded man stepped up to face the Trolls, protecting his home, and struck at the nearest of them with a rusty old sword. The blade snapped in half against the creature's hip, and then everybody watched the Troll pound the man to a bloody paste with a few quick blows. Then, it scooped up the red goo and shovelled some into its wide mouth.

The villagers screamed and scattered like cockroaches under light. The men rushed to grab their weapons, the women to grab their babies, the babies to grab their toys and teddy bears. Some fled Tamblin-Doon, heading east or west, avoiding Myrkvior Woods at all costs. Some barricaded themselves in their homes or hid in basements if they had them.

Conn just stared, open-mouthed.

His pa shouted him from the doorway of their house, "Conn! Get back inside now or the Trolls will get you! Hurry!"

Conn turned to look at his pa, then at Myrkvior Woods. His pa guessed his intent and lunged out of the house to grab him, but he was too slow. Slippery as an eel, Conn dodged his pa's reaching hand and hared off north toward the mountain and the black pines.

"Conn!" he heard his pa shouting. "Conn, come back!"

Conn did not turn or slow, but he did shout over his shoulder, "Don't worry, pa! I can save us!"

He ran up the mountainside, dragging himself up the steepest parts using the black trunks of the pines. His heart thundered in his chest, and his breath came fast and ragged, but he kept going as fast as he could. He collapsed in the thick snow a few times in his haste, but eventually he made it to the lightning-struck tree and passed it.

He started yelling at the top of his lungs then, "Driff! Driff! Where are you? I need your help! Please, Driff, answer me! Where are you?"

He ran and shouted, and ran and shouted, and was beginning to lose hope when he heard a faint sound on the bitter wind.

"Conn? Is that you?" a voice replied faintly from out of sight.

"Yes, Driff, it's me! I'm over here, Driff! Over here!"

He guided the Faun with his voice, and soon the two were face to face.

Driff smiled his sad smile. "It's good to see you again, Conn, but what is all this hollering?"

"Rock Trolls are attacking my village!" Conn blurted. "I need your help to kill them! You've got magic; you can do it!"

Driff frowned, his stubbly face severe. "Your fellow villagers would brook no help from me. And besides, I have told you I do not kill."

"But you killed the boar to protect me! Killing Trolls to protect villagers is no different, surely! The Trolls are no more than beasts!"

"I am not sure about that," Driff responded pensively, stroking his chin. "They exhibit some signs of bonding with one another on an emotional level – they live and hunt in families after all – and they often seem smart enough to avoid deadly confrontation. In my experience, they are cowardly creatures who will only attack when they think it safe to do so."

"No, they are just animals made of stone! Everybody knows that!" Conn raged, feeling helplessness rise up in his throat like bile, burning. "You have to help us, please! People are dying down there!" He thought of the big, bearded man with the sword and he felt sick. "You have the power to save us! Please, Driff!"

Driff looked away into the trees for a long time, clearly torn, but then he looked into the boy's eyes and sighed at what he saw there. "You are sure your fellow villagers will not kill me on sight?"

"I won't let them," said Conn stoutly. "You're my friend."

Driff smiled. "Very well. I will help you, my friend. Lead me to your village."

Conn raced back to Tamblin-Doon with Driff on his tail, but by the time they got back the sun was up and the village was ruined. The majority of the little lodges had been knocked down and lay in heaps; bodies littered the snowy streets, the steaming blood surrounding them unnaturally bright against the pure white snow, eye-catching. The Rock Trolls were still shambling around the village; they did not move very fast, but fast enough to trap most of the populace between them. The boy and Faun could see twenty people stuck between the half-dozen Trolls, penned in like sheep by sheepdogs. The village had contained almost a hundred people at last count, Conn recalled sadly. It looked like the Trolls were playing with their food, like cats before a kill.

Conn was wracked by sobs then, and hot tears rolled down his cheeks. He sniffled after a few seconds and said, "Quick, let's see if ma and pa are still alive!" Taking Driff by the hand, he dragged him toward the people pen. "Do something, Driff! Do something before they all die!"

Driff surveyed the scene grimly, while the six Trolls plodded around the twenty or so people, prodding them, roaring at them and knocking them back if they tried to flee. As he watched, one man tried to dart between two Trolls, only for one of them to smash his ribs like kindling with a punch. Falling in the snow, he convulsed and coughed up blood and died.

Conn knew the man and screamed out at the sight, "Derrick, no!" His sobs returned then.

Driff drew himself up to his full height, waved his arms in arcane patterns and muttered an ancient word in the language of magic, *"Yololoyo!"*

He pointed an arm at the Trolls and from his splayed palm flew a fist-sized, amorphous yellow globule of energy. Sizzling, the glob whizzed over the wreckage of a lodge and struck one of the Trolls in the back with a yellow splash. The creature of stone staggered forward a step from the impact, but otherwise seemed unhurt – as Driff had known it would be. He was not trying to kill them, but to scare them away.

The Rock Troll spun on the Faun then, let loose a bellow of rage and charged like an aged bull, slow and steady, destroying everything in its tracks. Whimpering, Conn hid a few steps behind Driff, ready to run. The Faun faced down the Troll, however, and gestured and spoke again, *"Yololoyo!"*

He pelted the stone creature with a little yellow blob, and then another and another, until they were shooting from both his palms as fast as Conn's eyes could follow. Driff hoped the sting of them would make the Troll rethink its charge and turn tail, but he was wrong. The Troll ploughed on.

Driff decided to try to freeze the creature. *"Chising!"* he shouted, pointing a palm.

An azure nebula of icy energy shot from his palm and swamped the Troll, but it paid it no mind. Driff realised then that it was not easy to freeze stone. He had to dodge out of the way or be crushed by the rampaging Troll then.

As he sidestepped, he said, *"Hummuhummshh!"*

A gust of arcane wind whipped from his hand to flay the Troll, but it failed to budge it an inch, much less send it running. Driff cursed himself for a fool; he should have known the Troll was too heavy to blow over, but he was running out of offensive spells, growing desperate. The Troll was waving its arms around, trying to pulverise Driff, as he wracked his brain for a way out of his predicament. He just kept dodging. Eventually, though, one big, rocky fist grazed his shoulder and sent him tumbling down into the snow.

Panicking then like a cornered rat, seeing his doom block out the morning sun and stomp toward him, Driff cried out, *"Elementera sciomboi!"*

He threw out an arm, and this time a spear of brilliant golden energy sprang from his fingertips to lodge itself in the Rock Troll, impaling it straight through the belly. The Troll stumbled to a halt and looked down at the spear in time for the magical weapon to fade from sight amidst sparkles. It looked up again in time to take the next golden spear in the face, and then it toppled, lifeless, to the ground with a thud.

Driff rose to his feet, trembling with fear and power and excitement. Conn saw only his profile, but the Faun's eye looked terrible; haunted and cruel. He advanced on the other Trolls, who had noticed him by then but were loath to leave their other prey.

"Begone from here, savage creatures," Driff commanded in a loud, cold voice completely unlike his usual singsong tones, "or I will wreak bloody murder amongst you."

The Trolls, of course, did not understand. Tiring of their game, eager to play with the newcomer, they began pounding the people in their pen to pieces with their massive fists.

Driff let out an animalistic shriek of anger and yelled, *"Elementera sciomboi!"*

Another lance of shining golden light materialised in his upraised hand, and he cast it like a javelin at one of the Trolls, skewering it high in the back, just below the head. The Troll didn't make a sound; it just collapsed, poleaxed, with a thump before the spear could even disappear. Seeing this, the remaining four Rock Trolls turned away from the remaining few people and bulled towards Driff, shaking the ground as they went.

The Faun stood his ground. He threw two more magical spears, and two more Trolls died. Then, they were upon him and he had no time or room for another throw.

He muttered different words, *"Chising wo'oriss!"* and a sharp, white sword made of sparkling ice appeared in his hand.

He evaded the Trolls' charge and ducked under a punching stone fist. Then, he leapt and spun and lashed out with his ice-sword at the apex of his jump. The magic sword cut through the solid stone like it was nothing more than smoke, and one Troll's head bounced on the ground a moment later. The last Troll came at Driff with a fury, having seen its whole family killed before its eyes, swinging its arms in wild haymakers that forced Driff to back away or be pulverised. Finally, learning the rhythm of the strikes and spotting his chance, the Faun skidded between the Troll's legs and came up smoothly to his feet behind it. The Troll tried to swing around to elbow the Faun, but Driff had buried his white sword in its back before it could move far. Like the rest, it fell, inanimate, in the snow.

Driff looked up at the cloudy sky and screamed until his lungs were empty. He couldn't precisely explain why he screamed, even to himself, except to say that he needed to. He turned then to see Conn watching him from afar. The expression on the boy's face was not one of gratitude, but one of horror.

Nevertheless, the boy approached sheepishly, not meeting the Faun's eyes, and said, "Y-you killed them."

"I did what you asked." The words came out harsh, biting – more so than Driff had intended.

Conn nodded and finally met Driff's hard gaze. "You're right. Thank you, Driff. Thank you for saving my village … what remains of it, anyway."

He stood still, staring at the survivors, who were grouped together, hugging and sobbing.

"Aren't you going to go and find your family?" asked the Faun.

"I already found them," Conn said flatly, "while you were killing the Trolls. They're back there." He jerked a thumb over his shoulder. "They're dead."

Though the boy was not crying now, Driff suddenly saw that he had been crying recently. His eyes were red and puffy, and his voice was croaky. The Faun didn't know what to say.

"Can I come with you back to the Woods?"

Driff was taken aback by the question. He hated himself for what he had done, what he had become, and he had been planning to hurl himself from the mountaintop. Now, however, it appeared Conn had become his charge.

He tried to fend off the boy. "Wouldn't you rather stay with your own people?"

Conn glanced at the survivors, then shook his head. "No. I'd rather stay with you. Can I come with you back to the Woods, Driff? Please?"

There was such sorrow in the boy's voice that the Faun's heart panged. "I'm not going back to the Woods," he said.

"Wherever you go, can I come with you? I just want to leave this place. I don't mind where we go."

Driff sighed. "Yes, you can come with me."

The two of them put the village of Tamblin-Doon behind them and wandered off out into the snow, into the wild.

So was born the pairing of Conn and the Faun, who would wander the world of Maradoum and the realms beyond and become legendary for their deeds of daring and heroism in later life.

A Deadly Present for the Khan

Moshi Usuru was nervous.

He was nervous about a great many things, in fact. For one thing, he was nervous about where they were; he was accompanying Ambassador Sifang south from Yuguanji, the final fort in Qin Xi Wall, leaving the Empire of Quing Tzu entirely. He had travelled before, of course – it was mandatory for a Wizard to visit the far corners of the Empire to fully understand it – but he had never ventured beyond its vast borders. He glanced back wistfully across the empty panorama at the fort; impressive up close, it was now a speck in the distance, hardly more comforting than the presence of a gnat. The Wall, so vast and indomitable when he had been in its shadow, now could not even be seen.

He was nervous about entering the land known as Chimanchu; it was a barren, dusty, lawless land, where there was no ruler, no oligarchy, no democracy, no system of government whatsoever. There were only clans forever at war with one another, riding into battle again and again on their fearsome steeds, fighting just as fiercely over feuds long forgotten as fresh ones newly made. It was a land of barbarism, a land where the strong took from the weak, a land where surviving until sunset each day was a challenge.

In short, it was nothing like Moshi's home. He still thought of Xi'Ping, the capital city of the province of Shaanchang, as his home. He had lived there for most of his thirty-two years, after all. That was where the Chi Academy could be found, where he had studied for more than a decade. The Viper Tower was there; that was where he had become a Wizard and received his staff. It was lush and beautiful up there in the north of Quing Tzu, green and vibrant, warm and sunny – nothing like Chimanchu.

Moshi glanced up at the broad blue sky and thought it a paler, icier blue than he was used to. Where Xi'Ping was green and wet, Chimanchu was brown and dry. Where Xi'Ping was fit to burst with people, Chimanchu was empty, devoid of life. Where Xi'Ping was order, Chimanchu was chaos. Moshi's horse lurched and almost threw him off and he let out a garbled cry, letting dust into his mouth, thinking all the while of how much he missed the quiet libraries of the Academy. He thought of the two books in his pack; they would have to suffice until he returned to civilisation.

He was also nervous about riding the horse. It was a huge, fractious, speckled grey gelding, bigger by far than anything he had ridden before. Somebody had given the monster the ironic name of Sweetpaw. It was supposed to make him look impressive, formidable, Moshi reckoned, but all it did in reality was churn his stomach. The ground looked very far away beneath him, and the cursed beast insisted on rearing every once in a while as though it didn't want to be ridden. He had never quite perfected the rhythm of riding, either, so when when they started trotting, he bounced around in the saddle like a sack of potatoes loosely tied down. Even at a walk, his bottom and spine were soon railing against the ache. So he was nervous, because knew he had a long journey ahead of him.

He was nervous, too, about the company he was keeping. Ambassador Sifang was not known for his easy-going nature or merciful tendencies. He was strict, by the book, and unforgiving as winter. He was the epitome of the politician, Moshi supposed, glancing the man's way anxiously. Lantang Sifang was riding beside him, pointedly ignoring him. Being far richer, more influential and generally higher up in the indecipherable echelons of Quing Tzu society, Sifang had every right to ignore those beneath his station – such as Moshi and everybody else on the mission.

Moshi was glad the ambassador was oblivious to him, in fact; it was better than speaking to the pompous buffoon. Every time the fool opened his mouth, it was to make a demand or sound an insult, or more likely both. Then, Moshi would have to grovel and nod and obsequiously get on with whatever infuriatingly nonsensical task he was assigned, like preparing the man's tea in the evening. Moshi wanted to throw the steaming hot tea in the man's face every night, but instead he bowed and gently poured it from the kettle into the little china cup the ambassador had brought along.

Being higher on the pecking list had its advantages, Moshi had to admit – like being able to make or break a simple Wizard in your employ. Moshi did not technically work for the ambassador, but when a first minister made a request of the Chi Academy, the Academy endeavoured to fulfil that request and impressed upon the Wizard it sent to do so that he would be excommunicated if he failed. So, for all intents and purposes, Moshi worked for Sifang.

If he failed here, his life as he knew it would be over. He

would be cast out of the Academy, his staff would be taken from him, and he would be tossed into the gutters. With the shame that would come with such an expulsion, it would be unlikely his family would take him in. They would not want their reputations tarnished. He would be ruined. He had been unable to say no to the mission, of course. One did not say no to the Academy; that would have been social suicide just as surely as failing would. Moshi smiled to himself nervously; he was damned if he did and damned if he didn't. The only way to continue living in comfort and retain his own and his family's honour was to succeed in this mission, to venture out into the wilds of Chimanchu and return. So, that was what he would do.

Lantang Sifang was a flower in that wasteland, draped in his finest, most colourful silks, purple and pink and rose from head to toe. His gauzy hat covered a bald head that looked too large for his bony body; a beak for a nose only added to his comically birdlike appearance. His eyes were squinty from counting numbers and reading ledgers all his life. In contrast, Moshi looked like a duck beside a swan, garbed in the simplest, and itchiest, of woollen brown robes and leather sandals. The wool was thin, but it chafed like fire and felt as hot under the sun, too.

That was another thing he was nervous about; the weather. It was said that Chimanchu was cold, and Moshi hated the cold. So far, it had not yet seeped into his bones, but he thought he could feel the temperature dipping further every night the further south they travelled. He subtly used spells to warm himself and prayed the thirty soldiers with whom he and the ambassador travelled did not know he could do so, lest they ask him to do the same for them.

The main causes for his fraying nerves, however, were Pai and the man to whom they were delivering her. Moshi turned to regard the Pai Tse, whom he had taken to calling Pai. She was a wondrous creature, which most believed to be entirely mythical. Pai Tse were the stuff of legends, or at least had been thought extinct for many hundreds of years. Then, the minister had found rumour of one and sent Moshi to capture it.

Moshi remembered the days of searching for her amid the swamps in the east, the heat and the mosquitos. He remembered the battle with the beast, remembered her deadly way with water. She had lashed the ship with supernatural waves and flayed the crew with stinking waterspouts, drenching them and killing more than one brave man. He remembered using a ghostly hand of mist to hoist the creature up out of the white marshes, separating her from her beloved home and weakening her. He remembered how she had writhed in dismay and how she had almost capsized the ship in her fury, able to control the bog even while she was in the air. Such innate powers of mastery of the water had stunned Moshi; he had thought he was going to die that day.

Fortunately for him, he had been able to read the beast's mind and understand her urges quickly. Moshi had always had a quick mind and found it easy to empathise with anyone and anything. He had sensed the creature's thought patterns and had understood how she manipulated the pools. Then, feeling like a torturer, like a cruel and vindictive master of evil, he had forcibly dampened the Pai Tse's mind, her energies, with his own, blanketing it with power and subduing it like holding a pillow over its face. He had not destroyed the mind, though; only dulled it to dim-wittedness, so that the legendary creature could no longer access her inherent powers. He had numbed her to the point that she could not think at all.

He hated himself for that. He felt like he had degraded and was constantly degrading this ancient, noble creature. He had to focus his energies on dampening her spirit with every waking moment, only snatching quick naps when she herself fell asleep lest she regain her powers. The idea of that made him nervous, too; so nervous he could barely catch a wink even when the opportunity presented itself.

Pai looked almost peaceful in her huge water tank on the back of the special-made flat-back wagon. She looked like a salamander, only on a far greater scale. Her wedge-shaped head was facing him, her tiny black eyes judging him. Her mottled orange-and-blue skin, bumpy with nodes, shone healthily under the sun's glow, but he knew she had no will to move, or to live. She lay still; her four stumpy legs did not so much as twitch. Her long tail, which could once have killed a man, now did not swish in the slightest. He shook his head sadly; a twenty-foot-long monster reduced to a prisoner, a plaything, a pawn in a game.

They had lashed the tank down with about a hundred straps, but it still jostled precariously as the wagon rumbled down the rutted dirt road. Gone were the paved roads of civilisation; they were entering the Badlands now. Moshi wondered if Pai could even survive out here; there was little water away from the river they were following.

Moshi thought anxiously of the man to whom they were delivering Pai: Nebaatar Khan, the most powerful clan chief in all of Chimanchu – or so he claimed. He claimed to have conquered and amalgamated half a dozen clans into his own; he claimed to rule more than a thousand men. Moshi doubted it; these chiefs were given to hyperbole, and he thought it unlikely from history's evidence that a thousand of them could be in the same place without starting a war with one another. Still, he believed that the man was not to be crossed, especially out here in his own home.

The first minister, Hong Maoa, had apparently been in contact with this Khan and – upon hearing rumour of its existence – had agreed to send him the legendary Pai Tse as a gesture of friendship, so that Quing Tzu and Chimanchu could improve their centuries-long hostile relationship. It had seemed like a noble mission when Minister Haoa had explained it to him, but now Moshi had a sour taste on his tongue and he was beginning to feel like the epitome of the evil Wizard the common people so feared. He felt like he had been used for politics, and he felt soiled by the experience. He would finish this mission, he decided, and then go somewhere far away. He would become a hermit in the mountains, perhaps; he would not be used again. For the sake of his own sanity, he would not be used again.

He mouthed to Pai, "I'm sorry."

Moshi, Pai, Ambassador Sifang and their entourage followed the Silver River south, tracking its meandering course through barren plains that gave way to scrubland. When the scrubland reluctantly abdicated the land in favour of grassland, Moshi was shocked. A single blade of grass was more than he had thought to find growing down here, however one day he could not see but for green fields. Chimanchu was more verdant than he had ever dreamed possible, it seemed. He wondered why he had not known; all the stories painted the infamous Badlands as a dusty waste, and yet now he saw the land was much the same as parts of Quing Tzu.

A few days out from Yuguanji, however, the promised cold did indeed materialise. Moshi awoke one morning shivering in his blankets, and the climate only worsened after that. Soon, spending a night out under the stars in Chimanchu seemed equivalent to spending a night in the Nether. Every night, Moshi went to sleep shaking with the chill, and every morning he awoke with it in his bones. Sleeping on the icy, rock-hard ground did not help; it was so hard-packed in fact that Moshi wondered that any grass could grow at all, forcing its way up through the unwelcoming clay. It was a symbol of the tenacity of life that the flora had found a way, marvelled Moshi.

After following the Silver River south for more than a week, deeper and deeper into Chimanchu, Moshi was slack-jawed one morning to see a little woodland rearing its hoary head in the distance. Nobody had told him forests grew down here!

As they neared it, all that day, Moshi kept thinking he must be seeing a mirage, hallucinating from sleep deprivation. When sunset came and they were standing in the shadows of birches and poplars, however, Moshi could not doubt his eyes any longer. He reached out to touch a tree in a daze, staring at it like a child at its first sight of snow. Chimanchu was not exactly how he had imagined.

"We'll stop here for the night!" Ambassador Sifang drawled when they reached the woods. "Set up camp!"

The ambassador had a large and exquisitely made tent of animal hide in which to bed down, while Moshi – being a simple Wizard and therefore living a monastic life – had no tent to his name nor money to buy one. He had imagined the ambassador would provide him a tent when he had set out from Yuguanji, but he had quickly been proven wrong. So, he learned to love the hard ground – or he tried to at any rate.

Sifang waved Moshi over once the camp was established, and the Wizard grudgingly put down one of his two books and moseyed over to sit next to the ambassador by the fire.

"Wizard! How is the Pai Tse?" Lantang Sifang asked, seeming like he could not care less about the answer.

"She is … well," answered Moshi. "As well as she can be in such circumstances."

"Seems like you're doing a fine job keeping her senseless, a fine job!"

Moshi bowed his head. "Thank you, Ambassador. I do my best to please."

"Indeed you do, indeed you do." Sifang seemed to forget Moshi was there then; he pulled out his pipe, stuffed some baui in the bowl, lit it and puffed until smoke swam around him like little white tadpoles.

"If I may, ambassador, how much longer will we be on the

road before we reach our destination?"

"Damn you, man!" burst out Sifang, spouting billows of smoke. "You're like a nagging old wife with your questions! Didn't I tell you we'd be there in a few days? We follow the river south, and then – when it veers east sharply – we are to keep going south until we find some old ruins. Didn't I tell you?"

"No, Ambassador, you declined to share that information. You only told me at Yuguanji that it would take 'a few weeks.'"

Sifang narrowed his eyes at Moshi. "Watch your tongue, Wizard. If I didn't know any better, I'd think that was insouciance in your tone! You don't want Minister Maoa to send anything less than a glowing report back to the Academy, do you?"

Moshi throttled the urge to throttle the man. "No, Ambassador."

"No ... I thought not!" he sneered derisively. "You Wizards think you're so big and powerful, but when it comes down to it you're just children compared to those of us with real power, aren't you? Do you know what *real* power is, Wizard? *Real* power is the ability to kill a man with a word. *Real* power is the ability to take what you want with a coin. *Real* power is the ability to influence the lives of thousands of other men and women, to influence a whole nation! *That* is real power, *Wizard,* and it is something that I have and you *do not!"*

Moshi imagined setting the man on fire, or boiling him in acid. "As you say, Ambassador."

"That's why these savages down south will never have any *real* power," Sifang continued, puffing on his pipe and staring into the flames. "Because they can never agree on anything, they can never accomplish anything. No one man among them is strong or clever enough to unite them." He shook his head. "Idiots."

Moshi frowned. "D'you know that if such a man existed – if one man ever did unite all the clans, all the thousands upon thousands – it is likely he could topple the Empire within a year? Those are the Academy's best estimates. One year. That's all it would take these *savages* to destroy Quing Tzu."

Sifang waved a languid, uncaring hand. "Well, thank the Gods they can't agree on anything then. Otherwise we'd really be in trouble, eh?" His tone was snide.

"You don't believe me?" Moshi said. "There are hundreds of

thousands of warriors down here, men and women both, warriors born. They can ride a horse from the age of five and shoot a bow from the age of seven and shoot a bow while riding a horse by the age of ten. They are some of the toughest people in the world, it is said. They have their own culture and their own language – did you know they don't even call this land Chimanchu?"

"Who cares what they call it?" drawled Sifang. "They are savages. They can call it what they please. We know it is Chimanchu."

"Devoid of life," Moshi translated the name roughly into Oracle Bone Script, the language found preserved on ancient oracle bones.

Just before dawn the next day, Chimanchu struck out at those infiltrating its borders. In the grey light of pre-dawn, horsemen burst, ululating, from the woodland, waving curved cavalry sabres. Moshi, who had been snoozing fitfully while he had the chance, woke to see fifty riders tearing toward the camp from the treeline. Some started shooting arrows, and hollering Tzunese soldiers began hitting the ground, shafts stuck in their flesh.

Sleep-fuddled, Moshi grabbed his short, straight ash staff, pointed it at them and shouted, *"Tikleytomtaum!"*

A hundred little shards of ice burst from the tip of his glowing staff, which bucked in his grip. The tiny icicles whistled through the air, too fast to follow, but their effect on the horsemen was noticeable. The front row of riders went down in a great, bloody spray as the little shards tore into both horses and men, shredding them to ribbons. The horsemen wore simple leather armour, which provided scant protection against the sorcerous shards. Not all died, however; some were left with ice stuck in them, paralysed on the ground. Their screams mingled with the horses'. As the riders behind the front line cleared those that had fallen in great bounds and came on at the camp, Moshi saw that they had the tell-tale sabres and hard, flat faces of Chimanchis. Bandits, perhaps. They were golden-skinned and black-haired like the Tzunese, but their eyes were flatter, less slanted, and their complexion tended to be slightly darker.

Waking fully and remembering where he was and his mission, Moshi cursed himself for a fool then. He should not have cast that spell; he should have been focussing his energies on containing the Pai Tse as was his duty. He turned his eyes and his will on Pai, but he saw that he was already too late. She was awake, and she was aware.

Having turned away from the Chimanchi horsemen, Moshi did not see them hit the camp like a hammer, rampaging through it and cutting Tzunese soldiers down left and right as they scuttled to grab their gear. What he did see was waterspouts form in an instant inside the water tank; growing in strength, they shattered the heavy glass lid in a second and towered up into the air like watery tornadoes. Pai, who had directed the liquid up with a bob of her head, now turned her tiny black eyes on the soldiers who had caged her for so long. Moshi was trying desperately to overpower her mind again, but she seemed to have grown smarter since their last battle. She had adapted, formed a rudimentary shield for her mind, and she was consciously blocking him, battling him for control. He started to sweat. He could get no hold; it was like scrabbling for a handhold on a sheer ice cliff. He could not stop her.

"No, Pai!" he whispered.

The Chimanchis were turning the camp into a slaughterhouse from the east and the waterspouts were rearing high to the west. The Tzunese men were caught in between them, between killers and a watery grave. Most did not even realise the peril at their backs, since they were focussed entirely on the enemy riders. The clash of steel on steel echoed out over the grass hills, and the river was stained red with blood. The Chimanchis were vicious, merciless, and they gave no quarter. The Tzunese were caught unprepared and were being culled like sheep by wolves in their own camp, trampled or ridden down and spitted on blades.

Then, the Pai Tze struck from behind and more men died. Five waterspouts – like giant blue fingers – reached out from the water tank and extended across the camp horizontally, swirling in a tight column and arrogantly defying the laws of physics. Speeding up as they went, the fingers lashed out at the backs of the nearest soldiers, throwing some yards through the air and catching others within the watery funnels and spinning them until they ran out of air. Those that had been tossed across the camp were soon trampled under the Chimanchi horses' hooves.

"Stop, Pai!"

The waterspouts flailed again and again, slapping soldiers this way and that or ensnaring them in a watery web to be drowned. Moshi noticed that not once did the waterspouts touch the

Chimanchis. They tried to get him, but Moshi summoned a magical, translucent barrier, forming a glimmering, green sphere all around him that protected him on all sides. He breathed a sigh of relief when it proved impenetrable to the deadly water; he did not even get wet.

Seeing the last few Tzunese survivors knot together around Ambassador Sifang out of the corner of his eye, Moshi refocussed his energies on dampening Pai's power, digging his psychic fingers into her mental wall and trying to prise it apart. He thought he could vaguely hear Sifang screaming at him – something about helping out and doing his job. He gritted his teeth; he was trying, but it was far from easy.

Now, the ambassador was shrieking for someone to just kill the creature, but it was too late. Moshi would not do that to the noble animal, and the soldiers could not risk attacking it now without turning their backs on the circling horsemen. A few of the Chimanchis lashed out at Moshi, but their blades bounced off his shining green shield, unable to pierce it. So, they left him alone and prowled around the survivors like a pack of wolves around a stag.

Moshi saw the soldiers' and ambassadors' end only in glimpses. From the corner of his eye, he saw them fall one by one in a scarlet haze, hacked to pieces bit by bit by the horsemen. Pai helped until she saw that her watery tentacles were only impeding the riders, at which point she retracted her watery limbs and thus refilled her tank. From there, she began to lift herself up out of the tank in which she had been kept captive, slowly pushing herself up with the help of the water. The Chimanchis, meanwhile, rode past the survivors again and again on all sides, flicking out their blades to score dozens of shallow cuts on every side of every soldier until the Tzunese men were on their knees, begging for a deeper cut, begging for death. The Chimanchis gave it to them heartlessly, spearing them through the lungs or beheading them where they knelt.

Then, the Chimanchis converged on Moshi, just as Pai was reaching the top of her tank. Moshi ignored the horsemen as their blades began to batter on his glowing jade aegis by the dozen, but each and every strike drained him a little more and he began to feel weak. His knees knocked together, his breath rasped in his throat, and sweat trickled down his face. He focussed the vestiges of his energy on a brute-force assault on Pai's mind, much as he hated to do it. He dug his fingers into her mental wall until he gouged out shallow holds with which to ply her, though it pained him to do so. Feeling like his skull was going to tear in twain with the effort, he finally ripped through Pai's wall and had access to her mind once more. His first instinct was to dampen her like before, but then he realised that he knew how she had manipulated the water in the tank. More than that; he could make her do it again.

Feeling every inch the evil Wizard, he wrenched her mind and forced Pai to follow his will. He commanded her to form waterspouts again and she did so, falling back down into the tank, though he could feel her trying to resist. It was too late now, though; he had hold of her mind, and he was not about to let her slip through his fingers. The pillars of water reformed, and the Chimanchis cried out in alarm. Moshi commanded the re-imprisoned Pai, and she directed her waterspouts at the riders, sweeping them out of their saddles, throwing them around, drowning them, crushing them, killing them all in moments.

Mere minutes after the skirmish had begun, Moshi was alone beside the woods with only Pai for company, surrounded on all sides by wet, bloody corpses. The Chimanchis, he noticed, were adorned with tattoos of spiders on their forearms. He let his shield fall and dampened Pai's mind then, suffocating her powers lest she try any more of her tricks. Then, spotting two horses fleeing into the distance, he used his energies to ease the beasts' panic, turn them and bring them back to him. They were well-lathered by the time they returned, but they had calmed.

The Chimanchis had slain most of the Tzunese horses, including the four that had pulled the massive wagon bearing the water tank. So, Moshi cut the dead horses free of their traces and hitched the two surviving mounts to the wagon. This was not easy, for the pervasive reek of death and blood constantly spooked the horses. Moshi had to use his power to calm them time and again, while also keeping Pai dulled.

Eventually, he managed it and then he took up the reins and cracked the dead drivers' whip over the horses' heads to get them moving. It was slow going, for the wagon was heavy, but the horses were able to get the wheels rolling. Moshi let them go slow, knowing the great burden they were dragging. He pointed them south and followed the winding river.

When the river veered east, he left it behind and continued

south. After another two weeks' lonely travel, Moshi made it to the ruins Ambassador Sifang had spoken of. The ancient, crumbling keep poked up out of a hilltop like a beige wart on the green landscape, an unwelcome stony crust. Ruins was the right word for it, Moshi saw; there was not a single building or wall left intact, only fragments of the past laid bare.

Amid the decrepit remains of the age-old keep, a Chimanchi clan awaited the Wizard. They too were garbed in leather, and they too stared at him with narrow, flat eyes. They too had black hair, and they too had tattoos of spiders on their forearms. Moshi approached them calmly, trundling the wagon into their midst amid gasps and murmurs of awe.

"Where is Nebaatar Khan?" asked Moshi loudly in Traveller's Tongue, pulling on the reins to halt the horses. "I have a present for him from Minister Maoa."

The men of the Hashimaji clan – or *Spider* clan in an ancient Chimanchi dialect – shuffled and turned to look as one at a particular man in their midst, a monster of a man. The man – Nebaatar Khan, Moshi presumed – was almost a head taller than any other in the clan and was muscled to the point of obscenity. He wore no leather armour, nor a top of any sort; Moshi suspected one would not fit over his massive shoulders and barrel chest. He had a bushy black beard trimmed into an arrow, and angular cheekbones gave his whole face a similar cast. His black hair was tied back in a long ponytail, and he stared at Moshi with angry, dark eyes from beneath low, heavy brows like storm clouds. His face and torso were scarred and pitted from combat and hardship; it was clear he had been through a great deal.

"So, you made it," he said in the same language, voice like a bear's growl. "And you brought the beast. I wasn't sure any of you soft northerners would get this far in one piece. I am Nebaatar Khan. Who are you?"

"I have come to decide I do not like Chimanchu," replied Moshi. "It is far too violent a place."

Nebaatar frowned. "Chimanchu is *your* word for this place. We here call this great country *Ogbun Nagali, Land of the Nagali*, and we do not call ourselves Chimanchis. We are the *Nagali.*"

Moshi stared at him. "Chimanchi, *Nagali,* it makes little difference. There were thirty-two of us when we left Yuguanji. Most of us did not make it here in one piece."

"Ah well," said Nebaatar Khan, carelessly waving a hand, "it's a dangerous world out there, you know."

"Indeed it is," Moshi agreed, nodding. "I wonder what the Emperor would say if he knew his loyal subjects had been murdered on the road?"

"The Emperor?" The Khan looked genuinely surprised, then barked a laugh. "Maoa said the Emperor didn't know anything about this little arrangement! So why would he care?"

Moshi was stumped for a moment, before the pieces of the puzzle clicked into place. Hong Maoa had been trying to befriend the Spider clan without the Emperor's knowledge or consent; Maoa had likely been thinking of somehow using the Chimanchis against the Emperor in a coup. It was just the sort of sordid thinking in which first ministers indulged – never mind the peril to the country; just let the Chimanchis in and pray they gave you what you wanted. Moshi gave a bitter bark of laughter himself then, surprising Nebaatar again.

"Why do you laugh?" asked the Khan.

"It's nothing," said Moshi. "I just figured something out, that's all. Let me rephrase my earlier question then: I wonder what Minister Maoa would say if *he* knew *his* loyal subjects had been murdered on the road?" Nebaatar did his best to look nonplussed. "Murdered by the very man he called friend."

Moshi took something out of his pocket and threw it at the Khan; it did not reach the other man, but fluttered to the ground at his feet. Nebaatar bent and picked it up, his eyes going wide. It was a scrap of skin that Moshi had cut off a man's forearm back at the forest after the skirmish, a piece of one of the dead Chimanchis. On it a spider was tattooed in black ink.

Realising the jig was up, Nebaatar Khan bellowed, "Kill him!"

It was too late, though, far too late. Moshi had released his dampening hold on Pai as soon as he had trundled to a stop.

Now, the Pai Tze created waterspouts once more. Hearing their howl, Moshi cloaked himself in a luminescent green shield and was therefore kept safe when they descended upon him in full wrath. Again, he did not even get wet. In her fury at being unable to take her revenge on the man who had singlehandedly imprisoned her, Pai turned her rage instead on the other men nearby. Her waterspouts soared up from the tank to tower in the sky, and then they dove down on the Hashimaji clan like localised storms, each spout sweeping up multiple men and churning them around and tossing them away through the air to fly for yards before landing in a crumpled heap. Nebaatar Khan himself was lifted some twenty or thirty feet into the air by a watery tentacle and then hurled even higher. He made quite the splatter when he hit the ground; Moshi averted his eyes from the spectacle, but saw the expansive bloodstain on the floor when he looked back.

Then, Pai hit the green shield herself, slamming her body down on it, and Moshi jumped in shock. He had not even noticed her escaping the tank, but she had and now she was pawing and biting at the jade bubble in which he was encapsulated, trying to get at him, to kill him for what he had done to her. He could sense her anger; he understood.

He mouthed to her again, "I'm sorry. But you're free now. Go. Be free!"

An arrow lanced into her rump; she had left some of the Hashimajis alive. Pai turned away from Moshi with a bestial roar and nodded towards the remaining men. Her forgotten foaming waterspouts reformed in an instant and butchered the last men like a blade on a chopping block, smashing down again and again until they were all broken or drowned. Moshi watched her; she was merciless in her fury. No one escaped; no one could outrun soaring water. Soon, all was still, all was quiet.

Pai turned her beady black eyes on Moshi again, who stared back at her through his translucent, glowing green shield. The Pai Tze was speckled in blood alongside her natural orange and blue hues. She raised a paw as if to approach him, but then turned away and waddled over to the river. She looked back one last time before she submerged and was lost to sight. Moshi watched until she was gone and then watched a while longer, feeling an unexpected sense of loss.

"Goodbye, Pai," he said.

A few months later, Minister Maoa returned to his home in Xi'Ping after a hard day's treachery to find Moshi sitting in his lounge, awaiting him. It was not the same Moshi that Maoa remembered, however. This was a different Moshi; a bearded Moshi, a tougher Moshi with crueller eyes.

Maoa gaped and gasped like a landed fish. "What are you doing here?" he spluttered. "I'll have you arrested! Get out at once, I say!"

"It is you who are under arrest, Minister Maoa," replied Moshi, "for the crime of high treason. Many good men died because of you."

Armoured soldiers smashed down the door behind Hong Maoa, clanked into his home and seized him by the arms. Then, they dragged him away to the dungeons while he wailed over and over, "No! No! No! I was going to be Emperor! No!"

The Emperor thanked Moshi for his service and offered him any reward he chose. Moshi declined any reward and vanished from social circles, never to be seen in Xi'Ping again. Some said he went south in search of a mythical beast living in the Silver River ...

Were-jackals

"My arse is sore," grumbled Daff Gamor.

He had been riding for three days straight, and there were another six or seven days of riding to look forward to. He was growing to loathe his pony; one of a particularly small species bred by the Dwarves for their own use. The poor beast was only doing as it was told, he knew, but he was growing sick of the sight of its black mane and grey-and-white dusted coat. The fiery face in the sky was nestling on the pillow of the horizon now, and shadows were creeping across the grasslands from the hills to the west. His arse had been sore since that morning – not that he wished to be walking. That would be just as bad. No, Daff would rather he was lying down in one of the wagons, sleeping amid the cargo.

He said as much to his friend, Chirri, who chuckled and replied, "Wouldn't be very comfortable lying on top of that lot, but I know what you mean. My legs are aching something fierce."

Daff and his fellow Dwarves were taking a shipment of metals across Shimyahein from the dwarvic city of Dwarrafug to the human capital, Eshimbranir. Shimyahein was one big, relatively flat savannah, so the journey promised to be an easy one, if tedious. It was one he had made many times before in his long tenure as a dwarvic emissary working for His Illustrious Majesty, the King of Dwarrafug, Albèr Olfonsso. He had visited Eshimbranir and its Glorious Emperor, Hadagosk the Third, numerous times, too, and so he was well-accustomed to the titles both rulers enjoyed the most. He also knew, from his interactions with humans on the road, of the surrounding countries' opinions of Shimyahein; that it was scarcely a country at all, more an empty expanse of grassland around which a few nomads enjoyed riding their horses.

Daff sighed. "Why do we do this, Chirri? Why do we do it? Why do we ride across Shimyahein day after Gods-damned day? Ferrying bloody metals and spices back and forth, back and forth between that dung-heap, Eshimbranir, and our lovely little hole in the ground. Why do we bloody bother?"

"We carry more than just spices back," returned Chirri, cheerful as ever. "We provide a vital service to our people, exchanging our wealth of metals for a wealth of foods, spices and fabrics. Unlike our cousins, we have learned to thrive on cooperation with the humans, Handaff. You ought to get on board."

"I am on board!" Daff mumbled, irked by the use of his full name. No one used his full name; no one but his mother, who had passed away earlier that year while he had been away. "I've been doing this for some fifty odd years, by the Gods! I'm just achy is all."

At ninety years of age, he thought he had earned the right to be achy. Dwarves lived to be more more than two hundred years old regularly, but ninety was still a respectable age, he thought – or it should have been. Chirri and the others, youths whose balls had barely dropped, nominally his bodyguards, barely paid him any heed. Chirri's eyes were full of the romantic naiveté of youth, Daff could see it, and it made him sick.

He had no one else to whinge to, though, and there was little else to do on such a journey. "Gods-damned pony is sending my arse all to sleep!"

Chirri chortled. "Why did you get into this line of work, if you don't mind my asking, Daff? All you do is complain about it!"

"That's my right as a Dwarf," Daff replied. "And I'll tell ya. I got into this mess, because I got married and had kids. After a few months of that, I just had to get out of the house more often. Ten hours a day down the mines wasn't cutting it, so I took to the road so as to have weeks of peace at a time. Then, you little snot-noses came along and ruined the tranquillity!"

Chirri burst out laughing at the sour look on Daff's face, which only soured his expression further.

A league later, as the road wound under the shadow of the vivacious, green woodland to the east, Daff muttered, "Gods-damned Eshimbranir! Rancid horsemen – all they do is stink up the place! Reeking of leather and horse sweat. Ugh. The whole place is one big shanty town full of pestilence and people who smell like shit! Some capital!"

Chirri was covering his mouth to keep from laughing out loud, but his shoulders were shaking.

"Last bloody place I want to visit," Daff continued, oblivious. "And it's where they send me every Gods-damned time! Andhrun must be sitting down there in the First Forge in the middle of the world laughing his bloody head off at me running around up here!"

Chirri let out peals of mirth at the thought of the God of the

Dwarves watching Daff ride around the country in cruel amusement. Daff almost smiled himself, but turned it into a frown.

"We do visit other places, as you well know, *vaunted emissary,*" Chirri said when his laughter had abated, adding a mocking emphasis to Daff's title.

Daff bridled. "You watch your tongue, you young whippersnapper! Or I'll … cut off your balls and feed 'em to a frog!"

Chirri snorted. "We went to Dwarhummer just a few months ago," he pointed out.

"Yes," Daff agreed ruminatively, stroking his long, grey beard. "Some welcome we got there, eh? They're a bunch of miserable bastards down there."

Chirri grinned. "There's no place good enough for you, is there, Daff?"

Daff held his head high, haughtily, for a moment. "Well, some of us are just too good for this world, I suppose."

Chirri snorted. "Yeah, right. Ever think that you might be the miserable –?"

"Watch your tongue, you little pest!"

Chirri smiled and shook his head, adjusting his own ochre beard, which was rubbing at his neck. Dusk had settled over the landscape now, inking it in mystery, and they felt the chill more in the forest's penumbra. Daff felt a shiver run down his spine as he eyed the shadowy woodland and shifted in his saddle uncomfortably before hawking and spitting on the ground.

"I hate trees," Daff announced not long later, still regarding the trees suspiciously.

Chirri laughed. "There's a shock!"

"Gods-damned forests. Could be anything hiding in there. Still, I can barely see my prick to take a piss, so I guess we'll have to make camp here for the night."

Chirri chuckled. "I guess so."

"Give the call then."

"Company halt!"

The six wagons rolled to a halt by the woods, and the score of armed men – Chirri included – pulled back on the reins of their snickering ponies, all stopping in perfect formation around the wagons. Daff almost smiled again, but scowled instead. He had trained them well. Each wore armour made from the bones of the subterranean eyeless creatures known as Rodici, whom the Dwarves kept as pets, of a sort. Each carried a steel axe and a dagger, too. Banditry was rife in Shimyahein. There were few laws, foremost among the few being that you only owned what you could hold on to. Daff put a hand on the haft of his own axe as his dismounted to ensure he didn't accidentally cut either himself or his horse. Unlike the others, he wore only a linen tunic and baggy pantaloons, having eschewed the armour's protection in favour of comfort.

"Why don't you give your pony a name?" asked Chirri as he jumped off his pony far more elegantly than Daff. "A pony should have a name, I think – something to complement its personality and solidify a bond between you."

"A pony does not need a name," Daff said, not even looking around as he stroked his mount. "His name is pony. That is what he is. That is what I call him. He is a good pony, as ponies go, but no more than that. When you have had several ponies, named them, fed them, reared them and watched them die, you lose interest in the naming. What is the point?"

Chirri shook his head in bemusement. "What is the point of marriage? Your spouse will likely die at some point, too. That does not mean the connection you make isn't worthwhile."

"Doesn't it?" returned Daff. "My wife's not even dead yet, and I can barely remember *her* name."

Chirri shook his head again, but his smile crept back.

The Dwarves built a fire by the side of the road – the opposite side from the forest, Daff insisted. They started cooking a couple of rabbits and a grouse that had been brought down by bow earlier that day. The smell made Daff drool like a hungry dog, and he had to keep wiping his lips. He took out his pipe, stuffed some baui into the bowl and lit it with a leaf-taper. He puffed on it until a goodly amount of smoke wreathed him like a mystical aura.

Then, he spoke, his voice deep and smooth and measured, lilting in the fashion of storytellers everywhere. "Did you ever hear the tale of the monsters of the woods of Shimyahein?"

Chirri and a number of others looked around to bestow their gazes on him at that.

"No," said Chirri.

"Well then, let me fill in this most egregious gap in your knowledge," said Daff. "Ahem. Legend tells of a breed of creatures so ancient and so evil that their name was forever spoken in a hushed whisper. More than a breed of creature. Legend tells of an infection – an illness that can be spread from person to person through the ingestion of tainted blood. These creatures were said to be human once, long ago – human Sorcerers who dabbled in magics too dark even for their black souls. It is said that these humans sold their souls in exchange for bestial power, but that they were tricked. They did not consciously get the power they sought, but they did get it *unconsciously.*"

He gestured up at the full moon rising in the sky, a silver coin flipping in the void. "Every month, at the time of the full moon, these human Sorcerers would transform in their sleep into monstrous beasts with no knowledge of the person they had once been. These beasts rampaged throughout the towns and villages where the Sorcerers lived, slaying and eating those closest to them. Then, when the full moon was gone and the sun had risen again, the Sorcerers would transform back into men. Upon seeing what they had done, many took their own lives with their dark arts on the spot. Those that did not wander Maradoum to this day, forever cursed, undying ... Unable to die, unable to take back what they have done, they seek only to spread their horrific blight in their spite. You know, of course, of whom I speak." He dropped his voice to a dramatic whisper. *"The were-jackals!"*

Silence roamed the camp for a moment, towering over them all like a spectre.

Then, Chirri chortled. "Full of old fishwives' tales, aren't you, Daff?"

Everybody laughed, and the spell of storytelling was broken.

Daff scowled. "T'aint an old fishwives' tale! That's a Shimmish legend, that is! I heard it from the stinky bastards over at Eshimbranir."

"Sure," said Chirri cheerfully, condescendingly, "and I suppose you believe in Mermaids, too? Haha!"

"As a matter of fact, I do," Daff mumbled, crossing his arms. "What's so funny about that? They're real, they are! That's why I'm never going near the ocean, not me."

This redoubled everyone's mirth, and they fell about laughing. One Dwarf almost rolled into the fire and had to be pulled back by his comrades, who then patted out the flames in his beard and chortled at the sight of his singed eyebrows.

The sound of a scuffle down the road made them all fall silent and spin to look out into the blackness, their eyes stifled from looking into the flames. First one human man appeared in the firelight, then two women followed him and all three stood in sight with empty hands raised, facing the Dwarves.

"Please," said the man in a pitiful, warbling voice, "will you help us? We were robbed by bandits on the road, and we have no provisions – no way to survive! Please, help us!"

Daff studied them. They certainly looked like they had been robbed. They were a mess, dirty and a little bloody, gaunt and ill-looking. Their clothes were in tatters, and they obviously hadn't seen a comb for a while. The man had black hair and a beard matted with dirt. One woman was skinny as a rake with short blonde hair; the other was more robustly built with long blood-red locks.

"Where were you going?" Daff asked.

"We were on our way to Harrow's Brook when we were waylaid," the man explained, wringing his hands. "They took everything, and … and they killed a number of us, my wife among them …"

Daff nodded slowly. Harrow's Brook was along this road; he had passed it many times. "Why were you going there?"

"I am a merchant," said the man, unable to keep from eyeing their food hungrily. "I was on my way to trade a few odds and ends." Daff raised his bushy grey eyebrows. "Leathers and furs mostly. Not much. I'm not a very *good* merchant." He smiled weakly.

Daff thought about it a moment longer, while the other Dwarves awaited his verdict.

"Oh, let them come over," said Chirri. "They look like they could use a fire right now."

Daff glowered at him and kept deliberating. Eventually, though, he waved the man and women over.

"Come," he said. "Join us. Sit by our fire. Eat with us. Be welcome, friends. But know this – if you seek to rob *us*, I will be forced to make you eat your own tongue, got it?"

The man gulped, nodded and beckoned his comrades. The Dwarves shuffled closer together. Nervously, the humans approached the fire and sat on the opposite side of it from the Dwarves.

"We understand," the man said, gesturing at the food on the

spit. "Smells good."

"It'll be ready in a while. I sure hope it's good," rumbled Daff. "Chirri here is a notoriously dreadful cook. Even worse than my wife – and that's saying something!"

Chirri punched the emissary on the shoulder, and Daff glowered at him. "How dare you, you – you – you young scallywag!"

Chirri grinned.

"So," said Daff, turning back to the strangers, "what's your name, friend?"

"I'm Blodnut Shearer," said the man. Daff nodded; it was a common name among the humans in Shimyahein, he knew, taken by those who excelled at sheep-shearing. "This is … was … my wife's friend and the wife of my friend. Both my wife and her husband perished in the attack. Her name is Cliassa."

Daff nodded to the blonde woman, whilst refilling his pipe. "Nice to meet you both."

Blodnut turned to the red-haired woman. "This is Roberta, a friend of the family. She too suffered losses in the attack."

"It's a pleasure, Roberta," said Daff, bowing his hoary head. The woman did not reply, barely met his gaze.

"And what is your name, Dwarf? I would know whom to thank for this welcome hospitality," said Cliassa, her voice soft, diminutive.

"I go by Daff, my lady." He lit his pipe and puffed smoke.

"Oh, I am no lady," she squeaked, "but thank you for the kind words. I mean no offence, my new friend, but it is rare to see your kind wandering the countryside. Do you mind if I ask where you and your caravan are bound?"

Daff eyed her for a moment. "I do mind, I am afraid, my lady. That is our business. Now, if *you* do not mind *me* asking, where are you all from?"

"We're from Ramhorn," said the man with the dirty black beard. "It's a village down south, if you've not heard of it."

"I've heard of it," Daff assured him, blowing blue-white plumes. "I'm sorry to hear about your wife, by the way. Did you lose many in the attack?"

"Yes, unfortunately," said the man, lowering his head. "When we left Ramhorn, we were a company of thirteen."

"How long ago did the attack happen?"

"Two days ago. We've been foraging berries and nuts for the

most part. We haven't been making very good time."

"And you say bandits attacked you?" asked Daff. "Human bandits?"

"Why – did you think it might have been the were-jackals?" Chirri said, chortling.

Daff glared daggers at the younger dwarf, said, "Shut up!" and then turned back to the humans. "Sorry about him. So, was it human bandits?"

Blodnut nodded. "Yes, yes, it was. Damn them to the Nether, how could they do that to their own people?"

Daff nodded; he had seen it many times on the road. "Damn them indeed," he agreed, drawing on his pipe and then coughing and spluttering and quickly wiping the spittle from his lips. "Ahem. Damn them indeed."

Chirri dished out the food on makeshift bark plates hacked from nearby trees when the meat was cooked. Since they had extra mouths to feed, there was little to go around and all ate what they had with relish. Daff burned his mouth on the hot meat, complained about it loudly, and then kept eating and complained about it again.

Chirri involuntarily spat a mouthful of meat into the fire as he burst out laughing, but then he frowned at the older Dwarf. "Damn it, Daff! Now, look what you've made me do! I've gone and spat out half my bloody dinner!"

The others all laughed at him, each careful not to make the same mistake. The humans were reticent for the most part – as well they might be, Daff thought.

Licking his plate clean, Daff then turned to the strangers and slapped his own thigh. "Well," he said, "I hope that quenched your hunger for a time."

"It did, thank you."

"It was our pleasure. Now, you'll be safe here with us tonight. You look like you could use a good rest so go ahead and get some sleep. In the morning, if you continue along this road the direction you were headed, you'll be at Dorrowset before dusk, I should think. It's a tiny little hamlet, but someone there ought to be able to help you."

"Thank you so much," said Blodnut. "We won't forget your kindness, friend Dwarf. Are you sure you don't want any of us to stand watch?"

"No, no," insisted Daff, seeing that the poor man could scarcely keep his eyes open and that one woman had already fallen asleep on the shoulder of the other. "We will stand watch. You get some rest."

"Thank you."

Daff assigned the watch-shifts for the night, taking for himself the longest stretch in the deep of the night. Then, he curled up under his horsehair blanket and went to sleep for a couple of hours while another Dwarf, Rodrigo, stood sentry duty.

Daff awoke to screams in the middle of the night. His eyes snapped open, but it was dark and smoky all around as though the fire had only just been extinguished, and the moon was veiled by clouds. There was a foul scent on the air; one he recognised. He could never forget the salty smell of spilled blood. He heaved off his blanket and scrambled to his feet, his ears straining to make out the slightest noise. There were plenty of subtle noises to choose from; the rustle of the trees, the sighing of the wind, the hoot of an owl, the gurgle of the dying and the scuffles of the quick and quiet killers.

Daff hefted his axe; he slept with it under the blanket like a lover. It had a three-foot haft with a crescent steel blade on one side and a counterweighing spike on the other. He darted glances this way and that, seeing shadowy figures writhing, grunting, in the gloom. Someone was attacking them, of that he was sure – but who? Bandits?

"Daff!" Daff recognised the strangled, frightened voice as that of Chirri. Gone was its normal joviality. "It's those bastards from Ramhorn! They're attacking us! Them and – ugh!"

"Chirri? Chirri!"

He bumbled toward the sound of the voice, toward the hissing shadows in the darkness. "I'll get you for this, Blodnut!" he roared at the night. "You fucking see if I don't! I swear by all the Gods I'll gut you for this!"

"Hahaha!" Daff heard a human laugh tinkling from close by. "But you cannot see, little Dwarf! Even with those beady eyes of yours that are so good at seeing underground, you cannot see me! But *I* can see *you* just fine!"

The moon broke through the cloudbank just in time for Daff to see Blodnut snarling and leaping at him. He gasped. The man looked strange in the silvery light, like he had claws for fingers and he was sprouting long, dark hair all over his body, even his face. His eyes were tawny, and his nose and mouth were elongated somehow, like a snout. Daff tottered backwards, alarmed by the sight, only taking a cursory swing at the man in his shock and horror.

Blodnut missed the Dwarf with his leap and then swayed back to avoid the arcing axe blade. Even as Daff stared at him, the human seemed to be morphing, sprouting more hair, his nose extending and turning wet and black. His eyes grew more feral by the moment, as did his bearing, as if he were more beast than man now. His shoulders hunched up, he crouched on bent legs, and he sniffed at the air like a bloodhound. Daff kept backing away, speechless, unable to believe his eyes.

"Were-jackals!" he whispered, eyes round.

Past Blodnut, he could finally see the camp illuminated by the moonlight, swimming in his vision like the scene was under silver waters. He had been wrong; the gurgling had not been the sound of the dying. It had been the sound of something much worse. Past Blodnut, he could see more man-beasts, more men with fur and tawny eyes and snouts and fangs. There were a dozen of them, at least. Surrounding them were Dwarf corpses; there were at least a dozen of them, too. Not far past them, there was a pile of dead horse-flesh, blood shining silver in the moon's radiance.

What made Daff feel like puking, however, was not the dead bodies or the stench emanating from them; it was the sight of those still living. The dozen were-jackals had pinned down about ten Dwarves, one of whom was Chirri, and were biting into their own hairy arms and then holding the wounded limbs over the Dwarves' mouths. The Dwarves were gurgling on the creatures' blood, Daff saw in disgust; they were being forced to drink it. Many tried to spit it out, and when they did, they were walloped for their efforts. Daff could only think of one reason why the were-jackals would be acting in such a way. They were trying to infect the Dwarves with their horrific disease, trying to transform the Dwarves into were-jackals just like them. That thought was what made him feel sick.

Blodnut saw where he was looking and grinned viciously. "Envious, are we?" he asked mockingly, now thoroughly transformed, a man no longer. His clothes had been mostly torn clear of his body by his engorging frame; only tatters remained around him. Speckled grey and brown fur coated his body, his hands and feet had become paws, and his snout ended in a wet, black nose and was full of yellowing fangs. Dog-like ears perked up. His eyes were jackal eyes. "Don't worry, we've got the same in mind for you!"

Daff felt hollow and cold and alone, but he brandished his axe in front of him and forced himself to rumble, "Stop your Gods-damned yapping, you mongrel!"

Blodnut bared his teeth and came at Daff again, claws swinging. He had been expecting Daff to back away some more, perhaps try to dodge the claws, but the Dwarf was in no mood for playing around now. Rather than back away or try to dodge, he waited for his chance between the swiping claws and then hurled himself forward. Though his arms and shoulders were raked bloody, his axe found Blodnut's skull and split it as easily as cracking an egg. The *snap* sound was reminiscent of a busting eggshell, too. The human-turned-monster stared at Daff for a moment with wild, tawny eyes, and then he slumped down to the ground like he was so tired he couldn't stay up an instant longer.

"Chirri! Rodrigo! I'm coming!" Daff cried out, setting off toward his pinioned companions at a run.

Seeing him coming, the two closest were-jackals, striped with brown and black fur, threw aside their victims and turned on him with snarls. Daff barreled toward them, and just before he reached the first, he dropped and let his momentum slide him forward on his rump along the ground. Skidding straight through the legs of the first were-jackal, the Dwarf held his axe high and felt and heard a thump as it clove deep into the creature's midriff. He twisted the axe to free it and shoved himself back to his feet hastily.

The second creature was on him as soon as he was up, slashing at him with claws and snapping at him with jaws. He tried to fend it off with the axe, but it knocked his arm aside and bore him to the ground with its superior size and weight. He could feel and smell its breath on his face; it smelled like carrion, like old rotted meat. He was barely holding its teeth away from him, his arm shaking, lodged in its neck.

He hurriedly cast aside his axe and tugged out the little knife at his belt; an eating knife more than anything else, but sharp. He plunged the little blade into the were-jackal's side again and again, feeling hot blood pump out over his fist and arm. The beast kept writhing, and its jaws kept snapping, though, so he kept stabbing. Eventually, when he thought he must have stabbed the creature a score of times, it weakened and then abruptly fell limp. Its dead weight on top of him made him wheeze for breath. Arms trembling, he slowly shoved it off him.

Standing up, he saw two more were-jackals toss aside the Dwarves to whom they were feeding blood and advance on him. He watched Chirri fall limp on the ground, and his heart panged. He scooped up his axe and switched his knife to his left hand. One of the creatures pelted at him; the other came more slowly.

The creature that pelted at him screeched as it came in a vaguely familiar voice, "Oh, Daff! Little Daffy! D'you remember me? Do you remember Cliassa, little Daffy? She will be the end of you!"

Cliassa – of course he remembered her. Apparently the women had been were-jackals, too. Tired, knowing he could not face her head on while she was going at such speed, Daff lifted his axe up over his shoulder and then flung it. It whirled end over end through the air, humming as it went, and then the blade caved in Cliassa's sternum, violently catapulting her back like she had reached the end of an invisible leash. She didn't even have time to squeal before she died.

Daff watched the second were-jackal come on more slowly, only his little knife in hand now, and wondered if it had once been the woman, Roberta. The were-jackal's eyes flicked to a spot behind him, and that was when Daff knew he was dead. Piercing agony suddenly bloomed in his side, and he gave a juddering gasp and turned his head to see Roberta. She was still in human form; she looked quite beautiful in the moonlight in fact with her red hair framing her voluptuous face. The beauty was only enhanced by her soft, loving expression, which was completely at odds with her hand wrapped around the hilt of the dagger buried in Daff's side.

"There, there, my handsome warrior," she cooed soothingly. "There, there. All will be well now. We've got you, don't you fret." She glanced at the dagger and pulled it out of Daff's body, making him whimper. "Sorry about that, but I had to slow you down. You were killing my babies. Luckily, you have provided me with new babes to suckle at the teat!" She glanced up at the were-jackal who had been advancing on Daff and who was now standing still, watching her with tawny eyes. "Bring him and the others into the forest. We will finish up there. Oh, and bring the horses, too. I could use a snack after the night's work."

Aflame with agony, only half-conscious, Daff saw the were-jackals sling the surviving Dwarves – who seemed as comatose as he – over their shoulders and bear them off into the woodland by the road, moving from moonlight to shadow. Then, a creature seized hold of him, and he screamed and blacked out.

He came to as he was dumped on the leafy ground in the middle of the woods. There were hoary trees on every side of him, and he had no idea from which direction they had come. The broad-leafed trees seemed to tower over him and press in on him like cruel overseers, blocking out all light from moon and stars and watching the proceedings with sadistic glee. The owl's hoot was much closer now, and there were scuffling sounds all around him.

He looked around through bleary eyes, seeing many shapes shift in the darkness. Then, a spark flew and a fire was lit, blazing to life in the middle of the small clearing where he had been thrown down. The trees looked even more sinister in the flickering firelight, like barky Demons with shifting faces of shadow in their gnarled and knotted trunks.

The were-jackals looked like monsters; all evidence of their humanity was gone. The firelight illuminated the blood flecking their predominantly ochre coats, and they licked it off their snouts contentedly. Daff thought of his wife and children; he would never see them again, he knew. He wished he had stayed at home then, rather than gone gallivanting, looking for adventure. A life in the mines did not seem so bad now.

"Finish the initiation!" Roberta commanded, her voice soft but ringing with authority.

The were-jackals resumed their ritual, forcing their blood into the mouths of the groaning Dwarves, forcing them to drink it.

Roberta crouched by Daff, leaves rustling as she did so. She looked him in the eye, and he saw then that her eyes were tawny too, just like the were-jackals'. She was one of them; he knew that now.

"Handsome Daff," she said softly, "I know you think this is all horrible and that we're terrible creatures. I know you think life isn't fair and that we're monsters. And you might be right. But I would like to point out that we are merely a different form of life to that which you understand. Wolves eat deer, but they aren't demonised for doing so. Men eat chickens, but they aren't demonised for doing so. I hear Dwarves eat dogs on occasion, but they aren't demonised for doing so … for the most part. So, what is so different about us eating you for survival? What makes you so much more worthy of life? Because your meal isn't sentient? How do you know? Just because it doesn't speak the same language as you? No, no, you've been misled, Dwarf. To live is to consume; there is nothing evil in that. Nothing evil in existing. So, now you know that, you can be happy with your new life here with us."

"What?" gasped Daff, his mouth desert-dry with fear. His heart drummed, and his head throbbed.

"Your new life with us," Roberta said again, smiling kindly. "You and your friends are to be a part of my family, Daff. It was your own doing, really. When I heard you telling our tale in such eloquent terms, I knew I had to have you for my merry little band! We haven't had a storyteller for years, and I'm guessing you know many stories. So, here you are now, and here you will stay."

"Stay?" repeated Daff dumbly.

"Yes. Stay. You will stay and be one of us."

Daff's world swerved upside down and he vomited, feeling like he was falling from a great height. When he looked up, a hairy arm was forced into his slack mouth and he gagged on the iron taste of blood. A hand gripped the back of his head hard and forced him to stay still.

Choking and spluttering, he heard Roberta's voice, even as a pond. "You were right about us in some respects, you know. The first among us, like myself, were Sorcerers once. Or Witches, or whatever you want to call us. Many of us did transform under the full moon first, and many of us did kill ourselves in grief at what we did when we transformed. Some among us, however, like myself, chose to keep living, and we found that in time we could learn to control the power, to transform at will. And you were right about our *infection,* as you put it. It is transferred by the ingestion of tainted blood. You were very vague on the origins of our powers, however. Shall I fill you in?" Daff choked and spat. "Tongue tied? Very well. I shall tell the tale. You just sit there and listen." Daff gurgled.

"We performed a ritual long ago," Roberta said, her voice lilting in the manner of storytellers, "we Sorcerers, under a full moon just like the one in the sky tonight. We took the souls of jackals, the wiliest of beasts, and tried to infuse them into our own. Yes, animals have souls – albeit simplistic, mangled things. The result was … not exactly what we had planned. We succeeded, though. We absorbed

Ross Hughes

the animals' souls, and we became … what was it you called us?" She grinned then, evilly. "Were-jackals! And now, you are one of us, Daff. Welcome to the family."

Kidnapping

Chun Lun swung his axe again with a grunt, and a shower of splinters rained over him as the blade bit into the soft, light pulp buried beneath the bark of the eucalyptus tree. Chun was a woodcutter in the village of Podang, old enough for his hair and beard – once soot-black – to have become more of a salt-and-pepper colour. His once-taut golden skin now had a few sags and wrinkles and his back ached when he worked too long, but he could still be found day after day up in the forest, chopping wood that would one day be made into sheets of parchment.

The tree he had been chopping creaked loudly and toppled to Chun's right, coming down amid its fellows with a swish and a crash. Chun stood still and watched it, leaning on his axe, then he took out a roll-up he had crafted earlier that day and struck a sulphur match. Soon, aromatic baui smoke glittered in the sunshine reflected off the snow. Chun was swaddled in stripy grey otter-fur to combat the cold, and the sweet smoke helped warm his insides. After smoking, Chun chopped up the eucalyptus into small logs for easier transport and then wheelbarrowed some back downhill to Podang. His back was starting to ache and he knew he was done for the day, even though it was yet early afternoon.

He was slogging through the snowy streets toward his home, looking forward to seeing his family, when he was amicably waylaid by a stranger in rich ermine fur bearing parchments. The man was unusually tall and skinny as a rake. He carried an ash staff and looked neater than anyone else in the village with oiled-back hair and a carefully trimmed moustache. Chun stroked his own dirty beard self-consciously.

"Excuse me," said the stranger in a voice as smooth and polished as lacquered wood, "but I wonder if you could help me locate a man by the name of Chun Lun?"

Chun eyed him suspiciously for a moment, being naturally wary of outsiders, as is any villager's prerogative. "And what if I could?" he replied at last. "What would you say to him?"

"I would tell Sheng Chun that he has been selected to represent Podang at the Shenzhan's son's wedding in Lamshambule in two weeks' time. I have invites for him and his family here."

Chun frowned. The use of the honorific *Sheng* suggested this man was from rather more civilised circles, unused to backwater villages like Podang where they rarely bothered with such niceties. The man and his message stuck out like a goose at a singing contest. Furthermore, the Shenzhan was the provincial governor; why would he want a woodcutter at his son's wedding?

"And what if Sheng Chun doesn't want to go?"

The oily stranger nodded, as if he had been expecting that very answer. "Then, I have his execution writ in my other hand and we will choose a new representative."

Chun's good mood had evaporated by the time he got home. He banged open the door and growled at his wife, "Hao, we're going to Lamshambule for the Shenzhan's son's wedding."

"Ooo," cooed his wife, Hao Nin, excitedly. "Why us?"

"I have no idea. I'm just a simple woodcutter, after all."

"The children, too?"

"Yes, I have their invites here," said Chun, looking down at the slips of parchment and remembering what had been in the tall stranger's other hand. "Even the newly born."

The children's screams of joy when they were told they were visiting the capital were ear-piercing. A week later, Chun and his family were packing their bags onto a horse-drawn sleigh in the snow and waving goodbye to their neighbours in Podang. They travelled along dirt tracks and then paved roads, skidded over frozen lakes and skirted gurgling rivers and rumbled up and down hills for days. A week after they left, they were in the capital of Foyan province, Lamshambule.

Chun, Hao and their three children were awed, slack-jawed, by the immensity of the city, the like of which they had never seen before. They were used to more space, so the rows of tall, terraced buildings and the packed streets and all the noise intimidated them. Hawkers were yelling, and people were shouting and arguing or singing and dancing in a riot of colour wherever they looked, caught up in the celebratory spirit that had possessed the city as the wedding loomed close. Chun's two older children hid behind him, crouching low as if to hide, as they strolled toward the Shenzhan's manor. His wife carried the youngest, a newly born babe less than a year old.

A palace in all but name, the manor house was an extravagance of architecture, a behemoth of a building crafted from timber, stone, gold, silver, marble, and jade. Its façade was decorated with stone gargoyles with vicious fangs and claws and eyes of ruby or emerald. A sprawling affair, its four central roofs could be seen rising high above the rest, great domes of jade topped with golden spires that glinted in the sunlight. Chun thought it looked like the highest of them was a golden wind vane. The amount of wealth contained within its walls was incalculable.

Two lamellar-armoured guards and a servant awaited them under a great, arabesque stone arch at the grand, golden doors, which were embossed with scenes of old famous battles from the long history of Quing Tzu. The servant bowed stiffly to them with an expression of disdain barely veiled; he was dressed far more smartly than them, after all. He wore neat black-and-whites, while the family from Podang was clad in stinky old furs.

"Welcome," he said nasally, as though he might be trying to hold his breath, "to the Shenzhan's home. May I see your invitations?"

Chun brought them out from the folds of his clothes and handed them over. The servant took them with the very tips of his fingers and studied them a moment, squinting with his thin face close to the invites, his beak-nose practically touching them. Then, he regarded the villagers with a hard look, clearly surprised that they had invitations and that all appeared in order.

"Go on through," he bit off the words at last with a false smile. "Give your coats to Harold over there. Enjoy the festivities."

The family entered the manor and gawked at the antechamber, which was beset with all kinds of luxuries, from patterned metal wire chairs with plump cushions to large portrait paintings and friezes to the stone mosaic floor depicting mermaids to the crystal chandelier overhead. They gave their coats to another servant there, Harold, a chubby man who took their garments in much the same fashion as the doorman had taken their invites. Chun saw that he was trekking mud and snow all over the mosaic floor and brushed his simple woollen tunic self-consciously.

His wife, Hao Nin, spoke to their children in Tzunese, a more formal language that they used less often than Traveller's. "Listen closely, you three. You must be on your best behaviour when we go in here, d'you understand? And you must only speak Tzunese from now on. Speaking Traveller's in there will draw the wrong sort of attention. Eat cleanly, don't wander off, speak only if you're spoken to – and then speak politely. Understand?"

"Yes, ma," they all said in Traveller's Tongue.

"Tzunese!" she hissed in Tzunese.

"Yes, ma," they all said again in Tzunese this time.

She looked their second-eldest, a girl with long, loose raven hair, in the eye and said, "Behave yourself, Fifi. There will be lots of handsome boys in here your age."

Chun rolled his eyes; his daughter was only eleven years old and already his wife was thinking about suitors and marriage.

Then, Hao turned to their eldest, a boy of fifteen with his father's dark hair and round face. "And you, Wulan, don't be a grouch! Nobody likes a grouch." Ironically, he scowled at her words.

She spoke finally to the babe in her arms in a high-pitched, singsong voice, "And you, Songba, don't you be a little squealer now, you hear? D'you hear me, sweet cheeks?"

She cooed for a moment more, then Chun laid a hand on her shoulder. Others were passing them by and giving them strange looks.

"Come on," he said and led them into the manor's main hall.

Chun Lun had never felt so much like a country bumpkin in all his life as he did standing there in that room. There were as many people in the manor as in his entire village, it seemed, and they were all dressed far more smartly than he. The women all wore silk and satin ball-gowns and dresses, despite the season. Chun wondered if the creamy colours were supposed to blend with the snowy surroundings. The men wore silk robes or fashionable shirts or velvet doublets of darker, autumnal colours as was the current trend.

The chamber itself was magnificent, too; twin sets of curving marble stairs on either side of the room rose to a mezzanine, where bookshelves gave the area the feel of a grand library. Down on the ground level, there was space for a hundred people to move and mingle among couches and little pools and fountains and tables and chairs. The creamy, marble walls were lined with more portraits and tapestries, like the antechamber, and china ornaments marched along a mahogany mantle on either side of the room above twin lit, grand stone hearths. The carpet was thicker and creamier than any Chun had ever seen, and he felt guilty just stepping on it with his travel-stained boots.

"What are we doing here?" he asked Hao.

"We were invited," she reminded him. "Forcefully invited."

A woman up on the mezzanine spotted them, waved and began to hurry down the marble steps towards them, beaming sweetly. She was the very picture of beneficence, in fact; small and petite, she was ageing with dignity with pale golden skin, a kind demeanour and the most charming of smiles. Her onyx hair, tied up in complicated knots, bounced as she sprang down the stairs one by one, almost childlike in her innocence.

She stopped before them and bowed. "Gods watch," she said in a high, warm voice; the fancy equivalent of saying hello or goodbye. "My name is Ada Yuongang. I am Shenzhan Tung's wife. Welcome to our home. I am so pleased you could be here to celebrate our son's nuptials!"

"You know us, my lady?" asked Hao, so taken aback she forgot to give the proper greeting, remembering late to bow in return.

"Of course!" Ada smiled. "You must be the Chun family from Podang. I am so glad you made it in time. I know it was a long journey. Come, come with me and I'll show you to refreshments. You must be hungry and thirsty."

They were, and they followed her happily to a nearby table laden with odd delicacies; little finger-snacks like clams and cold sausages that would do nothing in the fight against hunger one by one. Chun regarded them askew, and Ada laughed a tinkling laugh to see him so clearly ill at ease.

"Don't worry, Sheng Chun," she said, stroking his arm, "you can have as many as you please and there are roast ducks and pheasants scattered around on the other tables, too. Help yourself to as much as you please. You are our guests."

Mollified, Chun said, "Thank you, my lady. We appreciate the hospitality, don't we, children?"

"Thank you," the two older children chorused obligingly.

"What wonderful little darlings," Ada crooned, pinching Fifi's cheek with long, colourful nails. Fifi clearly didn't appreciate it and pulled away. "Just wait until they grow up and get married!" She sighed. "What a joyous day today is, for my son to wed his soulmate. I couldn't be happier! Please, enjoy yourselves and I hope to see you again later. There are others I must greet. Farewell for now! Gods watch!"

"Well, she was a delight," Hao observed.

Chun nodded. "You heard her. Help yourselves, Fifi, Wulan. Eat till you pop, that's what I say!"

They sat down and dug in.

Against tradition, the wedding itself was to take place in the manor, since it was so much larger than any of the temples nearby and there were so many guests. Shenzhan Tung was not one for tradition. He had, however, imported holy men from the Temple of Jiu Pai, the Goddess of Love and Fertility, to officiate the ceremony.

While the Chun family were still filling their cheeks like hamsters expecting a famine, one of the holy men struck a gong and its ringing soon put an end to all other noise. All eyes turned toward the front of the hall, where the brown-robed holy men stood beside the bride and groom in all their finest regalia on a raised, rug-laden dais.

One of the holy men, the lead officiant leaning over a lectern of convoluted golden wire, cleared his throat when the gong stopped ringing and then spoke in a dry, hoary voice, going through the blessings and benedictions for the bride and groom and their families and listing their duties as husband and wife. The ceremony proceeded without incident. The bride and groom kissed, the marriage was cemented, and the crowd's cheers shook the crystal chandeliers overhead.

Then, the revelries commenced in earnest and the Chun family found themselves in the middle of a zoo at feeding time as people bumped them from all sides in their raucous rush to fill their bellies with food and wine. Chun and his two older children soon had food-stains on their tunics, while his wife somehow managed to abstain.

A little while later, when the ambience had calmed somewhat and everyone was good and sozzled, Ada Yuongang visited the Chun family again, dimpling her cheeks with her friendly smile.

"Hello again," she said. "I hope you're having a good time! I have a treat for you. The Shezhan and I are about to give our speech, and I've reserved seats for you up front! Come along, come along!"

Reluctant, but unwilling to offend, Chun and his family followed the sweet old lady to seats by the dais. There, she left them to join her husband.

Not long later, the Shenzhan, Tung Fuo, stood up on the dais with his wife to make a toast. Tung Fuo was a big man with a stern, shaven face and grey hair, who had once been strong before his dotage, and he still maintained a straight spine and a snappish military conduct most of the time. Now, though, he too was giggly and wobbly from an excess of wine, which – like Chun – he had spilled over himself, staining his crimson doublet and fawn trousers. He made a slurred speech that few could understand, but at which everybody laughed when he did. Then, he stumbled off to one side of the dais to let his wife speak over the ornate lectern.

Ada Yuongang smiled sweetly out at all the happy, drunken faces beaming up at her. Her pink ball-gown was immaculate. "Thank you all for coming, thank you so much!" she began in her high lark-song. "What a day it's been! I'm surprised my husband can still stand, given how much he has drunk!" There were titters all around the room, and the Shenzhan happily saluted the room with his sloshing glass. "Then again, I'm surprised his cock is still in his trousers, given his sexual appetites."

The room went deadly silent, and someone dropped a glass, which smashed with a loud tinkle.

"What in the name of the –" Tung Fuo began, storming toward his wife.

She stepped to meet him and shoved him in the chest, sending him sprawling on the rugs. Old and drunk as he was, he wriggled there like an impotent upturned turtle, unable to right himself with ease.

"I bet he's been walking all around the room tonight, grabbing every woman by the pussy," Ada continued, looking around. "Sorry about that, girls, but at least you don't have to live with him, eh? I have had to live with that lecherous git for years. Now, it is time for his comeuppance. Behold what I have brought here tonight! Behold Shenzhan Tung Fuo's bastard son, Chun Lun!"

She pointed at Chun, who went still as a statue with his eyes bugging out of his head. He didn't know what to do; suddenly he was the goose at the singing contest, and everyone was staring at him. A few armoured guards were helping Tung Fuo to his feet by this point, and Chun prayed the Shenzhan would do something to take the attention off him. He never imagined that what Ada was saying could be true.

"Tell them, Tung Fuo!" Ada Yuongang demanded, turning to her husband, who was standing once more. "Tell them about all the bastards you've sired over the years! This one was just the easiest to find!"

Tung Fuo looked around at the room with a stony face, smoothing his doublet and somehow managing to seem dignified despite having been writhing around on the floor. He stared daggers at his wife, and then darted a look towards Chun that the woodcutter thought looked almost apologetic.

"Nonsense!" Tung said coldly at last. "I am a man of nobility and honour. I gave my word that I would be faithful to you, and I have kept it. You have no proof to the contrary! You are only embarrassing yourself and your son with your wild paranoia, woman!"

He struck her with the back of his hand, and the chamber erupted into cacophonic chaos as people bellowed approval or disapproval and rushed the dais to help or hinder the Shenzhan.

Chun rose to his feet. "Time to go, children," he shouted over the ruckus in Traveller's. "We've been tricked into coming under false pretences. That sow just wanted to use me to make a point! Come on, let's get out of here!"

Overhearing the woodcutter, Tung Fuo – protected by a ring of guards – rounded on him and shouted, "Yes, get out, you! Guards, throw this man out! He's no son of mine!"

Despite the fact that they were already leaving, the lamellar-armoured guards came for the Chun family then. They grabbed hold of them with painfully tight grips of their gauntlets, dragged them back to the golden double-doors through which they had entered and tossed them out into the street. Chun and his older children were thrown out on their faces, while the guards were kind enough to let Hao leave carrying the baby. They weren't complete monsters, Chun reflected, face-down in the muck of the street. Their coats were tossed out on top of them.

"Good riddance to the lot of you!" he cried, sitting up and waving an angry, but impotent, fist. "We never wanted to come to this bloody wedding anyway!"

The guards ignored him and went back inside, slamming the doors behind them.

"Well, that was … unexpected," Hao observed dryly.

"Weddings, eh?" Chun joked weakly. "They're always a hotbed for madness. And I don't think being rich and powerful makes it any easier. They're all nuts in there! I for one am glad I'm not the

Shenzhan's son. I'm much happier with you lot back in Podang." He smiled and held out his arms, still sitting on the ground, and Fifi and Wulan hugged him tight. "Come on, it's late so we're not going to travel tonight. Let's go find an inn and rest until morning, then we'll go home."

Unbeknownst to them, as they left, they were followed by a tall, slender figure cowled and hooded in the shadows.

Chun and his family found that the inns nearby were all full, so eventually they settled for paying an innkeeper for the privilege of sleeping on his common room floor.

Later that night, the door to the inn banged open and Chun and his family came awake with a start. Two figures entered through the doorway, silhouetted against silvery moonlight. As they came closer and pulled down their black facemasks, Chun realised with a lurch of the stomach that he knew both of them; it was the oily, moustached stranger who had given him the invites in Podang and Ada Yuongang. Both were dressed all in black and did not look polite or friendly anymore.

"Hello again, Chun family," said Ada, her voice cold and hard now, all trace of her former sweetness scoured away. Her face was bruised where the Shenzhan had hit her. "I know I have put you through a lot already tonight, but I need one more thing from you before you leave, I'm afraid."

"What do you want, you hag?" Chun hissed, getting slowly to his feet.

"My son, Tung Shaku, cannot bear children," explained Ada, "but he needs an heir, or else the head of another family will be made Shenzhan. So, I am going to take your new-born son and give him to Tung Shaku to raise as his own. We'll have to hide the baby for a while, of course, and the wife to give her time to pretend –"

"What?" interrupted Chun loudly, going red with anger. "No, you can't have him, you –"

"Sow?" Ada offered just as loudly. "You called me that once already tonight. Don't think I didn't hear you. And I am taking that baby, Chun, so you can make it easy for yourself or you can make it difficult. Either way, the result will be the same."

"I wasn't going to say sow; I was going to say bitch!" Chun raged. "You can't have him, I'll fucking flay you, you –"

He stormed toward her, intent on pummelling her stupid face.

The tall stranger moved like lightning; he pointed his staff and a small green globule of energy sizzled as it shot through the air and punched Chun to the ground before he could lay a finger on the Shenzhan's wife. Then, the stranger crouched quickly over the woodcutter and delivered a few fast, hard punches to the face. Dazed, Chun rolled around on the floor groaning. Hao was up on her feet now, clutching little Songba and whimpering.

Fifi was cowering behind her mother, but Wulan charged at the man who had struck his father, screaming, "I'll kill you!"

The man in black knocked him unconscious with one swift blow to the jaw.

"This is my associate," said Ada, "Sheng Chongyo. He is a Wizard, and he will be the one breaking your legs if you resist. Sheng Chongyo, the baby, if you please."

There was a puff of purple smoke, and a moment later Chongyo was across the room by Hao's side, his naked dagger held to her neck, his staff across her body. Chun forced himself to his feet, his visage battered and bloodied, but it was too late. Chongyo watched him knowingly.

"Let us leave with the baby," said Ada, "and the rest of you may live."

Chongyo was already forcing Hao towards the door, and Chun dared not stop him. One slip of that blade and Hao's lifeblood would be gushing all over the floor; the thought made him queasy.

"I just want to keep things in the family, really. It's what any mother would do for her son," Ada continued once Chongyo was by her side. She studied Chun for a moment. "You really are Tung's bastard son, you know. You even look a little like him around the eyes. That's why I expect your baby will be a perfect fit. And don't worry, we won't abuse the little darling. He'll be given every comfort – far more than you could provide for him, in fact, I am sure. So, in a way, I am doing you all a favour."

Chun wanted to rip her throat out with his teeth. He was shaking with rage, but he said nothing.

"Oh, and if you think of telling anyone about this," Ada added, "Sheng Chongyo here will skin you alive and make you eat your own flesh. No one would believe you anyway; you have no proof. If you think of coming for the baby, Sheng Chongyo will boil you alive and feed you to your wife. We are the richest family in Foyan, and like I said, he is a Wizard. We can get to you wherever you are, whatever you do. Remember that, Chun."

Chun wanted to bathe in her blood, but he did nothing.

"Come, Sheng Chongyo," said Ada finally, seeing that Chun was not rising to her bait. She took the Wizard's staff. "Grab the babe and let's get out of here."

Chongyo pressed the dagger deeper into Hao's neck, snatched little baby Songba out of her arms and then pushed her to the ground before fleeing out the door after Ada Yuongang. Chun stood still while Hao rushed to the door with a howl and watched the two figures disappear into the night.

"Why didn't you stop them?" Hao railed at Chun then, striking his chest while she sobbed. "Why didn't you do something, damn you?"

Chun ground his teeth and shook his head. His wife thought he was going to pop with rage, but when he spoke his words came out quiet.

"It wasn't the right time," he said, his eyes gleaming with intent. "I couldn't do anything without someone here dying. I didn't want that. This way, everyone is alive. This way, we can get Songba back and kill the rich pricks who took him."

*

Chun Lun was a patient man. It was what made him such an expert woodsman and effective hunter. Many were the days other men had failed to bring anything down and Chun had been the one to snag a buck or a brace of rabbits.

As Chun always said, "You need patience to be a hunter."

So, rather than go to the Shenzhan's manor looking for blood, Chun Lun took his family home to Podang. His wife, Hao Nin, raged against the idea at first, ranting and raving and striking Chun and then trying to run away from him to get her son back herself. Chun would not let her. Calmly, patiently, he ran her down every time and explained to her again and again that he would get their son back, but not by putting her in danger. He insisted that Hao keep their daughter, Fifi, safe, and eventually his wife agreed, sobbing and moaning. To make sure his family got home safe, Chun went with them on the sleigh, biding his time, never forgetting his wrath for an instant.

Once he had established Hao and Fifi back at Podang and told them to head to his half-sister's house in the village of Wushei with the next merchant caravan, Chun turned to his oldest son, Wulan.

He faced the boy in front of their little wooden cottage, put a hand on his shoulder and said, "You are almost sixteen now, Wulan, almost a man in your own right. As such, and as this is a time of emergency, I am going to address you as a man. As you know, your little brother, Songba, has been taken from us. Snatched by that sow, Ada Yuongang, and her blasted Wizard! I am going to get Songba back. Right now. I am returning to Lamshambule on the instant. Will you come with me? Will you help me rescue your baby brother? Feel no obligation to say yes, son. I will not lie to you. This is a dangerous quest I am undertaking, and it will most likely claim my life – and yours if you come. So, do not speak lightly and do not speak wrongly. I do not want you changing your mind halfway to Lamshambule. Speak honestly, my son. You do not have to do this; I will lose no respect for you if you say no, and I will lose no love for you either."

Wulan's mouth hung open at the shock of responsibility for what felt to Chun like a long time. Snow settled on Chun's grizzled hair and beard and his stripy, grey otter-fur coat, biting at his ears.

Then, his son set his jaw, hardened his eyes and said, "I'll come with you, pa. I'll help you rescue Songba."

Chun nodded, overcome by pride for a moment. He patted his son's shoulder to give himself time.

Then, he cleared his throat. "Ahem. Excellent. Thank you, Wulan. I do appreciate it. Now, go and grab my bow and all the arrows in the house. We will need them."

While Wulan readied the yew hunting bow, Chun grabbed his hatchet from where it was embedded in a tree stump and prepared the sleigh and the horses. The horses would be exhausted from all the travel, he knew, so he would not push them too hard for the first day or two. He could not let them rest, however; he had to get his youngest son back as soon as possible.

Chun and his family arrived in Podang at about noon, and the woodcutter and his eldest son were on their way again well before dusk.

Once more, they trundled down dirt tracks that eventually turned into paved paths. They slid over ice-locked lakes and dodged around rivers and crested and descended hummocks and ravines for days until the horses were lathered and shaking with exhaustion. In less than a week, they made it back to the capital of Foyan province,

Lamshambule.

They were a sorry state when they arrived, though; flea-bitten, gaunt from hunger, dark-eyed from sleeplessness and reeking of stale sweat. Wulan was suffering in particular; he had never gone through such rigours. His black mop was a tangled mess, his eyes were sunken, and his wolf-skin coat was worn and torn. Chun was proud of the way he had held up, though, hardly complaining at all through all the blizzards and late nights and early starts and uncomfortable beds.

Despite this, they did not stop to freshen themselves or to rest. They arrived at Lamshambule as the sun was dipping out of sight in the west, a blood-red rose on the horizon, and they went straight to the Shenzhan's manor.

The palatial manor no longer seemed like the apotheosis of wealth and extravagance it had when Chun first saw it. The second time around, it seemed like a massive mockery, a symbol of man's fallacy and folly. The gargoyles sneered at him from their roosts, and the jade domes with their pointless little golden spires held their heads high haughtily, thinking themselves superior. Chun scowled up at the place, thinking that it would be just as dead and gone as the Shenzhan in time. Time would level this leviathan of a building as it did everything else.

With his scowl still fixed, Chun stormed up to the embossed golden doors set beneath the superfluously frilly arabesque stone arch. He banged on the immaculate doors with a grimy fist.

"Open up! Open up in there, I say!"

"Pa, what are you doing?" hissed Wulan, trying to tug his father away.

"Open up!"

The doors clanged and then swung open smoothly, noiselessly, to reveal the same servant that had greeted them on the day of the wedding. The man looked just as neat as before in fresh black-and-whites, just as skinny, just as suspicious. He looked down his beaked nose at them.

"I recognise you," he said slowly, nasally. "You're the peasants from Podang that caused all the trouble at the wedding, are you not?" Before Chun could answer, the ageing man waved his arms around like a flightless bird flapping its wings and said, "You are not welcome here, Sheng. Good day!"

He made to slam the doors in Chun's face, but the doors were heavy and Chun was quick. The woodcutter sprang forward and bowled the servant over, bearing him down to the ground on the mosaic floor inside the manor.

Their faces inches apart, Chun growled, "Where is Ada Yuongang?"

"She is at the Shenzhan's winter home with the Shenzhan!" the scared servant squeaked. "This is their summer home! They only stayed here so long to hold the wedding here. They're gone!"

Chun was so angry he could have gouged the man's eyes out with his thumbs. Instead, he snarled, "Where is the Shenzhan's winter home?"

"Haipei! It's in Haipei on the Green River!"

"What in the name of all the Gods were you doing in there, pa?" Wulan demanded after they had fled the manor and cut through several alleys to lose any potential pursuit. They were now standing in a grimy little backstreet, leaning on a crumbling wall and panting. "You could've gotten us arrested! We're no good to Songba if the city guards take us to gaol, are we? I thought you had a plan, but you just walked up there like an idiot and banged on the door! What were you thinking?"

Realising he had called his father an idiot, Wulan froze, expecting retribution. Chun Lun stared at his son for a long moment, but then he hid his face and began to weep softly. Not knowing what to do, Wulan patted his father awkwardly on the shoulder.

"You're right, Wulan," Chun said eventually, his voice thick with sorrow. "I acted like an idiot. I pride myself on my patience, and yet I ran in there like a dumb wolf at the smell of blood." That was how they trapped troublesome wolves; with bait, with blood. "I just can't think straight with Songba missing! All this time, I've been getting so *mad* that when I saw the manor, the rage just burst out of me and propelled me up there!"

He took a deep breath, wiped his face and sighed. "But you're right, my son. I acted like an idiot. We are lucky, in truth, that the Shenzhan is not here, for if he was you are right – we may well have been arrested. Or killed. To get Songba back, we are going to need patience and cunning, the mind of a hunter. I will not let us down again, Wulan. From now on, every move will be carefully planned. We *will* find Ada Yuongang, and we *will* get Songba back!"

They rested that night in a barn with some chickens. They only

Chronicles of Maradoum Volume 1

A Fantasy Anthology

By Ross C Hughes

First Printing 2019
ISBN 9781702601610
www.rosshughes.biz

slept a few hours, though; before dawn, they were on their way again, heading for Haipei on the Green River.

As its name suggested, Haipei was situated on the Green River. The river was named so, for it did indeed gleam green under the sun, tinted by a unique algae in the waters. The river and its tributaries wound through Haipei in the form of canals shadowed by graceful, white arching bridges. It was a small, beautiful city, juxtaposing red brick against green waters, blue-slate roofs against white streets.

Chun Lun did not see the beauty as he entered Haipei, however; he saw its gluttony. It was a place for the rich and only the rich. The houses were all vain monstrosities, puffed up with their own importance – just like the people. Even the men poling along the canals did so in gondolas trimmed in gold with ornate figureheads. No ordinary man could afford to pole a gondola here. No wonder the Shenzhan favoured the place, Chun thought sourly. He had never seen anywhere so much the stark opposite of his simple village of Podang.

He knew where to find the Shenzhan at a glance, even before they entered the city limits. A proud crimson pagoda towered over all the other buildings in Haipei, in the middle of the city, its snooty nose raised high. That was where Chun decided he'd look first.

He and Wulan surveyed the city from a nearby hillside, lying flat in the snow and waiting for the sun to wane. It did so, silhouetting the city's skyscape, black mountains against a fiery backdrop. The journey to Haipei had been easy, passing by meadows and pastures for the most part; now would come the hard part, Chun knew.

He turned to his son. "Let's go."

The two slid down the hill, the sunset casting even the snow surrounding them in scarlet. It suited Chun; he had blood on his mind. The city was not walled, but its main roads were well-guarded by an elite force of mercenaries, nominally guards, that had been hired to protect the city. Seeing this, Chun and Wulan did not follow the roads into Haipei; they slipped in from the wilderness where a small copse bordered the city, using the trees for cover.

"Always use cover where you can," said Chun as they did so, darting glances around, "and if you can't find cover, you aren't looking hard enough."

Once on the streets, they tried to act natural, as though they belonged, but it was like strolling through a ghost town as they wandered the white streets. Haipei was practically empty, and it occurred to Chun then that perhaps there was a curfew.

As the thought struck him like a dagger in the back, he heard a gruff voice shout out, "You there! Halt! What's your business on the streets at this time of night, Sheng?"

Feeling sweat trickle down his back, Chun turned around. A guard in bronze laminar armour was approaching him, suspicion writ clear upon his sallow, bearded face. He laid his hand on the silver hilt of his katana as he swaggered over.

"I said," the guard repeated more loudly when Chun did not answer, "what's your business on the streets at this time of night, *Sheng?*"

The honorific did not sound very respectful at all; rather a waste of breath, Chun thought. His mind raced, searching for a plausible answer, but he could not think of one. It was obvious at a glance that he and Wulan did not belong. They were the filthiest things in the whole city, having been sleeping rough for days, penurious as paupers. They had been living off roots and bugs and whatever animals they could bring down on their journeys. They stank like dog breath.

"My son and I are just out for a walk, Sheng," Chun said, playing for time, trying to sound nonchalant. His voice shook, though. He tried a weak smile, but gave it up when he felt it wobble.

The guard frowned and looked them up and down. "Forgive my asking, but do you live here?"

The *Sheng* was gone now, thought Chun. "No. We're visiting my brother, who lives here."

"Mm." The guard did not relax one iota. "I think I'd best escort you back to your brother's house. There is a curfew in Haipei, you know. He should've told you. Come on, where does your brother live?"

Chun looked around for a moment as if lost. There was no one else in sight, and the sun was dipping fast, casting the city in mist and shadow.

He turned back to the guard with a firmer smile, feeling calm settle on him; the hunter waits for his chance, and then he strikes.

He reached behind his back and stepped closer to the man in armour, smile still in place, saying, "Hang on a second, friend. I think I've got the address written down here somewhere ..."

The man frowned. "Well, hurry –"

He was cut off mid-sentence when Chun's hatchet split his skull.

Little bone shards stung Chun, and warm blood dotted his face. Shaking with adrenaline, fear and excitement, he wrestled the hatchet free from the guard's face, which was cleft open down the middle. He saw surreal detail in the dying light of the sun; he saw that the cut was just to the right of the bridge of the nose, through one nostril. It had missed the right eye, but severed both lips. The guard, unsurprisingly perhaps, was still frowning, even in death.

Chun felt his stomach heave like someone was tugging at it with an invisible hook and rod. He gasped for breath and gulped back a mouthful of puke, but he heard his son behind him coughing up bile on the white street, retching until only spittle spilled forth. Chun had never killed anyone before, certainly never murdered them in cold blood before they could even draw a weapon. The act made him feel nauseous, sullied. In that moment, he never wanted to take another life again, but he knew it to be a vain desire; more deaths would be coming.

Though he felt like curling up in a ball and crying or throwing himself off a cliff edge, Chun forced himself to turn to his son. He reached out a hand to pat Wulan on the shoulder, but saw that the limb was stained with blood. So, instead, he stumbled numbly over to the river, knelt on the stone flagging and washed his hands. When he was done, Wulan was finally ready to face him and did so with tears in his eyes.

"Are you mad?" the boy whispered. "What in the name of the Gods have you done, pa?"

"What needed done," Chun answered shortly, grabbing the guard by the ankles, hauling him hastily into a nearby alley and dumping him in the shadows. He returned to Wulan and looked his son in the eye. "And I expect I'll do it again before we are done. I am getting Songba back, Wulan. I will do whatever it takes – and since you chose to come with me, so will you, do you understand? No hesitation. No mercy. Anyone gets in our way, they die. Understand?"

Wulan was round-eyed. "But what about –"

"But nothing!" snapped Chun, startling the boy. "We do *whatever* it takes. Do you understand?"

Wulan nodded. "I understand."

"Good."

"But surely you didn't have to kill him? Couldn't we have found another way?"

"No," said Chun. "Besides, I have a plan and it requires his clothes and armour. Now come, help me get them off him."

Once properly disguised, Chun set off for the grand red pagoda in the middle of the city once more, clanking as he walked openly down the streets with naked katana in hand and his bow slung over his shoulder. Wulan walked in front of him, hands seemingly bound. They passed several other armoured guards as they made their way through the town, but nobody accosted them again. In fact, the other guards waved to them, so Chun waved back and kept marching. He had been careful to clean the bloodstains off the armour in the river before donning it lest he be discovered a fraud. He worried for a second, in fact, that he had washed it too thoroughly when he saw the other guards' armour, but he kept going and told himself he was just being paranoid. Nobody stopped him, and he heaved a sigh of relief when he finally reached the pagoda.

As seen from a distance, it was gigantic. Its facade was colourfully painted with intricate patterns, geometric designs. Its seven sets of upsweeping eaves flared out over the adjacent buildings like brims on a hat, lording over them and casting them in that much more shade. Broad at the bottom, it gradually narrowed toward the top, where the peaked roof pointed accusingly at the sky, seeming to demand how anything could dare put itself above such a magnificent building. It was not the only one, though; the tall pagoda was surrounded by a whole complex of its smaller, squatter siblings, white bridges linking them over canals. All were hidden behind a seven-foot red brick wall.

Chun had loathed the pagoda at first sight, and he detested the whole complex up close. Nobody needed a house, or indeed a whole complex, that big – not even the Shenzhan. It was grotesque.

This time, however, he did not bang on the front door. This time, Chun and Wulan took their time, analysing every inch of the Shenzhan's home. They took a careful circuit around the walled-off complex and eyed it from every angle. Finally, they wound up back where they had started.

"No break in the wall except the gates," murmured Chun, "and they are manned. And we can't get at the walls to climb them without being seen."

"We could probably jump over the wall from one rooftop to the next," Wulan pointed out.

The houses were clustered enough that it would be possible, but Chun shook his head. "There's no way we could do it silently. Someone would hear us. No, I think we're going to have to bluff our way through."

Wulan stared at his father, and then opened his mouth to object.

Regardless, a few minutes later, under the last thin rays of the sinking sun, Chun was approaching the gate, prodding his son forward with the tip of his stolen katana. He prayed there were too many guards for them all to know one another.

When he reached the gate, he was sweating under his bronze laminar armour and his hands were shaking. He took deep breaths and tried to calm himself. The two guards at the gate, garbed similarly to Chun, looked relaxed as he approached; they did not reach for the swords at their belts, only watched him and Wulan as they came.

One of the guards halted the woodcutter and his son with an upraised palm. "Hold there. What's going on here?"

"Prisoner," grunted Chun. "I'm to throw him in gaol."

"Why not the city gaol? Why the Shenzhan's gaol?"

Chun blinked owlishly. He had not considered that. "He ... the offence was against the Shenzhan, so the Shenzhan specifically requested that he be gaoled within the complex."

The guard nodded knowingly. "Ah, not the first time." Chun breathed a little sigh of relief.

"What was the offence?"

Chun felt a bead of sweat trickle down his cheek. "Thievery."

"Typical," said the guard with a tut, allowing Chun to ease his tension a jot. "I dunno what the Shenzhan does with his prisoners, but we hear screams sometimes ..." The man shivered and turned his gaze on Wulan. "But I'm sure you'll find out all about that!" He squinted at Chun then. "Say, I don't recognise you." Chun's heart began palpitating. "You must be one of them Eagles, are ya?"

Chun's mind raced, and he came to the conclusion that the Eagles must be a mercenary group operating in Haipei, a group of which this guard was not a part.

He took a deep breath. "Yep. Best there is."

The guard chuckled. "Haha! They all say that. Go on in, Eagle."

Chun could not believe his luck and was unwilling to press it, so he prodded Wulan in the back. The guards opened the barred iron gates, and the woodcutter and his son strolled through.

They marched until they were out of sight of the guards, praying they had gone vaguely towards the gaols. Shaking, sweating, barely able to swallow his mouth was so dry, Chun sagged against a wall for a moment once they had rounded a corner.

"Come on!" Wulan urged him on. "We're so close now. Songba is somewhere within these walls!"

Chun gritted his teeth and nodded. Together, he and Wulan – still pantomiming that the boy was a prisoner – made their way slowly, carefully through the complex. They ducked back out of sight several times when they saw guards patrolling in pairs, but fortunately they were not seen. Chun did not want to risk another encounter if he could avoid it; the risk of detection increased exponentially every time.

Dodging past one last wandering pair of guards, Chun and Wulan reached the grand red pagoda at the heart of the complex, the seven-tiered, garish monstrosity. Two more guards awaited them in front of the old oaken doors; seeing them, Chun spat. He gestured to Wulan, and the two of them slunk back into the shadows, back around to another street to try from another angle. The hunter must be patient.

Just as Chun was about to give up hope and storm the front door, Wulan began pointing urgently. Following the boy's finger, the woodcutter saw a small side door set into the pagoda, painted over so as to be almost indistinguishable from the patterns around it. The door was locked, but Chun was running short on that most valuable of traits now – patience.

He shoulder-barged the door, and when that did not work he stuck the curved blade of the katana into the narrow gap between door and frame and tried to jiggle the lock. When that failed, he tried to prise the door open with the blade. With a clang and a creak, the blade and the door gave way at the same time. The door swung open. The blade snapped in half, and Chun fell on his rump. He sat there, frozen, for a moment, listening for sounds of the alarm being raised. After a minute, though, he came to the conclusion that nobody had heard him break in.

"Come on, Wulan," he whispered, "and be silent inside!"

He cast aside the broken sword and took his hatchet out of his belt, where it had been lying against his back, and he and Wulan padded into the pagoda.

Staring at all the doors branching off of the initial corridor and the stairs beyond, Chun realised aloud, "We're going to need a guide."

So, they began checking rooms. Some doors were locked, others were not. All the rooms they checked were empty at first, looking like they were used as pantries for the most part. Eventually, though, they found somebody.

An old man was sleeping on a straw cot in a small, misbegotten room. Chun guessed he was far from the favourite servant. He poked the old man awake with a finger. The old man rolled over, sat up and peered at them through watery eyes. He had grey hair ringing a great bald spot and thick, bushy eyebrows.

"Who are you?" he croaked.

Chun showed the old man his hatchet. "I'll be asking the questions here. Now tell me, where is the Shenzhan's grandson?"

"Grandson?" The old man gaped up at him in confusion.

Chun cursed himself for a fool; of course they would not have told this old man about the secret grandson and the false pregnancy. Reframing his question, he said, "Do you know the way to the Shenzhan's son's quarters? Tung Shaku's quarters?"

The old man nodded, his fearful eyes on the axe. "I do, I do. I know this place like the back of my hand, every nook, every cranny."

Chun pondered on that for a moment. "Excellent. Then, you also know where to find the Wizard, Chongyo."

The old man baulked. "I do, but I've no wish to go there. He's a madman!"

"What's your name, old man?"

"Qindong."

"Listen closely, Qindong. If you don't do exactly as I say, I'm going to cut you in half. I've already killed one man tonight, and I don't mind adding another to the list. Got it?"

"Mm!" Qindong squeaked a terrified affirmative, nodding violently.

"Excellent. Now, take me to Chongyo."

Chongyo awoke as the door creaked open; whether he awoke

at the noise or from some magical alarm, Chun would never know. The woodcutter flew across the room at the Wizard even as the tall, thin man rolled out of bed and grabbed his staff. Chongyo raised the staff and started to babble in a tongue that gave Chun goosebumps. It did not matter, though; before he could incant more than two syllables, Chun had reached him and cut off his arm at the elbow, severing him from his ash staff, the source of his power.

The Wizard whimpered and cowered before the woodcutter. "Please don't kill me!" he sobbed. "I'm sorry for what I did to you, to your son! They made me do it! She made me do it! Please –!"

Chun split his skull like splitting a log with one smooth motion of the hatchet. He spat on the corpse, and then turned to see Wulan and Qindong staring at him from the doorway, moon-eyed.

"Come, Qindong," Chun growled, feeling hot blood drip off his chin. "Lead us to Ada Yuongang."

"You … you want to go to the Shenzhan's quarters?"

"Is that where she will be?"

"Well, yes."

"Then, that is where I wish to go."

The old man squeaked assent and started leading them upstairs. They had already climbed to the fourth floor to find the Wizard, and now they climbed higher still. Their luck ran out on the sixth floor, where they spotted two armoured guards making the rounds, coming their way along a maroon carpet between tapestries on the walls.

Chun yanked his head back before he was spotted and held his son and Qindong back behind the corner, out of view. He turned to his son and laid both hands on the boy's shoulders, glad not to feel them tremble.

"Son," he whispered, trying to think of the best way to phrase his words, knowing he had to be fast, but also knowing that this was no small moment in the boy's life. "You volunteered to come with me, and I appreciate that. Now, I need your help. Songba needs your help. There are two guards ahead. I need you to use my bow to shoot an arrow into one of them while I kill the other – and you must be careful not to shoot me. I know this is a lot to ask of you, my son, believe me, I know. I am sorry for asking it. But it is necessary. Think of Songba. Think of our family. Do what you must. And remember, I'm proud of you, Wulan. Take out an arrow. Do it now. When I go around the corner, you do the same. Do not think. Just aim and shoot. And you, Qindong – do not move a damned muscle or I *will* find you, and I *will* kill you. Got it? Good. Ready, son?"

Wulan was holding an arrow to his father's bow, looking positively green.

Chun did not wait for an answer; what would happen would happen. He sprang around the corner and sprinted at the two guards, some fifteen feet away. Chun moved fast, keeping to the left-hand side of the narrow candlelit corridor, his shadow cavorting capriciously, flickering in the firelight. He could see in the guards' eyes that they were confused; he was dressed as one of them, after all. They took a step back, and then he saw their eyes dart behind him, where he guessed Wulan must have stepped out from behind the corner. He knew what they must be thinking then; it must have looked to them like he was running away from the boy with the bow, fleeing for his life.

By the time they realised the truth, it was too late. Chun heard a twang and, out of the corner of his eye, saw a thin black blur streak through the air alongside him. He felt the wind of it as it passed. A split second later, the guard on the right doubled over and staggered back, groaning, with an arrow in the gut. A heartbeat after that, Chun reached the second guard, who was frantically trying to tug out his katana. The guard moved as Chun sought to stove in his skull, so instead the woodcutter's hatchet clove into his collarbone and down into his chest, eliciting a sharp cry and a geyser of blood. Chun wrenched his axe out of the man's torso and turned on the other guard, who was backing away slowly, bent over and holding his side where the arrow had punctured him. Chun's axe took him in the cheek and smashed his face all to pieces. Once again, the woodcutter was sprayed with bits of bone and gore.

Chun wiped his face with bloody hands and turned to his son, who was standing behind him with another arrow nocked. He could feel warm blood trickling down his face, clotting in his beard. He paced slowly over to the boy and laid a gentle hand on his head.

"Well done, Wulan. And thank you. You did what you had to do. Come now, let's –"

Wulan suddenly doubled over and retched, but he had already vomited and he had nothing left to regurgitate. Chun let him gag for a few seconds, looking up and down the corridor nervously. He checked around the corner and was surprised to find Qindong there, sitting against the wall, hugging his knees and muttering with eyes wide. He looked like he had leapt clean off the precipice of sanity into the murky depths beyond. Chun pulled him to his feet.

When the boy finished spluttering, his father patted him on the back and said, "Come now, let's find Ada Yuongang. Qindong, take us to her."

"Yes, yes," the old man murmured, eyes vacant. "Ada Yuongang. Of course."

He led them on and up. At the bottom of the stairs on the seventh floor, Qindong turned to Chun and Wulan and whispered, "Up there are the chambers of the Shenzhan and his wife. There are guards there, though. You'll never get in alive."

Chun nodded thoughtfully, staring mournfully at Qindong. The old man could not be allowed to leave; he would raise the alarm, and then they would never escape with Songba. He thought of what he had said to Wulan; do what you must. He sighed and whispered in his son's ear for a second. Then, he put an axe-sized dent in Qindong's face, and the man fell without a sound except the thump as he hit the floor. Wulan did not puke or scream or make any noise or acknowledgement whatsoever, having been forewarned. He did, however, turn a touch greener.

"There are probably two at the top of the stairs," whispered Chun to his son. "So same plan again. You shoot one, I club one. Be ready when we round the corner."

The stairs went up in front of them and then turned out of sight in a switchback. The two of them crept up the stairs, Chun hefting his axe and Wulan with an arrow nocked and ready. Chun rounded the corner at a tight angle and took off up the stairs at full pelt. It was lucky he tripped and fell, for a crossbow bolt hummed through the air where he had been standing, fracturing the stone beside Wulan's head as he rounded the corner. There were indeed two guards at the top of the stairs, both wielding crossbows, and the second loosed a bolt at the boy as Wulan drew back his father's bow.

Wulan went down before he could loose his shaft, punched from his feet by the crossbow bolt. Slammed into the wall, he wheezed and slumped to the ground. Not seeing what had transpired, Chun sprang up and faced the two armoured guards, who were throwing aside their crossbows and laying their hands on the hilts of their swords. Roaring and pouncing like a great cat, like a madman, Chun was on one of them before he could draw steel, and he clobbered the man down with a hefty blow that caved in his ear, and skull and brain beyond.

Chun tried to dodge as the second guard stabbed at him with a snarl, but he did not move fast enough. He spat and growled as he felt the shudder of cold steel pass through his flesh, lancing through his insides like a red-hot poker. The katana took him through his left thigh, however, so the woodcutter was not slain on the spot. Spitting and hissing, Chun lurched at the guard, brimming with fury. This man would not stand between him and his child. He got his hands on the guard's neck and bore him to the ground with brute force. The guard let go of his sword and punched and flailed and wriggled and tried every trick he knew to escape Chun's hold. The two writhed on the floor in eerie silence for a minute, both red in the face with effort, frothing at the mouth, their eyes popping out of their skulls.

Then, the guard's arms stopped flailing and flopped to the ground, limp. Chun looked down into the guard's eyes, which seemed to be staring at a far-off point, waiting for them to blink. They would never blink again, though; he had crushed the man's windpipe. The man was dead.

Chun felt again the pain of the stabbing then, tearing through him like a wildfire, setting his innards ablaze. The katana was still inside him, penetrating his thigh. Its point was poking out of the back of his leg, dripping with gore. The pain was as nothing to the agony he felt when he turned, however, and saw his son slumped against the wall with a bolt high in his chest.

"Wulan!" he gasped, wincing with the effort.

He made to move toward his son, but the sword caught against his dead foe and he ground his teeth as he spasmed in pain. He knew he could not move until he got the sword out of him. With great difficulty, he slipped off one stinky boot and bit on its leather. The boot was cold and grimy and gritty against his tongue. Then, he tugged the katana out of his leg, slowly but surely, wheezing and snorting with agony every step of the way. Tendons in his neck stood out stark, rivulets of sweat trickled down his face, his eyes bugged, and his face turned plum-purple.

After what seemed like a torturous age, he removed the blade and cast it aside to land with a soft thump on the dead guard's legs.

Spitting out the boot and putting it back on his foot was one of the most challenging tasks of his long life. Gritting his teeth, he tried moving. Excruciating was far from the right word, but it was the most appropriate, the best of a poor lot, for the sensation that gripped him then. He felt like he would have welcomed death as an old friend had he rounded the corner at the bottom of the stairs just then.

The only thing that kept him going was the thought of his children. He had to get to Wulan. He had to get to Songba. He had to protect them. He had to keep them safe.

He wasn't sure how he made it back down the stairs to reach Wulan, but when he did he found that the bolt had pierced the boy's shoulder. Wulan was pallid and wan, sweating and shivering, but still breathing.

Wishing he could tell the boy he loved him, that he was proud of him, that he was sorry, but not having the breath, Chun grunted, "Hold still," and yanked the bolt out of his son's shoulder. Wulan would have cried out then, but his father had smothered his mouth with a hand, and so he only groaned and snuffled. "Good lad," Chun mumbled, watching the wound gush blood with trepidation. Every motion was an agony. He could see that his son was worse off than him, though, so he said, "Stay here. I'll be back for you, son."

Wulan nodded tiredly, seemingly capable of little more. Chun turned his back on his eldest son and set off back up the stairs to retrieve his youngest, his injured leg dragging behind him awkwardly. The stairs were like a nightmare climb, but he found that with each step he trod, his rage redoubled. When he took his axe in hand once more, the knobbly wood of its haft felt comforting in his calloused hand, even dripping with blood as it was. His wrath when he reached the top had him trembling from passion rather than pain, and he vowed to himself not to leave this place without both his sons. He would take back Songba, and he would kill those that had taken him from his family.

The door at the top of the stairs was unlocked, and Chun slipped inside like a wraith. Ada Yuongang and the Shenzhan, Tung Fuo, were making love on the bed; Chun could see their outlines through the gauze that hung around the four-poster bed, and hear their amorous moans.

In a terrible, hoarse voice, the woodcutter said, "Father, I have come home."

The Shenzhan and his wife sprang up like startled chickens, clucking the same way, demanding in shrill, violated voices to know who dared to trespass in their chambers at such an hour.

"My name is Chun Lun of Podang, and I have come for my son."

Silence stretched across the room then, taut as a drum-skin. The discomfort and the fear were as palpable as the axe in his hand; Chun thought he had the vaguest inkling of how some predatory beast might feel then, stalking its prey, smelling its fear on the wind. He drank it in like a fine wine, savoured it, let drops of blood drip from his axe onto the Shenzhan's plush carpet. The room was an exercise in needless opulence; there wasn't a single functional object in the room, except perhaps the bed, despite the fact that the room was littered with expensive furniture and sculptures and candles and ornaments and potted plants. The room confirmed Chun's suspicions; he hated these people.

Dressing themselves hurriedly behind the gauze, the Shenzhan and his wife then tentatively emerged, like rabid butterflies from a rancid cocoon, resplendent even in their night-attire. Their old, golden-skinned faces were pictures of contrition.

Ada Yuongang spoke, her tone wheedling. "Chun Lun, please put down the axe. You must understand that what was done was for the best for all inv-"

"Tung Fuo," Chun spoke over her loudly, "I do not know if you know what your wife has done to me. I do not know if she speaks the truth when she says you are my father. But I pray you are an honourable man, Shenzhan, and so I will give you one chance to right the wrongs that have been committed. Return my son to me now, and I will leave you be."

Tung Fuo looked affronted and drew himself up to his full height, bristling with indignation. "Look here, young man," he said sternly, "do not presume that you can come into *my* bedchambers and make demands of *me*. Whatever your grievance, schedule an appointment and we can discuss it in the day time like civilised folk."

Chun shook his head. "No, we will discuss it now. Where is my son?"

"I will not give in to these wild demands!"

"Give me my son, Shenzhan, or I will kill you and your wife."

Tung Fuo sprang to his bedside table and pulled out a knife

from behind it, before bouncing back to where he had started, brandishing the blade.

"Kill *me?*" he sneered. "I don't think s-"

Chun had always been a champion axe-thrower among the woodcutters of Podang. They would hold impromptu little contests now and again to see who could fling their hatchets furthest and most accurately. Chun almost always won for accuracy.

Now, in those stuffy bedchambers, Chun imagined the Shenzhan's face was a knot in a bole he was aiming for, and the hatchet took him between the eyes, blade-first. The axe split him open like a pumpkin on the Day of the Dead. He fell, poleaxed, and his brains splattered the carpet, the bed-gauze, the ceiling and his wife.

Ada Yuongang's scream reminded Chun of an eagle's screech; high, raw and warbling. She flew at Chun like a raptorial bird then, clawing at his eyes and face with her talons. He shoved her off him with his bare hands, grunting at the effort and the stitch of pain it caused in his thigh. She slipped, tripped and toppled over backwards with her arms flailing wildly. She landed on her husband, and from the clunk as she went down, Chun was confident she had knocked herself out cold on the haft of his hatchet.

He stood staring at the two of them for a moment, and then he looked up. A heavy iron-cast chandelier was dangling over the two of them, and he followed the rope that supported it down to a metal sconce on the wall. He tugged his hatchet out of his father's face with a gruesome sucking sound and a red spray, and then he turned, strode across the room and cut the rope. The chandelier clattered down to the ground behind him, crushing the two figures splayed out on the floor.

Chun stared at them again for a moment, their forms cracked, crumpled and bloodied, and he said, "Goodbye, father."

Then, he turned and left, wincingly. He stumbled down to the bottom of the first set of stairs, where surprisingly he found Wulan in a much-improved state. The boy was on his feet, leaning heavily against the wall and staunching the flow of his own blood with his fur coat as best he could. He was still pale and shivery, but at least he was standing, marvelled Chun. He guessed the bolt must have hit closer to the shoulder than the lungs and thanked the Gods.

"Come, Wulan," he breathed, "we still must find Songba. It looks like there is little else on this top floor; let us check the next one down."

So, they descended, leaning on one another like a pair of drunkards, both cursing and griping and spitting with agony at every step. Circumventing Qindong's body at the bottom, they approached the nearest door. Luck was finally on their side; it was opened by a face the woodcutter recognised.

"Tung Shaku," growled Chun Lun, barging into the room and seizing the Shenzhan's son by the throat, "where is my son, you son of a bitch?"

Tung Shaku hit at Chun's arm, but otherwise seemed too shocked to retaliate. He soon started turning blue and wheezing, though, and he gasped, "In here! He's in here!"

Chun looked around the room. It was almost as lavish as the Shenzhan's, but the woodcutter's eyes saw nothing but the babe in the young woman's arms. Chun smashed Tung's head against a wall and tossed him aside like a child discarding a toy. Then, he crossed the room in three great strides and was by the bedside, by his son. The whimpering woman offered him the child, and he took Songba wordlessly from her arms, enchanted by the child's handsome little face. Songba smiled up at him sleepily, chubby cheeks bunching up. Chun moved to stroke the child's head, only covered with the slightest dark fuzz, with his hand, but saw that it held his axe and that it was coated in gore, so he refrained.

He turned and passed his youngest son to his eldest, who slung his father's bow over his shoulder in order to take the baby swaddled in blankets. Chun turned back to the woman whose name he did not even know, who was cowering in terror and mewling incoherently.

He sighed. "I am tired of killing," he growled. "I am going to gag you and tie you up now, but I will not kill you if you do not resist. Lie down on the bed."

She was too scared to resist; he did not blame her. He could only imagine what he looked like by now; a blood-drenched monster come from the night, a vengeful spirit, a Demon. So, he lashed her to the bed with her own belts and sashes and stuffed a wad of cloth in her mouth so that she could not raise the alarm once they left. Then, Chun poked his head out of the room, looked this way and that, and then beckoned his son to follow him. Wulan staggered along behind his father, carrying his little brother.

Chun's memories of their escape afterwards were fuzzy. He thought he remembered getting into at least one more brawl within the pagoda, perhaps two. He had no idea how he survived them in his condition; the next thing he remembered, he was dripping with fresh, hot blood and sneaking out into the cool night air with Wulan. He was carrying Songba by then, he recalled. Together, they snuck through the complex once more just as they had done on their way in.

They headed for the gate through which they had entered, but just before they got there, Wulan collapsed in the snow behind the final corner. Chun tried to rally him, to lift him, but to no avail.

"I cannot move," said Wulan through chattering teeth. "You have to leave me here, pa. I cannot move, but I can provide a distraction so that you and Songba can get out the gates."

Chun had refused and protested, as any parent would, but in the end the boy's logic was irrefutable. He could not move, but he could still be of use as bait. So, eventually, with dawn not too far away, Chun agreed with tears in his eyes and slunk away from his son, first giving him a final kiss on the forehead.

After he had hidden himself close by, Chun heard Wulan start shouting in a hoarse, broken voice. The boy called out to the guards, calling them turd-pots and dung-beetles and all sorts of inventive insults. Chun heard the guards responding and, from his hiding place, saw them vacate the gate to venture toward the hollering boy. He knew he was looking at his chance; he had Songba in his arms and the gate was unguarded. He could not leave his eldest son behind, though, and the gate was still locked.

So, Chun set Songba down on a barrel under a wide eave, placing a hemp sack of unknown contents beside him to prevent him falling off. Then, he went back for Wulan.

The expressions on the two guards' faces as he pelted at them was comical, their fumbling for their swords less so. He hacked his axe deep into the neck of one before the man could unsheathe his sword, and the guard died with a gurgle. Thinking ahead this time, Chun swung away from the second guard so that the corpse of the first was between them. So, when the second guard lashed out with his katana, he struck only his dead friend.

Then, Chun wrenched out his axe and the dead guard crumpled to the ground between the two fighters. Guard and imposter snarled at one another for a moment, brandishing blades, but then the guard's concentration was broken when Wulan abruptly howled like a wolf. The guard's gaze flickered to the side as he thought of turning, and by the time his eyes flicked back, the blade of Chun's axe was shining like bright moonlight in his face.

Chun checked the dead guards over and took their keyrings. Then, he crouched by Wulan and said, "Come on, son. I've got you."

Without waiting for an answer, ignoring the boy's objections, Chun forced his son back to his feet. Then, supporting Wulan with an arm under his shoulder, Chun tottered back to where he had left Songba. Tucking his trusty hatchet into his belt then, he carefully scooped up the baby so that it was cradled in the crook of his spare arm. With a son in each arm then, he limped to the gate. He had given the keyrings to Wulan, who tried different keys until he found the one that worked and the gate opened with a click. Chun let out a sigh of relief; he had been expecting sounds of alarm and running guards behind him at any second while they waited.

The woodcutter and his sons slipped out of the complex, unnoticed, into the streets of Haipei on the Green River. Not long later, despite their injuries, they were slinking out of the city limits the same way they had snuck in; through the copse bordering the paved streets.

Once in the woods, however, disaster struck. Wulan collapsed, coughing blood. Seeing the end in his oldest son's eyes, Chun laid Songba down gently on the grass and cradled Wulan's head in his lap. "No!" he moaned softly, over and over, stroking his son's face. "No!"

"It's alright, pa," Wulan whispered as his face drained of blood. "It's alright ..."

Chun sniffled and said thickly, "I am so proud of you, my boy. Never has any father been prouder of any son, I swear it! You are everything I have ever wanted and more, Wulan. Don't leave me, please!"

"It's alright, pa." The boy's voice was faint now. "We got back Songba. We killed those that took him. We did ... what we had to do. It's alright."

"No, it isn't!" Chun groaned in anguish. "It's not alright. I don't want to lose you! I love you, Wulan! D'you hear me? D'you hear me? Wulan? Wulan? Wulan! No!"

Chun was grief-stricken, grief-smitten, grief-maimed, grief-killed. Grief gnawed at him from the inside out, stripping away his very core and leaving him empty, utterly spent.

When he could finally breathe again past the sobbing and see again past the tears, he looked up at the sky, at the cruel Gods. What was he going to tell his wife? How could he tell Hao Nin that he had saved one son but lost another?

Phut and the Blood Worms

The Day of Hrumdrum was a day like no other, for it was a day the people summoned giant blood worms by beating drums and beating their feet on the ground.

That was the origin of the day, anyway. It was said that, in ages past, all the clans of Ogbun Nagali had been terrorised by the *Congols* – ancient, giant blood worms. So, in order to appease the beasts and save the majority of their peoples, the clan chiefs had come together to organise a sacrifice. They had honoured those they sacrificed by holding a grand celebration in their honour; the celebration had also served to awaken the worms. Then, when the worms had come, the festivities would end abruptly and the clans would flee for their lives, leaving behind the sacrifices, who had been bound at wrists and ankles. That was the origin of the day, anyway.

Then, one day, a long time ago, the festivities had not been interrupted. The clans had feasted and drank themselves into a stupor all night long, and not once had a blood worm reared its head. Those that had been bound to be sacrificed were cut free the following morning. Since that day, not a single blood worm had been seen and they were presumed extinct. The annual celebration, however, had continued. So, every year at the start of winter, all the nomadic clans would gather together on the plains of Horrok-Muur and try to awaken the worms.

Phut of the Sujjuks was far more concerned with the annual wrestling tournament held on the Day of Hrumdrum than the worms. He had been training for it all year, after all. He refused to be beaten by that pompous arse-face, Yamen of the Kirrus, again. Squatting down on one leg to stretch out the other, he coloured with shame at the memory. He had not even made it to the quarter-finals. He glanced up at the overcast sky and prayed to the Sky Father that it would not rain; that would ruin his footing.

Seeing Phut's young face tighten with angst, his father ruffled his son's curly black hair. "You'll do better this year, Phut. You've been working hard."

Damn right, he had been working hard. Phut had been up at dawn almost every day this last year, running with the horses instead of riding them, climbing trees and hefting logs. Then, when his brothers finally awoke each day, he would practise his wrestling moves on them, whether they were willing or not. It was better practise if they were unwilling, after all. In the afternoons, he would help his father with the clan harras, or herd, wrangling the horses and checking them over. He would clean out their hooves, brush them down, feed them oats and show them to troughs of water. As a result, he was pleased to have seen a change in himself. His sixteen-year-old body was noticeably bulkier than it had been a year ago, broader in the shoulders, taller and tauter. He stroked the soft skin on his chin and pursed his lips to one side ruefully; still no sign of a beard like the magnificent specimen his father had grown.

"I'm going to go for a jog to loosen my muscles," said Phut, eyeing the fight in progress where two boys of his age were grappling one another, trying to heave each other out of the dirt ring amid the grass.

"Don't over-exert yourself. Your fight is soon!" his father barked after him as he set off.

"I know. I won't."

The Nagali were here in force today, drinking fermented mare's milk and smoking baui out of leaves and pipes. All the clans had shown up; all had survived the last winter. Thousands of people milled around a wide open expanse set in the middle of a sea of white yurts dotting the grassy landscape, looking like a colony of ants amid a cluster of cotton at a distance. Up close, the people were infinitely more colourful than drab ants, however. Everyone was in their finest regalia, prettied up in patterned robes, also called dels, or adorned in their most garish cotton or hemp trousers and tunics. Fur overcoats abounded, for a chill wind bespoke the plains at this time of year, and everyone was wearing their favourite fur hat.

Phut, on the other hand, was dressed in blue and red breeches that reached only to his knees, and was barefooted and topless. His golden skin was gleaming with sweat that had little to do with exertion, but paid its dues to nerves. He was facing Yamen in an early match this year; if he beat him, he might be able to make it to the quarter-finals this time, maybe even the semis ...

Running past colourfully garbed folk from all clans, Phut swerved in surprise and almost tumbled into a yurt when the crowd let loose a howl to shake the skies. Swerving again, he passed the yurt and tried to sneak a peek past the press of people blocking his view of the wrestling match in progress. It looked like one of the boys had slammed the other to the ground and was now taunting him.

Phut shook his head; a waste of breath.

By the time he had completed a circuit around the open expanse in the middle of the sea of yurts, the fight was over; the taunter had won. Phut shook his head again; the victory would doubtless enforce poor lessons in the boy's mind. One did not waste breath until one's enemy was defeated.

His father evidently thought the same thing, for he could be seen frowning at the boy, shaking his head and muttering, "Fool of a boy."

His father saw Phut coming. He did not smile, but his grey beard twitched as though he might be thinking about it.

He patted his son on the shoulder when he arrived by his side. "One more fight, then you're up. Relax now, conserve your strength."

Phut stood by his father, amid the people of his clan, and watched the next wrestlers square off. He didn't know the wrestlers; two boys from other clans, also topless, barefoot and wearing breeches similar to his own. Both were relatively sparsely built, whip-lean but small. Phut thought the weight seemed evenly distributed across the ring; it would be a fair, interesting fight.

The boys' names were announced as Kult of the Anjaks and Tirin of the Hassumats. Then, the announcer – a big man in a black coat – called for the match to begin in a booming baritone.

The two youths hurled themselves at one another, crashing together like headbutting rams. It occurred to Phut that they did it for the same purpose as rams, too – for prestige and to impress the ladies. More than wrestling matches were arranged on the Day of Hrumdrum. Phut felt his pulse quicken as his eyes wandered from the fight to scout out a few girls about his age opposite him across the great open expanse of grass. They saw him watching and giggled and pointed. He blushed and looked away, forced his eyes back to the fight, pretended that was where they had always lain.

The two boys were tugging one another round in circles, arms interlocked, heads knocking. They acknowledged the stalemate and separated, then clashed like cymbals once more, trying to get a new hold with better leverage. Tirin went especially low and tried to grab at the other's waist, which is normally a good tactic, for it is easier to upheave someone from lower down. In this instance, however, the ploy did not work. Kult grabbed, twisted and tripped his opponent cleverly and the crowd hollered, thousands of feet thumping the ground in approval.

Tirin went down, but stayed in the ring. As the rules require, Kult let his opponent rise again. They faced off once more, then Kult charged in, evidently overconfident. It was Tirin's turn to skip to the side and grab his opponent, using his momentum against him and trying to fling him out of the ring by one arm. It was a common, effective strategy, but Kult seized Tirin's arm even as it gripped him. So, they whirled together, both teetering on the edge of the ring for a moment while the watchers cheered them on in a deafening, discordant chorus.

Finally, Kult threw Tirin out of the ring to sprawl on the grass and the clans whooped and hooted and booed and cried out in a thousand conflicting voices. The very earth shook with their stomping. Kult turned in a slow circle, panting and grinning, his arms raised above his head.

"You're next," said Phut's father.

As if Phut needed reminding.

Kult exited the ring, and the announcer called out, "Continuing with the same age group, the next match will be between Yamen of the Kirrus and Phut of the Sujjuks!"

Phut and Yamen made their way to the dirt ring in the midst of the onlookers. The sky was still woolly, but it was not spitting, for which Phut thanked the Sky Father. His heart felt like a bird fluttering, trying to fly away. His stomach dropped out of him as he crossed into the ring, and his knees wobbled. He gritted his teeth and ignored the sensations, reminding himself that he had been training hard all year for this moment. He would not fail.

He looked Yamen up and down. The damn boy had gotten bigger over the last year. He was a head taller than Phut, just as he had been the year before, and built like a gorilla with a barrel chest and massive arms, shoulders and hands. His round face was grinning arrogantly, just as it had been the year before. He too wore only breeches, his black and yellow.

"Phut!" he said, as if they were old friends. "It's good to see you again. Hard to believe it's been a whole year since I put you on your back, eh? How've you been? Hope I didn't cause any permanent damage, haha!"

Phut wanted to smack that stupid smile off his stupid face. There are rules in wrestling, though; no punches, only grappling. So, he ignored Yamen, waiting for the announcer to call the start of the match. The announcer was taking his time, though, chatting to a friend between bouts. Phut's stomach was full of butterflies.

Yamen was still grinning. "So, how quick d'you think you'll go down this time, little Phut? A minute? Two? I don't think you're likely to last much longer than that, to be honest. Let's say two, shall we? Let's be optimistic, haha!"

Phut ground his teeth. His rage was like a furnace in his chest, but he would not waste breath on this fool.

Eventually, the announcer turned back to the combatants and called out, "Yamen of the Kirrus, Phut of the Sujjuks, are you ready to begin?"

"I am!" they said together, not taking their eyes off one another.

"Then, begin!"

They both crouched into fighting stances, lowering their centres and making it more difficult for the other to lift them or get a hold. They began to circle one another like prowling wildcats, movements lithe and smooth. For all his brawn, Yamen did not move like a dumb animal. He knew how to fight – more was the pity, thought Phut.

Then, like frisky young rams, they butted heads. Their shoulders smashed together, arms interwoven, hands scrabbling for a hold. Their faces were so close together Phut could smell Yamen's breath and musk. He snarled and heaved, trying to heft his opponent off-balance, even as Yamen did the same to him. As a result, they spun together, staggering like a pair of drunks clutching one another for support. The roar of the crowd had dimmed to background noise now, muted in Phut's mind. His whole world had become the little dirt circle that he could not be thrown out of.

The purity of the fight made his heart swell and his eyes focus more sharply than ever. The purity came from singlemindedness. In a fight, there were no extraneous thoughts; only necessities. Sometimes, in a perfect fighting state, there were no thoughts at all; only instincts and reflexes, action and reaction. Such transcendence felt akin to enlightenment to the boy, and he knew it was a common trait across all the Nagali. They were warriors born, his father had always said.

Battle was in their blood.

His lungs heaved in breath quickly and easily, and he felt flexible and strong. His body moved in the patterns to which it was attuned; the patterns to which he had trained it. Despite this, he fell back a step. Knowing he could not overpower the other through sheer force, Phut turned the pushing contest into a scuffle. Spinning and pulling his opponent with him, trying to trip him and keep him off-balance, Phut darted around the ring while Yamen lumbered after him. Phut felt like a possum taking on a black bear, but Yamen could not get a decent hold on him as long as he kept moving, so that was what he did. Like Tirin had done to Kult, Phut tried to use his opponent's momentum and weight against him, tugging him by the arm toward the edge of the ring.

Yamen refused to be defeated by such simple tactics, however, and Phut found – to his ire – that he had hissed, "Sky Father!" invoking the Nagali's God.

Yamen was grinning again as they squared off once more. "Getting annoyed, Phut? Thought you had me there, did you? Haha, I don't think so, my little friend! You won't get me so easily."

Yamen came at Phut low, but being naturally shorter, Phut simply lowered himself and met the attack head on, twisting and trying to throw Yamen down as he did so. Yamen stumbled, but did not go down, and Phut cursed inwardly. How could the damn boy be so tall and yet so balanced?

He tried again, but he was getting desperate and he overbalanced in his excitement. He realised too late, when he was already off-balance and he felt Yamen's leg sweeping his own. The sky whirled above him, and then the ground struck him on the back, hard. He wheezed for a moment after his wind abandoned him. He glanced to one side and saw that, thankfully, he lay in the dirt ring. His pride was wounded more than his body; he hated that Yamen had put him on his back again.

Waiting until his breath returned, he then got back to his feet, barely aware of the cheering surrounding him, although he could feel the ground vibrating beneath his bare toes from the pounding of a thousand feet.

Facing Yameg again, he forced his anger down and reprimanded himself. One must not fight with anger, one must fight with skill. He had allowed his emotions to dictate his movement, and he had made a mistake. He resolved that it would not happen again. He waited patiently for Yamen to attack, but when he did not, Phut decided to take the initiative himself. He darted at his foe low, lower than Yamen could comfortably go and quick enough that he could not stop the smaller boy. Phut managed to hook his thumbs into Yamen's breeches, and though the larger lad grappled him from above, Phut was now in a position of power with the lower leverage.

Bending his legs, he hoisted the other boy up with all his strength, wedging Yamen's breeches up his buttcrack. He barely managed to heft the heavy boy off the ground, but – with red face and tendons popping out – he just managed it, tottered forward a step and slammed Yamen down to the ground on his back, hard. He cursed inwardly when he saw that he had not gone far enough to throw the bigger lad out of the ring, but he recognised that he had gone as far as he could and that he had done well. The other boy would be weaker now.

While Yamen lay gasping for breath, Phut finally heard the cheers. It felt good to be cheered, and he was tempted to look around, to bask in the adoration, but he knew he must not lose focus. One must not lose focus until the fight was over. So, although he heard the hooting, he did not acknowledge it in any way. He stood still, sucking in ragged breaths and watching Yamen do the same on the ground. He felt the earth shaking beneath his feet, shaking so violently that he wondered if another thousand people had joined the celebrations while he wasn't looking.

The cheers died down, but the shaking continued, which was odd. Why would the people still be stamping if they weren't shouting? The ground was distractingly turbulent, juddering visibly now as if in the grip of an earthquake. Phut wished the clans would stop their damned stomping before he lost his balance and fell on his arse. Realising he had been looking at the ground, Phut guiltily returned his gaze to Yamen and saw something strange in the boy's expression. Yamen was not looking at him; he was looking past him, and he was deadly afraid.

Phut was convinced it was a ruse to trick him into looking away so that Yamen could jump up and seize him from behind. He kept his eyes on the boy a while longer, but then he could take the ignorance no longer. He turned and looked, knowing his father would give him a smack for doing so.

What he saw made him forget about any punishments his father might have for him, made him forget about his father, about Yamen, about the fight, about almost everything in fact.

What he saw was that the Nagali were not stomping, not one of them. They were not shaking the ground. The ground was shaking on its own.

Phut's face fell slack with fear like thousands of others as they all stared in mute horror at the ground beneath their feet. The shuddering increased until Phut could barely keep his feet, and though Yamen tried, it looked like he could not rise. He looked like a beached whale. From the look on his face, it was clear that he too had forgotten all about the fight. Juddered from his position, not even realising that he had just lost the match, Phut staggered out of the dirt ring and managed to steady himself on the grass.

A heartbeat later, the dirt in the ring exploded upwards and Yamen was engulfed in ochre dust, removed from sight. As the dirt began to spread and disperse in the air, it became possible to see through it and Phut's eyes almost popped out of his skull in fright.

A worm, as wide as a man was tall, was erupting up out of the ground, and Phut could see Yamen's screaming torso hanging out of its top, his legs hidden inside the worm's mouth. Strangely, Phut's first thought was to be furious at the worm for denying him his victory; he had been so close to finally beating Yamen, and now he would never get the chance. His second thought was that he had never wanted Yamen dead and that he was sorry to see him go. His third thought was to run away.

He was rooted to the spot by fear, though, unable to move a muscle. Like everyone now living, he had never seen a blood worm, had thought them extinct, in fact. To see one in the flesh was both awe- and dread-inspiring. He was not sure why but he had expected the worm to be red, perhaps because of its name. It proved to be bone-white, covered in little black bristles, and segmented like any common earthworm, albeit a hundred times larger. Already ten feet of it was sticking out of the ground, and more was still emerging. Fortunately for Phut, the worm turned away from him and snaked across the grass towards one side of the crowd. By the time it had fully emerged from the ground, it was at least fifty feet long, Phut reckoned. The young wrestler realised the worm was wriggling toward his father and the rest of his family, and his feet finally unglued.

"Father!" he cried as he flew across the grass, chasing the worm.

People were scattering in all directions now, screeching and fleeing for their lives in a mass uproar. Pandemonium ensued with people being shoved aside, knocked down and trampled by their own clansmen. The Nagali, all of the clans, were natural riders; most kept large herds of horses throughout the year, constantly shifting grazing pastures. Now, they all made for their horses, or for any horse they could find, regardless of ownership. Had anyone stolen a horse under normal circumstances, it would have been cause for a blood feud lasting years. That day, no one cared. Everyone who could grabbed a horse and made for the distant hills.

Many did not reach the horses, however. Many did not get far at all before the blood worm caught them. Unfortunately, the Sujjuks were at the heart of the travesty, hemmed in by other clans, unable to make a hasty egress. The worm meandered across the grass and was on them in seconds, even as they turned and ran.

Being behind the worm, Phut could hear the people screaming and could see them vanishing in a scarlet haze as the worm caught up to them, but he could not see the intricacies of their deaths, for which he was grateful. The worm's head was turning red now with the blood of its victims; it was living up to its name. It slithered surprisingly quickly, and Phut had a hard time keeping up. He lost count, but he thought the worm devoured more than a score of people while he was pursuing it.

Finally, realising they were not going to escape, a few men shouted out to each other and banded together. They turned, drew their swords and faced the great beast head on. Phut's heart swelled with pride and then spasmed in fear to see his father among them. The sabre he held – three feet of curved steel attached to a bone handle – had once seemed like a mighty weapon to the boy. Now, it seemed like a pin with which to fight a giant anaconda.

The worm slowed and reared up high over the small knot of gathered warriors. A dozen men looked up at it in mortal fear as it drooled blood and saliva on them. Then, the worm lunged down and Phut saw an unknown man disappear in a crimson flash. The others hacked at the worm with their blades, but it hardly seemed to notice or care. Phut's father swung his sword two-handed with a vicious snarl on his face, but it looked like the steel barely bit in an inch. Then, the sabre was yanked out of his hand as the worm lifted its head once more.

Seeing his father defenceless, Phut's heart began to pound and he somehow quickened his pace, despite the burn in his legs. He was close to the back of the worm now. He prayed to the Sky Father that his own father would survive just a little longer.

He felt like the Sky Father laughed in his face, pulled down his trousers and pissed all over him.

Barely had he thought the prayer when the worm coiled up like a snake. Then, it spun rapidly, uncoiling as it did so, and used its tail to whip all of the remaining men. Every one of them was sent flying through the air, and many of them lost their grips on their weapons. Phut was still too far away to help, and the worm had knocked his father yet further away. His heart panging, roaring with rage and anguish, Phut pelted after the creature. Before he could get close, it was casting its sinuous shadow over the surviving men and then biting down at them, one by one. Each time it did so, a man would vanish from sight in a crimson spray, eaten in an instant.

Time seemed to slow for Phut as the worm converged on his father, who was lying prone in the grass amid yellow flowers. Phut was not sure if he was breathing. The worm reared up above the fallen man, but Phut was close now and he swept up a dropped sword as he ran. The feel of the sabre was unfamiliar in his hands, but its weight gave him confidence. He was sure it could cleave through a man with such weight, so why not a worm? He forced himself to calm as he ran – one must not fight with anger, one must fight with skill.

As the worm was about to bite down at his father, Phut pelted up behind the creature and leapt at it. Mid-air, he brought the sabre scything down on the worm and caught it, completely by luck, where its segments joined. The worm's leathery hide was weakest there, little did he know it, and the blade bit deep into the joint, parting the segments and unleashing gouts of stinky white ichor all over him. He fell to the ground then, sword yet in hand, and stepped back lest the worm whip him with its tail while it wailed.

It gave a high-pitched keening and writhed in pain, and Phut almost smirked at the sight. Then, he reminded himself – one must not lose focus until the fight was over. He thought about shouting out to his father, but then remembered – one did not waste breath until one's enemy was defeated. There would be time to see to his father if he survived.

Phut squared off against the worm, finally witnessing its unpleasant face. Flecked and dripping with gore, its nub of a head had no facial features other than a small white lobe of unknown purpose beside a cavernous, circular mouth with round rows of jagged teeth. Its breath stank of rotten meat and death. Phut gulped and forced back a mouthful of vomit.

The worm lunged at him like a striking snake, but it seemed slower now that it was wounded. Sidestepping, Phut hacked at it artlessly and gaped in astonishment when the blade bounced off its thick, white hide. He dodged its mouth, but was knocked down by its bulk anyway. He rolled backwards and came up smoothly with the sabre held before him. He grasped it with both hands and watched the worm rear up with a shriek and come down again, its mouth open wide, seeking to engulf him. He thought he could see bits of the people it had eaten lodged in between its teeth.

He dove to the right and rolled on his shoulder. The worm bit the earth alongside him, the impact almost juddering him from his feet. Nevertheless, he came up fast and lashed out with his blade, this time aiming for the joint between segments, realising the creature's weakness. The blade bit deep. Hot, white goo spurted over the boy, and the giant worm shrieked. Wiping blood out of his eyes, Phut almost didn't see the worm coming for him again with a quick snatching bite. He staggered back to avoid it, tripped on a little hummock in the grass and tottered away from it as its round jaws snapped shut like a sphincter barely a foot away. He flailed his arms for balance, and the worm bit at him yet again. He was off-balance; there was nothing he could do.

The jagged agony as the circling rows of teeth sank into his right arm was beyond any words Phut could conjure; it was almost pleasurable it was so excruciating, as though the two sensations were somehow linked and he had come full circle between them. He thought he might have laughed out loud in hysteria, in fact, when the bone snapped beneath the grinding teeth.

The wrenching pain as his arm was torn off beneath the elbow was equally indelible. Blood blossomed there, along with the pain, both spurting out together, burning hot and numbing as ice. Despite his fury at the Sky Father earlier, Phut now tiredly thanked him that he had been born left-handed. His left hand was untouched, and it still held the sword.

Ironically, the tug at his right arm had helped him regain his balance, and so even as the worm bit off one arm, his other brought the sword round to spear into the creature's head, in the top joint between segments. The skin burst beneath the steel like ripe fruit, and the blade sunk in to the disc-shaped hilt, again spattering Phut with gore. He did not care this time; he was finished.

As his arm was torn free, the sword was pulled from his grasp and he fell back to lie in the grass. The long green fingers tickled his face, cushioned his back. He thought he heard incongruous laughter somewhere, and a moment later he realised he was giggling uncontrollably; it was the only thing that kept him from sobbing as death came for him, tunnelled his vision.

The last thing he saw was the worm raising its head directly above him, silhouetted against the cloudy white sky, slobbering its own blood and that of his people on him. Then, its head came down and Phut closed his eyes, accepting his end.

*

When he reopened his eyes, it was dark and there was a fire nearby. He could still feel the grass tickling his face, soft against his back. He was roused by a hubbub of many voices, and when he tried to move, he croaked in pain. Only then did he remember that he had lost his right arm. He groaned again, and a dark, blurry figure hurried over to him. As Phut's eyes came into focus and he struggled once more to lift his head, he saw that it was his mother.

"Mother!" He was glad to see her alive.

His mother embraced him and whispered in his ear, "It's alright, son. You're alright. You're going to be okay."

"What about father? Is he okay?"

He felt a shiver run through his mother, and he knew the answer in the pit of his stomach before she answered, "Your father … he did not make it, Phut. I am so sorry."

Phut buried his face in his mother's collar, feeling tears burn his eyes and sobs wrack his chest.

"Some of the other men survived, though," his mother continued, obviously trying to hold back from crying herself. "You saved them. You saved us all, Phut. You did so well. You were so brave. I'm so proud of you, my boy! The boy who slew the blood worm! The boy who laughed at death! Phut Wormbane! All the Nagali are telling your tale already. Half of them saw it with their own eyes! You're famous, Phut!"

"Really?"

"Yes! They'll be telling your tale for generations to come!"

"Can I have some water?"

"Of course!"

Phut drank sparingly and then laid his head back on the grass and closed his eyes. He was famous, apparently – something he had craved since childhood. Fame and glory – he would trade them in a heartbeat to have his father back, he knew. He stared up at the clouds.

The Sky Father had a twisted sense of humour.

The Waystation

Drew Farrinson had never seen a snowstorm like this.

He could not see for it, could barely breathe for it. He could not hear for the wind. Big fat flakes smothered and saturated him anew with every passing second, cold as ice. His whole body was shaking as he walked down the road, scarcely able to see the dirt track. He led his horse by the reins, unwilling to ride the poor beast in such weather. He figured the gelding was suffering enough; it had been dun once, but the storm had coated it in white powder. It tried to shake it off now and again, but by the time it shook any amount off, that same amount had fallen again.

It was a hopeless battle; Drew knew how the horse felt. He had given up trying to shake off the snow and now simply plodded on, eyes slitted against the stinging flakes and howling gale. When he made out a dark blur up ahead of him, he decided that he would be stopping for the day no matter what sort of building it was. Fortunately, it was a waystation; a resting spot for weary travellers, one and all.

Drew scowled at the simple wooden shack; he had been hoping for someplace slightly more durable. The waystation looked as old as his great-grandfather, like a good gust could bring it down at any second. Nevertheless, he needed shelter like he needed to relieve himself, so he led the horse to the stables. They were well-kept; there were empty stalls, freshly lain with straw, and troughs of water. Drew rubbed the horse down with frigid fingers on the brush and then fed the beast some oats. He was tempted to curl up in the straw beside the horse and go to sleep, but he did not want to be trampled. So, he exited the stables, braved the blizzard and made his way to the waystation door.

The wind yanked it out of his grasp as soon as he unhooked the latch, and slammed the door open. He had to put his back into it to close it again, and by the time he had done so, a smattering of snow had spilled onto the welcome mat and wooden floor of the shack. Leaning on the door once he had closed it, Drew surveyed the waystation.

Two people looked back at him, a man and a woman, both sitting on poorly carved wooden chairs by a fire in the stone hearth.

Drew breathed a sigh of relief at the sight of the flickering flames. Besides the chairs and the fire, there was little else inside save for an old, scarred table, a door Drew was confident would lead to a pantry, and piles of pots and pans and tools cluttering up two corners of the room. Dusty hoes sat beside rusty shovels; Drew wondered if whoever lived here fancied themselves a gardener.

"Well, it looks like you were wrong," the man said to the woman. "Someone else was daft enough to be travelling today." He turned to Drew. "Welcome, friend. Come in out of the storm; make yourself at home, please. My name is Radda Ulvarson; I'm the waystation officiant. I make sure everyone's as welcome as everyone else here."

The man beamed at Drew; he was perhaps twice Drew's age, but still spry for his size. He had a fatherly manner, ruddy cheeks, a receding hairline and a pudgy face. Drew wondered how he could have gotten so pudgy out here in the middle of nowhere; some people were just pudgy, he supposed. Radda's gut strained his belt and pressed up against his red wool tunic.

"What's your name, traveller?"

"Drew."

Radda turned to the woman, and Drew saw a huge tuft of grey hair sticking out of his ear. "Not much of a talker, I suspect," he said jokingly. "You two ought to get along famously." He turned back to Drew. "Where you headed on a night like this, eh, lad?"

Drew stared at him and stopped slumping against the door, stood tall. "Is it a requirement now at a waystation that travellers must divulge their destinations?"

The man blinked, taken aback, his smile withering. "Well, no, I was just being polite."

"Being polite?" asked Drew. "By prying into my business? If that is so, I'll thank you to be impolite in future."

Radda frowned. "Alright, lad, no need to be so on guard. We're all friends here."

Drew shook his head. "I just met you. You're no friend of mine, old man. I will, however, make use of your waystation for the night."

Radda nodded, though his chipper glow had dimmed. "Of course, of course. Like I said, make yourself at home."

Drew nodded and swept past him. Dropping his pack by his

side, he knelt by the fire and warmed his shivering hands, not caring if he blocked the heat from reaching the others.

The woman watched him wordlessly with round green eyes, while Radda asked, "Do you have a horse, Drew?"

"I do. He's in the stables."

"Very well. I'll just go and check on him and the others. This young lady is Mina, by the way. She was as forthcoming with her last name as you were, Drew. Alright, I'll leave you two to get acquainted a moment. Won't be long."

With that, Radda clad himself in a big bear fur coat and opened the door. The wind and snow had been waiting for just such an opportunity, and they pounced inside and almost toppled the ageing officiant. Head down, body bent, he staggered out of the door against the wind and – after a minute of trying – managed to slam it shut again behind him.

Drew took off his fox-fur coat and hat and tossed them on the floor, where they began to seep water into the old, pitted wood, steaming at the same time. He shivered, but the fire's warmth soon embraced him again, more fully now that he had removed his drenched coat. His fingers tingled and prickled as feeling returned to them; a sensation somewhere between pleasure and pain. He took off his boots after a few minutes and laid them by the fire, the mud on their soles dirtying the worn rug there.

All the while he sat by the fire and disrobed, he never once took his eyes off the woman Radda had named Mina. She was young and pretty, slim and pale, with big eyes and long, blonde hair tied up in a bun. She wore tartan trews and a green tunic. She returned his scrutiny with implacable ease, until he was the one who felt uncomfortable.

Older than her, bigger than her, stronger than her, he knew he should not have been afraid of her, but he was. He had been afraid of all women since leaving Thetis. He had been on the road since then, on the run. He was constantly looking over his shoulder for signs of pursuit, but he didn't think it unfathomable that the Witches could have gotten ahead of him somehow. They were Witches, after all.

He had not even believed in magic until recently, had thought it extinct along with the Convent. What he had seen in Thetis had opened his eyes, however, and he had realised how blind he had been. He wondered what else could be real – Wizards, old Elves, Giants, the

Prophet, Dragons? There were a thousand legends, and he began to think now that maybe each had at least a grain of truth to it.

Now, not knowing what the Witches were capable of, but knowing that they would likely do whatever they could to get back what he had stolen from them, Drew's neck ached from craning to look behind. Looking the woman, Mina, in the eye, he asked himself whether she could be a Witch. She did not look particularly like a Witch; she had no warts or evil grin. She looked ordinary enough, but Drew kept his suspicions cloaked about him regardless and resolved not to let his guard down around her. He could not leave now, though; he was stuck there, Witch or no. It was getting dark, and he would be lucky to survive this storm in daylight, much less night time.

Eventually, presumably growing sick of him staring at her in silence, Mina said, "Would you like some water?"

"No, thank you," said Drew.

"We don't have much to eat, according to Radda, but he says whatever is in the waystation is for travellers such as us. So ... help yourself if you are hungry."

"I'm fine."

She nodded and stared into the flames. "Is it still as bad out there?" she asked after a while, nodding vaguely towards the door banging on its frame again and again.

Drew nodded. "It's a bloody nightmare."

She nodded again, still staring into the cavorting flames, which whipped back and forth now and again when a strong gust snuck through the door frame. "There hasn't been a storm this severe in the Fringe as far back as I can remember. Up in the Highlands, of course, but not down here in the Lowlands."

"You've been to the Highlands?" Drew blurted, surprised.

"Oh, I may look young," she replied with a slight smile, "but I've travelled extensively. I've seen every corner of this land we call Fjelburg ... from Titan's Pass to Baldr's Safe, from Dogoda and the Parapet to Thetis and Skalda's Teeth."

Drew started at the mention of Thetis, then cursed himself for a fool. Had she noticed him jump? Had he given himself away? Even if she was a Witch, could she have known who he was before that foolish twitch? Maybe. He cursed himself again regardless. He told himself that she was just comparing the southernmost points of Fjelburg with the northernmost, but his suspicions redoubled at the mention of Thetis. He wondered if she was testing him, trying to decipher his identity.

"That is … extensive," he said at length.

She nodded. "And never have I seen a storm so bitter. Anyone would think the winds themselves were riled." The windows rattled from the force of the wind just then, as if to punctuate her point.

Drew narrowed his eyes at her; was that a rebuke? "Where are you travelling to, Mina?"

"Odendroth. I have family there."

"And where are you travelling from?"

"Thetis, up in the north."

Drew's every muscle tensed, but he forced himself to breathe calmly. It could be a coincidence, he told himself, even while another part of his brain screamed at him that he was in mortal danger, that she was a Witch, that she was here to assassinate him. He took a deep breath.

"I haven't been to Thetis in a while," he said, trying to seem nonchalant. "What's it like up there nowadays?"

She finally turned her gaze on him, making his guts squirm. "It is in upheaval." Drew clenched one fist. "What with the freak storms, the populace is positively riotous. Supplies are running short. Thieves are growing more and more common."

Drew clenched the other fist. Trying to keep his voice even and flippant, he said, "They're an epidemic. They're everywhere, like rats."

"True," she said. "They are fiendish folk." Drew ground his teeth. "What about you? Where are you travelling to?"

"I've come from White Cliffs," he said. "I'm heading to Pottle Bay to meet a business partner."

"A merchant, are you?" she asked, arching an eyebrow at him.

"A merchant in the making," he said. "Looking to get rich quick – you know the type."

She chuckled at that, a tinkling sound. "I do indeed. I've met a few. You know, it seems to me that you're taking the long way around. Why didn't you just travel straight down the coast?"

He had worried she would pick up on that. She was right, of course. The journey from White Cliffs to Pottle Bay did not require the inland detour he was claiming to have taken.

"I … got lost," he said lamely.

She arched that eyebrow at him again. "Lost? All you had to do was keep in sight of the sea."

She was right, of course.

He blushed and snapped, "Yeah, lost! I got caught in the snow and took a wrong turn. It could happen to anyone!"

She nodded, looking on the verge of laughter. "It could indeed."

They chatted for another hour, and Drew began to relax. They were laughing, joking and swapping stories. Drew still did not trust her enough to take anything she offered, but he ate some mouldy bread and strips of meat from his pack and drank from his own wineskin. He had water, too, but he hated the stuff. Sozzled was the way he liked to live his life.

While Mina was telling a story about the farm she had grown up on and her father chasing after pigs and falling face-first in the muck, Drew crumbled some baui and rolled it up in a leaf. Then, he lit one end in the fire and puffed on the other, producing great billows of thick blue-white smoke. Mina asked for a drag, and Drew gave her the roll-up, relaxing even more; surely Witches did not smoke? Surely they could not cast spells if they were inebriated on narcotics?

After that, he inwardly berated himself for his childish behaviour earlier on. He had been a fool to suspect her of anything. She was just an innocent young woman, who had grown up on a farm near Thetis and was travelling to meet her aunt and uncle in Odendroth. If she was a Witch, if she had meant to assassinate him, surely she would have done so by now. An assassin would not have sat and chatted with him for more than an hour.

After they finished smoking, Mina said, giggling, "I think I saw an old, corked bottle of wine hidden among the pots and pans earlier. D'you want to crack it open?"

Drew grinned. "Be rude not to."

Mina snuck over to the pile of pots and pans and gardening tools, darting glances at the door lest Radda come back. She rooted around for a moment and then pulled out a bottle of red wine, coughing at the dust spurt.

"Found it!"

"Pass it here. I'll open it."

Mina gave it to Drew, who saw that it was indeed full and corked. There was no way she could have tampered with it … unless she was a Witch … but she wasn't. He was sure now. He took out a little knife and quickly pried off the cork, before tucking the blade away in his belt again. Then, he sucked at the neck of the bottle, glugging.

"Hey, don't hog that!" Mina complained, holding out a hand.

Drew reluctantly lowered the bottle and smacked his lips. "That's a good vintage, whatever it is," he said with a grin, grudgingly handing it over.

Mina took a long pull, swallowed and then pursed her lips thoughtfully. "Mm, fruity, with hints of chestnut and drunkenness." She cracked a grin; so did he.

They passed the bottle back and forth for the next half hour, both guzzling the wine like it was water. By the time the bottle was empty, Drew felt like he had come to know Mina well. He also felt a warm glow in his belly and a comforting fuzziness at the edge of his brain.

He hiccupped. "Wish there was another bottle."

He was still on the rug on the floor by the fire, where he had set himself down. Now, Mina got off her chair, lurched forward and intentionally fell down beside him, shoulder to shoulder.

"It's so nice and warm down here," she said with a smile. "I'd been wanting to lie by the fire all day."

"So why sit on the chair?"

She puckered her lips. "I don't know. Propriety, or something stupid like that, I suppose. Women are supposed to be proper." She giggled.

Drew smiled. "You're no ordinary woman, though, are you?"

She smiled back, coyly. "Have you known many? Women?"

Drew's smile stretched further as the memories came flooding in. "More than a few, I reckon. I've been singularly blessed. But, alas, no one has yet claimed my heart or my hearth."

"Aw, poor Drew," Mina said mock-piteously, pursing her lips. "Perhaps you just haven't found the right woman yet."

"Perhaps not. What about you? Have you known many men? I don't see a wedding bracelet on your wrist."

Mina's smile faded, and she leaned away from Drew a little and rubbed gently at her left wrist. He wished she would lean closer again.

"I was married once," she said quietly, with a sad look in her eye, "not so long ago."

Drew felt a lump in his throat. "I'm sorry," he rasped. "What happened? If you don't mind my asking."

"No, it's natural to be curious, I suppose," she said, staring into the fire again. "I was young and naïve, and I still lived with my parents on the farm. I ran off with a young man called Brett, and we were married in secret by a priest in a little village called Springswallow way down south."

"You *have* travelled far," said Drew, impressed.

She nodded. "Anyway, I had to run away, because my family did not approve. They're very controlling, my family, and they would never have let us be together, be happy together, if I had stayed at home, I knew. So we ran, and we started a new life in Springswallow and things were wonderful ... for a time." Her face morphed into a slight snarl. "Then came the ... brigands." Drew wondered at the pause, but supposed it was painful to speak of. "The brigands," she repeated numbly. "They came to Springswallow, and when we refused to pay them tribute, they burned it to the ground, every building, every beam, every stable, every hut. They killed most of the men and children and enslaved the women. I was not caught luckily; I managed to escape in the ruckus, and I watched my village burn to the ground from a nearby copse. I saw the ... brigands ... swinging babies by the ankles and bashing their heads in against the ground, against the rocks."

Drew thought she might vomit for a minute, she looked so green; he thought he might vomit too. Neither did, but both felt a wrench in their guts at the image. Knowing his own picture was entirely fabricated, Drew could not imagine the wrench Mina must be feeling, having real memories to gaze upon.

He opened his mouth to say how sorry he was, that the world was a disgusting place full of horrible, terrible people, but she continued speaking, her voice breaking slightly.

"They did not kill all of the men, though. Some of them, the brigands took to be tortured. Why, I do not know. Bastard Justiquans!" she hissed suddenly.

"Justiquans?" Drew was surprised.

Mina looked startled, like a child caught by a parent with its hand in a forbidden cookie jar. "Yes ... The brigands were Justiquans."

"Mm, strange." Justiquans were far from known for coming to Fjelburg to take up crime, but it was possible, he supposed.

"Anyway, the brigands took my Brett, and they tortured him … For days, I waited for them to finish, to leave, to give me my Brett back. I hid in the woods, and I waited and I watched. I ate leaves and berries – and bugs, I think. I suppose I was half-crazed at the time, so the memories are a little fuzzy. After three days, they were finished pillaging and burning and raping and killing. Finished torturing. So, they moved on to the next town, passing close by my own little copse as they went. Luckily, they did not find me.

"When they were gone, I rushed back into the blackened husk of a village and found half a dozen men there, all mutilated, all dismembered, all mangled, all in horrific states. I could scarcely recognise my Brett when I saw him lying naked right in front of me. He was a mewling wreck of the man he had once been." Her eyes filled with tears, and her voice was thick with emotion.

"They had cut off every other finger and every other toe and ripped out every other tooth. They had burned his tongue to a crisp inside his head. They had mauled the muscles in his arms, so he would never be able to lift a hoe again, much less a sword. They had … cut off everything *down there!* They had … they had made a eunuch out of him and left only a blackened stump between his legs!"

She covered her face with her hands, and Drew reached out and awkwardly patted her on the shoulder. To his relief, she seemed to take comfort from the contact and leaned into it.

After a minute, she stopped trembling and weeping softly. She wiped her eyes and said, "That's when my family found me, kneeling in my burned-down village beside my ruined house and my ruined husband. They dragged me away from Brett and the other tortured men, wouldn't let me help them. They dragged me away by force and slung me in the back of a wagon, where they held me down. They took me home. They forced me to leave my husband, alone and maimed, whimpering among the ashes of our village … I never saw him again. By the time I could have escaped again and gone back, I knew he would have died. He would not have survived the night, much less the days and weeks I was away. My family told me it was a mercy to let him die, that it was what Brett would have wanted … They were probably right, but still … It was heartless. Not to even let me say goodbye."

She leaned into him more, and he put an arm around her and hugged her close. She nestled her head against his. She turned to look at him after a few minutes' silence, tear-tracks streaking her beautiful face. He noticed then that she was dusted with light brown freckles across the nose. Odd how he had not noticed it before.

"So, to answer your question, Drew," she said with a sad smile, "I have known only one man – in that sense."

"Only one?" said Drew, his voice husky. "A beautiful young maiden like you ought to have suitors tripping over each other trying to get your attention."

"You think I'm beautiful?" Their faces were very close now.

"The most beautiful woman I have ever seen," said Drew. It was a good line – it nearly always worked.

She kissed him, and he kissed her. Her lips were soft, warm and wine-flavoured. Her tongue, when it darted against his, was even softer, pliable as an eel. He licked the wine off her lips, and she did the same for him. Then, they were pressing against one another, tugging at each other in a sudden frenzy, holding one another tight and close. Their faces were mashed together, their lips and tongues working frantically, their faces cocking side to side. Drew grabbed a handful of Mina's firm buttocks and felt her tangle her hand in his hair. She was feisty, this one.

They turned fully toward one another, and she wrapped a leg around him. He pulled her close and began to grind against her, kissing ferociously. She wriggled against him just as enthusiastically, and so he slid his hand under her tunic to feel the curve of her breast. It was smooth and squishy. She tucked her hand down the front of his trousers and found him hardening fast.

They rubbed at one another for a few minutes, and then they began yanking at each other's clothes. Drew snatched the tunic off Mina's back, and she tugged his own tunic over his head. He pulled down her trews, and she tore off his trousers. Within frantic seconds, they were naked in front of the fire, lips pressed together, flesh slapping against flesh.

Drew rode her slow, then fast; gentle, then rough. By the time Drew climaxed, both were slick with sweat and panting like dogs. He wasn't sure if she had climaxed, too; it was hard to tell sometimes. It wasn't like he was particularly bothered, either way. They clung to one another while they spasmed in pleasure, with him still buried inside her. Then, he pulled out and rolled over to lie on the rug beside her, chest heaving.

"I may have been with many women," he said, "but it's been a little while. That was amazing!"

"D'you know what's amazing? *Adheraras invico lumbi'isim.* That you thought you could get away with it."

Her alien words made his skin crawl and break out in goosebumps, and he realised to his horror an instant later that he could not move a muscle. He was entirely paralyzed, stuck to the rug.

His eyes darted around manically, and Mina laughed at him and, waving a hand, said, "My apologies, Drew. You may speak."

He found his mouth abruptly unglued, though the rest of his body remained inanimate. "What is going on?" he squawked in alarm.

Mina held up a purple-blue crystal that fit snugly in her palm. It was pulsating with an eldritch phosphorescence. Drew's mouth went dry, and gongs of terror resounded in his mind. He recognised that crystal; he had been carrying it in his pack for the last week or so. She must have snuck it out of the pack while they were having sex, he realised, wheezing with fear.

"D'you even know what this is, thief?" Mina asked calmly, staring into the gemstone's swirling depths.

Drew's guts were ice-cold. He had been right to suspect her.

"This," she proceeded when he did not respond, only vainly tried to free himself from her spell, "is a shard of *Kun-Yao-Lin,* a soul crystal. And a very special one at that. D'you know that it is possible to entrap souls in crystals such as these, to confine a person's mind and energy inside this little rock? It's true. Many centuries ago, one of my order, a woman named Ellevrei, imbued this particular crystal with all her energies and all her knowledge – all of her soul – just before death. It has been a sacred relic to my order ever since, and a beacon of power to any with arcane abilities. We could never lose this soul crystal, don't you see? We could sense it wherever it went, follow it wherever you ran. There was no possibility of escape, Drew; there never was. You tackled the wrong job this time, thief. We Sisters do not take kindly to strangers stealing our belongings."

Her eyes were hard as emeralds now, cold and unyielding. "D'you remember that story I told you earlier – about my husband? Well, I may have gotten the sequence of events a little muddled. And the perpetrators. In truth, I *did* run away from my family – the

Sisterhood – with a man called Brett, almost a century ago. Then, one day while I was out picking herbs to make medicine, the Justiquans came on their Great Crusade to burn and proselytise, not realising the two do not go hand in hand. Follow our ways, they said. Obey the Word of the Prophet or die, they said. It was not me who hid in the woods, but Brett. I found him alive and unharmed, and we went into our burned-down village together, weeping. Then, like I said, my family came for me. The Sisterhood had hunted me down; they could not let me go rogue. They captured both Brett and I, and they forced me to torture my husband to death, or else be tortured and slain myself. I cut off his every other finger. I cut off his every other toe. I ripped out his every other tooth. I burned his tongue to a cinder inside his skull. I brutalised his arms, and I cut off his dick and balls with a red-hot blade. My Sisters let me rejoin them. My loyalty was proven. Then, we left him there, crying in the ashes, and we returned home."

Though his tongue was free, Drew was speechless, gawking like a simpleton. Fear shrivelled his manhood and hollowed him out. She had been a Witch all along.

He suddenly remembered Radda then, the ageing officiant who had been gone for hours, and he decided to play for time in the hopes the man would return. His tongue finally found some words.

"Why didn't you just kill me earlier?" he asked, his voice small in his own ears. "Why chat with me and sleep with me? What's the thinking, you heartless harridan? And why do you say you got married almost a century ago? You look no older than twenty-five!"

She smiled nastily. "My, my, we are full of questions all of a sudden, aren't we? Hoping that old fool, Raddagan, will come back, are we? I *can* read your mind, you know. Tch, tch. So sorry to disappoint, pumpkin, but poor Radda is dead. Some of my Sisters are outside, you see, and they will have cut his wrinkly old throat by now. But, since you asked so nicely, I will answer your questions. First of all, believe me, I am far older than twenty-five. I watched the Time of Witches come crashing to an end 300 years ago. I witnessed the bastard Knights crusade all across the lands, trying to spread their message of peace by force of arms. I witnessed the fall of the last King and the rise of the current one. I am older than you would believe, thief. Now, why sleep with you? Well, in part, I was distracting you while I searched for the crystal, but there is another reason. I have told many lies tonight, but when I told you I had only been with one man, I spoke the truth. It has been decades since that time. So, in essence, you filled a need; you satiated a craving, nothing more."

"Didn't it mean anything to you?" Drew begged, clutching at straws.

"No. The crime you have committed against my order is beyond forgiveness. Your punishment for this crime is death."

She drew his knife from his belt and laid it against the bobbing lump in his neck, stopping his pleading abruptly.

"Shh, now. I will make it painless. I pray you rot in the fiery pits of the Nether, Drew Farrinson. Breathe your last."

She slit his throat.

The King's Own Tournament

A fever filled the air in Baldr's Safe. An excited hubbub swelled as people took their seats, looking down on the granite courtyard where the spectacle would soon take place. Folk were so jubilant they did not even mind the uncomfortable stone seats or the frigid wind. As they sat down, they joked and laughed and swapped tales of the last time this event had been held, speaking in tones of awe and admiration for the winners and ridicule for the losers.

It was the day of the quadrennial King's Own Tournament.

While hundreds of people slowly shuffled through the courtyard and took their places among the tiered stands, the King of Fjelburg, Bolegard Njordson, looked on patiently from the top tier with his wife, Queen Finnig Havardax. He glanced up at the blue sky being slowly smothered by waves of white cloud and grimaced, hoping the rains would hold off – often a vain hope in the Highlands. He would not get wet, being under a canopy, but a change in the weather could ruin his visibility, not to mention saturating the other spectators and causing the fighters to skid around like ducks on ice. He was sat on a cushioned wooden chair in a large, open-fronted red-and-yellow striped pavilion – which was a little gaudy for his tastes, but Finnig loved it. A whole retinue was squeezed into the pavilion behind the royal couple; mostly the Queen's entourage, including a make-up woman, a seamstress, two advisors and several servants.

Bolegard tugged his speckled, golden snow cat fur mantle tighter around his neck as the wind nipped him, and was glad he had brought along his elk-hide jerkin too, even if his wife said it made him look like a commoner. He knew nobody could mistake anyone wearing a mantle of snow cat fur for a commoner. She had insisted he wear his crown too. He usually forewent the pomp of it, but she had nagged until he had caved like a worn hammock. So, the uncomfortable, heavy, cold stone circlet niggled at his brow.

He glanced sidelong at his wife. "Here, Finnig, everybody's facing the other way now, so –"

"Keep your crown on!"

He sighed. "Yes, dear."

He glanced at her askance. She looked as young and beautiful as the day they had married, decades ago. She had skin like milk, tresses of rich auburn hair and dark, mysterious eyes, and wore a maroon wool dress beneath her ermine fur coat. Bolegard, on the other hand, was past middle age with grey hair, a bulging gut and the beginnings of wrinkles. He often wondered how Finnig had contrived to stay so youthful. She had also survived eight successful pregnancies and a miscarriage – a rarity for women in the Highlands.

Thinking of offspring, Bolegard looked to his eldest son, Einar, down in the courtyard. The young man was the spitting image of his father in his youth – or so his father liked to think. Seven-and-a-half-feet-tall and thick as an old pine, Einar was a great fighter. He was young, though, and had yet to prove himself a capable warrior in anything beyond training bouts. Bolegard had helped train the young man himself, when his exhaustive duties permitted. He and Einar would spar in one of the courtyards with weighted wooden swords – they had sparred in that very courtyard in which his son now stood – and so the King had watched his son's skills grow. When his monarchic duties demanded his time, he delegated Einar's training to the Major of the King's Own, his elite bodyguards.

He glanced up toward Major Osto Valinson, who was stood beside him like he had an unbending iron rod for a spine. He was swathed in fur just like everybody else, and far from the cleanest specimen present, but he exuded steeliness. Bolegard imagined punching him would be like hitting a rock. His face was scarred and crooked, broken and mangled. A shock of white hair ran through his greying umber locks by his left temple where an Elf had almost brained him years ago, and a vicious scar ran along the right side of his neck from a wound he had received whilst fighting the Crawlers. He was still a deadly warrior, though; Bolegard knew that from their occasional sparring sessions. Osto could swing the mighty claymore strapped to his back faster than anyone the King knew.

"Osto!" the King spoke loudly over the surrounding hullaballoo, gesturing to the sixteen fighters arrayed in the courtyard. "Who's your pick to win?"

"His Majesty's son is a very capable fighter," Osto grunted, not taking his eyes off the warriors below.

"I sense a 'but' in there," prompted Bolegard good-naturedly.

Osto nodded slightly. "But I have scouted some of these youngsters before, considering them for the King's Own, and I know some of them to be ferocious. They have been to the North; they have been to the Wald. They are blooded."

"Is Einar not ferocious?"

"Einar is ... untried, Your Majesty."

"True," admitted the King, before smacking his armrest. "A wager then, Major Osto! I wager you a hundred Fjolins that my son will win!"

"As you say, Your Majesty."

"Just you watch, Osto," said Bolegard. "Just you watch."

By his side, Queen Finnig rolled her eyes and puffed on her slim, elegant, white pipe. Baui smoke wreathed her like a cloud. She had been married to the King practically as long as she could remember – certainly long enough to have come to detest him to the core. She had been so excited when she was younger at the thought of marrying a great warrior king, but now she regretted ever taking this mission from her Sisters.

Bolegard had proven to be a paradoxically shy, brash nincompoop, in her opinion. A doormat of a man, his face was always scrunched up in thought and he was always considering the best way to pander to everybody's feelings. She wondered if he had ever had a backbone. She shuddered to think of their amorous interactions, preferring to bury them under baui and wine. In the moment, she tended to squeeze shut her eyes and imagine he was somebody else.

Somebody like Lampton Odorson.

She subtly shifted her gaze towards Lampton; he was one of the fighters gathered below, clad in mustard and blue. She felt her pulse quicken as her eyes roved over his muscular, rippling physique and she recalled the feel of his hands on her body. He was far younger than the King, far fitter and more handsome too, she thought, stroking her neck. Lampton caught the gesture and smiled up at her, running a hand through his long blonde hair. She could guess what he was thinking. She licked her lips at him.

"-wouldn't you say, Finnig, my dear?"

Finnig jumped, realising the King was talking to her, and blinked at him. "What was that?" Once, she would have apologised for failing to be attentive; now, she barely bothered to veil her disinterest.

"I was saying," said Bolegard, unperturbed, happy as a pig in muck, "we have faith in our son to win, don't we, dear?"

"Of course," Finnig agreed out loud.

Inwardly, she thought that if Einar ever managed to win anything, it would be a small miracle. The boy was a witless panderer like his father, out of his depth and unsure which way was up. She loved him, of course, but she was not sure 'proud' was a word she would use in conjunction with him.

Down in the courtyard, Einar Bolegardson waved to his parents in the red-and-yellow pavilion up on the top tier. His mother and father waved back, beaming, making him smile. His smile was shaky, however, and he suspected a whole hornet's nest had taken residence in his gut somehow. He felt queasy, like he might puke, so he stood still and took long, deep breaths. His fellow competitors – men and women alike – tried to talk to him from time to time, but he mostly ignored them, scared that if he opened his mouth to talk, the vomit would come spilling out.

He adjusted his breeches and wished he had time to void his bladder. The wind howled by, and goosebumps stood up on his flesh, making him wish he was wearing more than a woollen tunic. His naked feet felt like blocks of ice and he wondered why the fighters were forbidden from wearing boots. Cases of frostbite were relatively common in the Highlands; going barefoot was inviting trouble, in his opinion. Nevertheless, he obeyed the rules.

He swept his gaze over all the hundreds of faces in the stands, all sat on stone seats behind sculpted limestone balustrades, all hooting and hollering at him and the other fighters. Women called out to him alluringly, men threatened and encouraged him, and children just squealed in excitement. He rubbed his aching ears and hoped they would quiet down during the bouts.

He looked back to his father and hoped he would make him proud. He felt as though the whole competition was on his shoulders; like everybody, including his father, was there to see him win, expecting him to win. The King had taught his son himself at times, so Einar knew he was heavily invested. Bolegard had been a great warrior in his youth, so it was said, and Einar prayed he could live up to his father's reputation. He could feel its shadow stretching, trying to cast him in its shade, and he vied to stay ahead of it, to stay in the light.

As he had the thought, Osto Valinson swept down from the pavilion on the top tier of seating, leaving behind several other bodyguards to protect the King. He looked daunting and dramatic with his ceremonial white cloak billowing out behind him. He sauntered down the left staircase of the two, beside the railed dividing aisle, which was a slope of patterned stonework depicting Gods and men. When he reached the bottom step, he halted.

"Warriors," he barked, "you know why you are here. You have been selected for your skill, strength and potential. Today is the day of the King's Own Tournament. Today, one of you will be chosen to join the elite bodyguard, the King's Own. Who will be chosen will depend on you. There will be a series of elimination bouts, wherein if you are defeated you will be eliminated from the competition. A defeat will be signalled when a competitor yields, bleeds or is knocked unconscious. The last fighter standing will be the victor."

Einar grinned, ready to begin, buzzing with energy, but Osto droned on. "The King's Own Tournament was begun by King Ulbard, son of High King Ulle himself, in this very courtyard before this very Temple, many hundreds of years ago. The exact date was lost – as was much of our history – during the Time of Witches, when they invaded Fjelburg and put our places of learning to the torch. Baldr's Safe and his Temple, however, survived. Praise be."

Osto gestured up at the great temple looming over them all. Conical and two-tiered, with a black roof and black eaves on the lower tier, it resembled the God of War's hat. The circular band of wall between the eaves and the roof was blue, while the bottom band beneath the eaves was maroon. Both stretches were covered in gilded patterns, depicting men fighting men and Gods fighting Dragons. A golden ball topped the roof, a little second sun.

Osto continued in monotone, "King Ulbard began the Tournament in order to be sure he was surrounded by the finest warriors in the Kingdom at a time when civil war looked likely. His father had held on to the crown with a precarious grip, juggling all the warchiefs of the various clans and trying to force them to forget old feuds. Ulbard's grip was even more tenuous as questions about inheritance arose; should the crown be inherited or should it be earned? For a time, it looked like the newfound Kingdom of Fjelburg would crumble. Ulbard, however, refused to let it, and as luck would have it, the Gods were on his side.

"They gave Ulbard enemies. People say the first year he was King was a dreadful year, and they are right. The Crawlers poured out of the North and passed Northbane – the only time they have ever done so – and the Elves came out of the Alfa Wald in a flock of thousands to terrorise the towns and villages in the west. Despite his youth, Ulbard was a master strategist, however, and he corralled together the warchiefs and brought them under one banner just as his father had done. He managed to constrain and harry back the Crawlers with one half of his force while building the Elfguard forts in record time with the other half, even while under attack from the Elves.

"Some say he designed those forts himself and that his tactics are the ones we still use today. Some say he used magic to defeat the Crawlers and erect the fortresses, that he was in league with Witches, but these are incorrect. He was a tactician and a great leader, nothing more. He died just before seeing the final Elfguard fort, Najuzna, built, but he secured the lineage of the Stonebrow line. His intelligence and fortitude cemented the inheritance of the crown and the continuation of the dynasty. His son, Faragon, was crowned King and took over the construction of Najuzna and saw it built within a year after his death. So, we continue the noble tradition of the Tournament not only to honour the finest warriors, but also to honour King Ulbard, to whom we owe so much. Thank you, King Ulbard."

He and everyone else bowed their heads for a second.

"Now," shouted Osto, "the Tournament will begin! When I shout out your names, pair off – and remember, the fight is to yield, first blood, or until one is unconscious. We don't want any deaths today."

The Major began barking out names in pairs, and Einar waited with bated breath for his own moniker.

"Kamor and Einar!"

Einar stepped out of line and surveyed his opponent as he did the same. Kamor was a seven-foot birch whip, wolf-lean to the point of being skeletal. His dark hair was tied back in a ponytail, as were Einar's fiery red locks. He walked off to one side of the courtyard with a smooth, rolling gait, and Einar saw he had a longsword in hand.

Major Osto came over and set them in place, taking up one half of the courtyard while another fight took the other half.

Then, he resumed his position on the bottom step and barked, "Fighters, ready?"

"Ready!"

"Then begin!"

Einar was so nervous he almost tripped over instantaneously when Kamor leapt at him, sword singing out. Einar managed to get his own short sword in the way, and there was a screech of steel as the blades met. Kamor came at him again, and this time Einar dodged to the side to regain his balance. That done, he forced himself to stand his ground until the last possible moment as Kamor's sword sought him out again, even though every instinct screamed at him to move out of the way sooner. Sweat dripped in his eye. The sword came down and Einar stepped smoothly to the side just in time to avoid it, watching it clang on the stone flagging. He swung the hatchet in his other hand and Kamor leapt back, abruptly ungainly.

Seeing this, Einar felt a grin contort his face as he took the offensive. He swung his sword and axe in a fast, rhythmic pattern that had them humming and had Kamor backing away across the courtyard. Concentrating, Einar waited until his pattern led him to a high blow with his sword and then he broke pattern, stabbing with his axe at Kamor's belly unexpectedly. Einar smelled Kamor's breath as it all whooshed out of his lungs, and then he kicked his opponent down to the ground and stood over him with his sword at Kamor's throat. Kamor was unhurt, thanks to the flat top of the blade of the axe, which was why Einar had selected a hatchet. For a real battle, he would have chosen a war axe with a larger blade that swept up above the haft with a counterweighing spike for balance; such a weapon could have potentially disembowelled his opponent.

"Do you yield?" asked Einar, feeling the grin tug irresistibly at his lips again, smelling the musk of sweating bodies.

"I yield," gulped Kamor, eyeing the blunted blade tickling his neck.

Einar's grin fully bloomed once he let it. He withdrew his sword and offered his opponent his hand; Kamor took it and Einar pulled him up. While they shook hands, the crowd went wild, cheering and whooping. Einar blushed with embarrassment when they chanted his name.

He had a break then while the other warriors fought their bouts, during which time he did nothing more than sip a little water and then sit twitchily on the steps between the seating stands, awaiting his next fight. He was half-deafened by the surrounding ruckus. The shouts did not, it seemed, die down during the bouts at all. He reflected that he had been so focussed, however, that he had not noticed the noise during his first fight. He had become sweatier than he would have dreamed possible in such a short span of time, though, and now the wind chilled him to his bones. He could not have sat there for longer than a few minutes, but it felt like an age was passing him by. By the time Osto called his name again, he was prancing with eagerness and sprang up from his seat like a startled cat.

"Einar and Grindul!"

Grindul was as wide as a cart, and short for a Highlander, peaking at less than seven feet. The resulting impression was one of stockiness and sturdiness; the mien of a mule. He was hairy as a mule, too; covered in umber curls on his head and face. He carried a beastly axe with big, blunted blades on both sides of the short haft. Einar noticed he had not taken flat tops into consideration.

When Osto called, "Begin!" Einar charged in recklessly. He was pleased with himself for his performance in the first fight and thought he could easily replicate the feat against a smaller opponent.

Grindul hit him in the face with his axe haft, making him stumble back, blinded for an instant by shock and pain. It was not a heavy blow – not enough to break the skin – but it broke Einar's confidence in a flash. Suddenly he felt like a small fish in a big pond, surrounded by men who were bigger, faster, stronger, more talented. He gulped as he went on the back foot, dodging and parrying, trying to tell himself it was all in his head. Osto and his father had told him the crisis of confidence assails every warrior when he falters, and that if he gives in to it, he has already lost. He told himself again and again that he must not give in to it, but it was already inside him. He could feel it in his chest, in his gut, squirming, growing, thriving.

He gritted his teeth against the feeling of helplessness, practically running away from the littler man now, circling around the edge of his half of the courtyard. He could feel the loss of confidence hollowing him out like a pumpkin on the Day of the Dead, and he knew it was getting worse. He knew he had to do something soon before he lost the ability to fight back at all.

So, he decided to lay it all on the line, risk it all for glory. He was going to duck an axe swing and go for Grindun's legs, but then he realised that if he did not duck low enough, the axe could shatter his spine. Suddenly rethinking his plan, he almost had his sternum caved in and had to leap away. He decided to wait for a better opportunity; the Tournament was not worth his life, after all. He saw his opportunity a moment later and hurried to take it. As Grindun drew back his axe for yet another swing – one in a long flurry – Einar barged into the big weapon, sword first, well aware he could easily take a cut to the arm if he made a misstep. He shoved the big axe aside as fast as he could and then smacked Grindun in the forehead with his hatchet haft. It made a *clonk* noise like hitting solid wood, and Grindun fell over backwards with his eyes crossed.

Einar raised his weapons in the air to cheers from the crowd, grinning from ear to ear. The sun peeked through the clouds and shone down on him, bathing him in a golden aurora. His confidence was restored, and he resolved not to let it become arrogance again. No matter who was his next opponent, he would treat them as though they were twice the fighter he was.

His next opponent was a woman with short-cropped black hair called Hama, who wielded a spear. He had seen her fight with it in the earlier rounds; she was quick. Her charcoal-smeared eyes made her look demonic.

"Begin!"

She came at him fast, jabbing, jabbing, high and low, faster than his eye could follow. He could follow strategy, though, and he could follow her muscle movements. Somehow, the two combined were enough for him to vaguely predict her movements; enough to deflect her blows on reflex. He was thankful then for all the hours of training he had put in, realising the practise had given him the mystical, rumoured muscle memory that older warriors were always speaking of.

Whirling hatchet and short sword, he backed away and circled, keeping her at bay with parrying strokes and lashing out occasionally when she came too close – which she did very rarely. Hama was a smart fighter, he had to admit; she knew distance was her friend, and she would not let him take it from her. With two weapons to hand, he knew he might have tried hurling one at her in a real battle, but he did not want to hurt her for the sake of a Tournament. Plus, he did not want to lose a weapon. So, he kept circling and dodging and parrying, searching out his chance.

It struck him like an arrow in the back that he was being stupid, concentrating on the wrong thing. He should not be focussing on Hama, he realised; he should be focussing on the spear. More specifically, he should be focussing on the weak wood of the spear haft. As soon as the thought hit him, he saw the fight in a whole new way and it was a cinch to sidestep a stab and cut the spear haft off near the tip with his axe. The wood splintered messily with the force of the blow, and the spear tip clanged to the ground.

Einar was about to hold his sword to Hama's throat and celebrate his victory when she surprised him by attacking him with her spear haft like it was a quarterstaff. She whirled it around and lashed out fast with the splintered end, presumably hoping to draw blood and so win. He barely dodged in his shock, and he reminded himself to treat his opponents with the respect they deserved. The fight was not over until it was over.

Still, she was left with only a stick. So, when she attacked again – having little other choice than to try to catch him off-guard – he swatted the blow aside with little difficulty with his sword. He aimed for her hand where she grasped the spear as he did so, though, so that she was forced to let go with one hand. Thus, when the sword hit the spear haft, it batted it aside easily. The blunt blade of his axe was at Hama's throat a blink of an eye later.

She stayed still, not wanting to be cut, and said clearly, "I yield!"

He grinned and they shook hands while the crowd went wild, hooting and carousing. This time, Einar did not blush. He was starting to feel like he had earned his place, after all, that he had shown off his talents admirably, even if he did not win the competition. His father's smile was so broad it looked like it might split his face in half. His mother was watching the other fight in progress. He followed her gaze and watched Lampton Odorson triumph over his opponent, Lignum Harrakson, with a well-placed punch to the face with a hand holding a sword hilt. Lampton was fast and adroit, he had to admit. Both he and Einar would advance to the finals now.

Osto stepped in and pompously announced, "The finalists have been selected! The final fight is at hand at last! But before we get to that, I will first commend all the competitors for their valiant efforts! Your displays of skill and swordsmanship were most impressive! All of you performed admirably, and all of you deserve my – and all of our – commendations."

"Hear, hear!" barked King Bolegard, toasting with a silver

goblet and encouraging his wife to do the same.

"Having said that," Osto continued, "on this day, Prince Einar Bolegardson and Lampton Odorson have proven the most skilful by winning the most bouts. Therefore, they will now fight to determine the one that is to join the King's Own. Prince Einar, Lampton, are you ready?"

"Yes."

"You bet."

Bolegard watched the fight from the pavilion on the top tier, scowling. His son had fought his earlier bouts with such skill, waving his sword and axe fast in well-practised patterns, leaving few openings and predicting counter-attacks with surety. Now, he bumbled around the courtyard, flailing ineffectually at Lampton with hatchet and sword, always seeming to be aiming in the wrong place. He was constantly missing, tripping over his own feet and barely hopping out of the way of counters. It was like he was moving through treacle all of a sudden, thought Bolegard, watching.

Inevitably, Lampton began to gain the upper hand. He danced around the Prince like a mountain lion nipping at an elk, lashing out at him with quick, precise movements of his two longswords. Slowing further still, Einar started to spin on the spot, trying to keep up with his circling foe. Now, it seemed like he only avoided taking a blow by chance; he kept stumbling back from a sword swing and missing the blade by a matter of inches. Bolegard felt like covering his eyes, but he continued to watch, eyes glued to the courtyard.

He could see his son's anger growing with each misstep. Knowing Einar's temper, he guessed it would not be long before his son ran out of patience and did something rash. He was not wrong. Not long later, Einar went on a rampage. His swings were wide and wild, but fast enough that Lampton could not riposte between moves. Lampton was suddenly on the back foot, dodging away and trying to gain some distance. Like a bear with a headache, Einar blundered after him, cleaving madly at the air like it had done him some injustice.

Lampton was beginning to slow himself now. He was clearly growing desperate and weakening, Bolegard saw; his parries were slower and less effective with each repetition, and he was not springing around with such vigour as he had done earlier. Bolegard leaned forward in excitement when it became clear that Lampton could not go on for much longer; each dodge, each block, each parry was taking its toll on him. His blades barely lifted before they were swatted down again, and he was shuffling rather than stalking now.

Bolegard watched Einar press Lampton back against the wall. With his swipes still erratic, the King's son nevertheless managed to corner his opponent and prevent him from slipping out to either side. Urging his son on at the top of his lungs, Bolegard grinned to see Einar lift his axe above his head for the finishing blow. Before it could land, however, Queen Finnig twitched at his side, her hand jerking. One of the flagstones in the courtyard abruptly tipped, lifting an inch on one side, just in front of the Prince's foot.

Einar stumbled on the uneven floor, hissing a curse as he stubbed his toes, and slammed face-first into the wall while Lampton sidled out of the way. The Prince's axe clanged harmlessly on stone. An instant later, Einar's blood was spraying through the air and pattering on the flagging as Lampton's sword arced across his back and carved a shallow cut. Bolegard didn't think Einar would take that well, and indeed his son spun with wrath written plain upon his face to confront his opponent, weapons gripped tight. As Einar stalked forward, however, Major Osto Valinson inserted himself between the two fighters, shouting loudly, "The Tournament is over! Lampton Odorson is the winner!"

Einar came to his senses with obvious reluctance, tossing his weapons down on the ground like a petulant child, where they clanged and rattled. Bolegard grinned to see it; likely he would have done the same. The Stonebrow Kings were not known for their good grace. He resolved to lecture Einar about it later, nevertheless.

"Finalists," he boomed, standing and spreading his arms, "approach the pavilion!"

Major Osto led Einar and Lampton up the steps to the top tier above the rows of seating.

Once the finalists were standing in front of him, hands clasped respectfully behind their backs with Osto behind them, Bolegard spoke again, his deep voice resonating around the courtyard and the tiered stands.

"Lampton," he said, "you appear to have won. Appearances, however, can be deceiving. Osto, now."

Major Osto kicked Lampton Odorson viciously in the back of the legs, seized the younger man's blonde hair and put his knee in his back. Kneeling and helpless, with his back arched painfully, Lampton looked up at King Bolegard with wide, frightened eyes, his breath coming fast.

"Did you think I did not know what you were up to, Lampton?" growled the King, leering down. "Did you think you could get away with bedding *my* Queen?"

Lampton's eyes flicked to Finnig, and he squeaked, "He knows! Help me, my love! Help me!"

"Oh-ho," chortled Bolegard without the slightest mirth, "she cannot help you now, adulterer." He turned on Finnig with a scowl. "Can you, dear?"

"You bastard!" she cried, flying at him with claws extended.

One of the King's bodyguards shoved her roughly back down, and then two of them held her in the chair.

"Tch tch," reprimanded the King, "that is no way to speak to your husband, you whore!"

"Ragia ellyriamv!" she spat at him, eyes wild with hate. *"Ragia ellyriamv! Senza bumbada!"*

"Haha," Bolegard laughed. "I wondered if enough time had passed for the drug to work … It seems it finally has. I only wish it would have worked sooner so that I could have seen my son beat your buffoon lover!"

"Drug?" Finnig snarled. "You finally discovered the uses of Witchbane, did you?"

Bolegard nodded. "Indeed I did. We were fortunate enough to capture one of your Sisters. We kept her insensate through beatings at first, until we discovered the plant that did the trick, nullified her dark arts."

"You spiked my wine," Finnig accused.

Bolegard nodded again. "Indeed I did. I wanted you awake to see this, but not so awake that you could use your heinous powers, of course. Did you think I would not see what you did to the flagstone during the fight? That was a bold move, tripping Einar like that. You must really feel something for this young fool, eh?" He gestured to Lampton, who was snorting frantically, snot bubbling on his upper lip.

Finnig jerked her arm, and a knife slid out of the sleeve of her fur coat. In an instant, she had slashed the hand of one of the men holding her and stabbed the other in the leg. While both reeled back instinctively, she launched herself at the King knife-first, screeching, "I'll show you!"

Einar had seen it all happen in the blink of an eye. Acting on reflex, he yanked Osto's longsword from its scabbard at the Major's hip and moved to protect his father.

Finnig groaned and staggered to a stop as the Major's sword slid between her ribs. Heartbroken, she stared into her son's face, only inches distant, and saw his hand upon the hilt.

"My son," she whispered.

Then, her eyelids fluttered and she swooned. Einar, horrified at what he had done, let the sword fall with her and stumbled back. He clasped his hands to his face, then realised he had smeared her blood all over his cheek and cringed and stared at his red fingers. He felt like he could not breathe, like the air was a dagger in his throat, and his eyes burned. His heart panged, and his knees wobbled.

Bolegard was equally shaken. Pale-faced, he clapped a hand on his son's shoulder. "Thank you, Einar. You did well."

His words were quiet, almost too quiet to be heard, and far from comforting to his son.

The King turned his eyes on the hundreds of faces staring at him in mute horror; the faces of all the spectators who had come to witness the Tournament. He cleared his throat.

"Ahem, hark unto me, good people, for I have dire truths to tell! I recently discovered, much to my chagrin, that my wife was a Witch and that she was conspiring with this man to dethrone me!" He pointed to the whimpering Lampton.

It was an atrocious cover story, Einar thought numbly; half the attendees had heard the King accuse Lampton of nothing more than adultery. Whether it was adultery or treason, however, all knew what would become of Lampton now.

"My son was only performing his duties," Bolegard went on, "protecting me – your King – by slaying Queen Finnig. Her crime was treason, and her punishment was death. Lampton Odorson," he turned on the man, "I find you guilty of the same crime and deserving of the same punishment. You will not be joining the King's Own. We will erect a gibbet and hang you in the morning. Take him away."

Two bodyguards took custody of Lampton from Osto and dragged him away while he howled that he was innocent, that he had not committed treason, that he had never touched the Queen.

Hundreds of eyes watched in silence.

"The Tournament is over," said King Bolegard. "Go home."

The Wish-Bird, the Qilin and the Demon

Abdul Popollop had a spring in his step on his way to his Granny's house. He always did.

Granny's house may have been in the middle of a thick, green forest – it may have been halfway up a mountain, too – but still Abdul found the journey more carefree than a stroll in the opposite direction, downhill towards civilisation. There was just something about the black mountain that he enjoyed; perhaps feeling like he was challenging and somehow conquering this primordial force of nature, this colossal pile of pebbles with its head in the clouds.

The wind whispered to him as he waddled, ruffling his sooty hair and drying the sweat on his cocoa-skinned face, cooling him slightly even as the sun glowered down at him, heavy and stifling. Despite the humidity, the sky was a pool of water in which only a few patches of white algae grew. Abdul wafted his loose shirt, appreciating the feel of the air against his clammy skin. He soon left the hard-baked earth of the road behind and trod the softer loam of the forest, and he made good time despite his tendency to dawdle and daydream. Abdul knew he'd have hours with Granny before he was due home for supper.

So he made no desperate rush. Slowing, he found a good stick, curved like Ishambrian warriors' khopesh swords, and pretended it was such a blade. Dashing through the undergrowth, kicking up dead leaves, bush-whacking and slashing at trees as he went, Abdul fantasised that he was a mighty warrior the like of Nashim Snakeblade. He imagined scything through hundreds of warriors with dual katanas just as Nashim had done at the pass of Taj-Rassan when he had held back the wildlings for days with only a token force.

Caught up in his imaginings, Abdul did not see the tree root poking up out of the ground, but he did feel it when he tripped on it, bumbled and fell on his palms, jarring his wrist. He hissed, wrung out his hand, got up and plodded on. There was no dampening his spirits for long today; today, he was visiting Granny.

He found a bigger stick next; one perfectly suited to the notion of being a young boy's Wizard staff. Dreams of summoning sinister sorceries so powerful that the entire world trembled at the sound of his voice flitted through his mind like migrating birds, leading him to his next pantomime. Trees were zapped with apocryphal blasts of lightning, set aflame and withered and rotted by the staff's invented abilities ... Imagination was a powerful thing. Abdul allowed himself to fancy that he was following in the footsteps of his great-grandfather, the feared and famous Ishambrian Wizard, Lanssa Hartma; attending the Chi Academy, studying in the Viper Tower and proving himself one of the most dangerous people in the world, capable of sundering it with a thought.

With staff in hand and ideas running riot, Abdul soon emerged from the forest into a little glade where Granny's house squatted among the ferns with the mountain rising up behind it. It was not yet noon and the rising sun glimmered on myriad dewdrops in the grass, like the forest was encrusted with jewels.

Abdul rapped on the door, the skin on his fingers even darker than the portal's teak. The sound snapped and echoed in the air, stark and abrupt. The door creaked open after a few minutes, and there stood Granny on the other side, dishevelled in her white nightie and faded pink sleeping gown. Her snowy white hair, fine as a dusting of powder, was spiking up in all directions like a porcupine's spines.

She fixed her grandson with a crotchety glare, looking down her long crooked nose at him. "What are you doing here, Abdul? Your mother will be looking for you, I shouldn't wonder, looking for you to help out with the family business!"

"The family business?" Abdul wrinkled his nose and withdrew his head. "Carpentry isn't the life for me; it bores me to tears! I'd rather come see you, Granny. At least you don't force me to fashion dovetail joints at all hours of the day. At least here I can think. I'm meant for greater things than carpentry, Granny, much greater things. I'm sure of it."

"Greater things?" Granny snorted. "You don't know what you're meant for – you're only thirteen."

"Fourteen," Abdul corrected.

"Fourteen then. There's nothing shameful about carpentry, child – or any other means of making money. Why, it is a positively noble endeavour which will allow you to provide for your family one day."

"I wouldn't want to provide for my family like that," said

Abdul, "and I wouldn't want a family that would want me to. I want a life I can be proud of. You understand?"

Granny smiled, one side of her lips quirking up. "I do, as it happens. Come on in, child, come on in. Got yourself a walking staff, have you?"

"It's not a walking staff! It's a wizarding staff. I'm going to be a Wizard like Lanssa Hartma!"

Granny chuckled. "Like Lanssa Hartma, eh? My, my, that would be a sight to behold and a sound to hear and no mistake. Not many like my father, Lanssa. Not anymore."

Granny led him through to a room full of iron cages hanging on chains from the low ceiling beams. Other than the cages, the room resembled a library or study, with a writing desk as the focal feature and brimming bookcases against every wall. It smelled musty, like old, undisturbed dust. In the cages squawked a plethora of birds, a smorgasbord of species. Tiny yellow canaries chirped beside cooing grey pigeons, beside yapping ducks, beside a honking white goose, beside screeching eagles. None of the birds were as they seemed though; Abdul knew that much. These were no ordinary birds; they were magic birds.

"You know tricks, don't you?" asked Abdul, eyeing the avians. "Could you teach me to be like Lanssa?"

"Only in the most rudimentary sense," replied Granny. "To truly rival Lanssa Hartma, you would need the same training he received; training at the Chi Academy."

"D'you think I can go there one day?"

"One day, perhaps. There has not been a Wizard in the family since Lanssa. Perhaps it is time for another. You would have to leave Ishambria and travel a long way, you know, to reach such a dream."

"I would go as far as it took!"

"Of course you would. Tea?"

"Yes, please."

Granny bustled off into the kitchen and hung her black kettle on its hook by the fire. Abdul followed her and watched it begin to steam. He had always loved water vapours; they swirled and curled in the air like intertwining lovers, like tangled string; slow, graceful and mesmerising, rising up the chimney and filling the room with haunting spirits.

Where the library had been spartan, the kitchen was more of a festering stain. Grease and dirt clung to the walls and surfaces, unwilling to be easily scoured away. Dust lined the window ledges all along one wall, overlooking a small, open courtyard set in the middle of the domicile. The air smelled of oil and spices and old, mouldy food. Like Granny's own aura of lavender and chamomile, the room's perfume was heavy and cloying in Abdul's throat, making him gag.

Once the kettle was whistling, Granny picked it up with the help of a thick cloth and poured chamomile tea for both her and her grandson in little white china cups marked with detailed blue flower panicles. That done, she led him out into the paved agora in the middle of the dwelling.

Abdul adored that little courtyard; full of caged birds hanging from the branches of the central tree, it seemed a magical place untouched by time and the elements, unsullied by the surrounding world. The tree – a gnarly old apple – was always both blossoming and fruiting whenever he came, impossible as it seemed. No matter the climate outside the front door of the house, it was always a tropical summer in the courtyard, with a gentle breeze. Today was no different. Abdul shivered as the courtyard's warmth struck him, as if the sun had only just revealed itself when in fact it had just ducked behind a cloud. Nevertheless, Abdul could still somehow feel the great orb's rays on his skin like a gentle caress. He sipped his tea; it was hot and delicious. Granny and Abdul lowered themselves carefully onto rickety, old, rotten chairs with termite-ridden slats.

Granny blew on and then sipped at her tea, slurping up a minute amount and then breathing a sigh of satisfaction and leaning back – putting altogether too much faith in the mouldered old chair in which she sat, Abdul thought.

"A new bird arrived yesterday," she said, gesturing carefully at a new cage Abdul had not noticed; a large silver cage more ornate than the rest, containing a white-plumed bird with yellow wing tips, yellow tail-feathers and a yellow crest on its head. "I had it delivered from a faraway land called Chilpaea when I heard of its existence. It is called a hamsa. It is possibly the last of its kind; its previous owner was glad to take it away from the island, where apparently it has been hunted to the point of extinction. He was happy to think the bird might be safe from abuse here – and safe I shall keep it."

The hamsa was staring at Abdul with beady black eyes through which ran a shock of blue when the sun hit it. It snapped its golden beak, flapped its wings a little and cawed, harsh like a crow.

"Why has it been hunted so much?" asked Abdul, unable to take his eyes off the impressive bird.

"It has another name," said Granny, setting her tea down on a side table and pulling out a white bone pipe from a deep pocket in her sleeping gown. "Wish-bird. In Chilpaea, the legends say this bird can grant wishes if you pull its tail-feathers, like a Genie."

"Wow!" breathed Abdul.

"Yes. Wow," said Granny shortly, stuffing the pipe's bowl with baui, a supply of which she kept stored in a white bowl in the courtyard. "Or it would be wow, except that the legends are wrong in this case. I must have tugged on its tail-feathers a hundred times and made a hundred wishes, and none have come true."

"Wait," said Abdul, frowning and turning back to Granny. "I thought you said you would keep the bird safe from abuse. Surely the man who sold it to you meant for you not to use its powers?"

"Oh, he did," agreed Granny nonchalantly, lighting the pipe. Abdul did not see how she did it, for she cupped her hand around the pipe; she had no matches or tapers, though. "And I assured him I would not. But here's the thing, child; people lie."

"You lied?"

"I did. And I'd do it again." Abdul looked horrified, but Granny pressed on, blue-white plumes billowing from her mouth. "More to the point, I shan't be killing the beast prematurely, guzzling its gizzards and adorning my house with its organs for good luck and prosperity – which is what they do with the hamsa in Chilpaea. Savage land." She sniffed disdainfully. "Why, in comparison, I'm practically a benevolent shepherd. I feed her daily and clean out her cage and give her a little exercise. What has she to complain about? She'll live longer than I will at this rate; they live to be hundreds of years old, or so say the legends. Could be another thing they got wrong, of course."

Abdul was wide-eyed at mention of the birds' fates in their homeland and forgot that he had been chastising his Granny.

"Surely they don't do that to the poor birds!" he said, touching his hands to his cheeks, his forehead wrinkling in concern.

"They do," said Granny remorselessly, puffing on the pipe again. The herb smoke smelled sweet and acrid at the same time, thought Abdul. "I just told you they do. The man who sold me the bird told me so." Seeing that she had successfully side-tracked him from questioning her moral compass, she piled on more distractions to keep him lost. "Now, would you like to hear a story of Lanssa Hartma – since you seem to be so interested in him today?"

It was not just that day; Abdul was always hungry for stories of Lanssa, his famous great-grandfather. "Yes, please!"

"Very well." Granny paused expertly and sipped her tea for a minute, letting the anticipation mount until Abdul was practically jumping with excitement, twitching and fidgeting in his seat. "Have you heard the story of the time Lanssa Hartma tamed a Qilin?"

She knew full well he had not. It was her least favourite story.

"No! Tell me, please!"

"Very well." She sipped her tea again, savouring the taste of the chamomile, then puffed on the pipe. "When Lanssa was an old man, long after his famous adventures were over, he retired from his teaching post at the Chi Academy in Quing Tzu and returned home to Ishambria to take up a well-respected position in politics. To spite him and his mounting popularity, the Raja convinced the government to charge Lanssa with capturing a legendary beast that had been spotted in the jungle in the west of Ishambria. As you may know, young Abdul, the jungle in the west is extensive. It should have been an impossible task.

"Ironically, the Raja of the time – a petty man named Ofuul Umari-Kishnan – knew that he would win either way with such a scheme. If Lanssa found the Qilin, it would be taken as an auspicious sign for the Raja – a sign that his rule was blessed by the Gods. If Lanssa did not find the Qilin, the Raja would have cause to call him a failure and lower his social standing. I have long suspected that the Raja was jealous of Lanssa's popularity and concerned that the Wizard would replace him one day.

"Anyway, Lanssa bade farewell to me and my mother and set off for the jungle, staff in hand. He was gone for months, and the Raja began to imagine – happily, I might add – that the famous Wizard had been slain by some wild beast in the heart of the jungle. Ofuul hoped his name would soon be forgotten ...

"But Lanssa returned to the capital after about five months, leading a Qilin as you might a steed, with a rope tied loosely around its neck. It was like a winged horse, all covered in scales. He took it and stabled it in the royal stables, but insisted on looking after it

himself, saying that it had taken him months to form a bond with the
beast, to earn the beast's trust. The Raja could hardly say no; he did
not know how to care for the wonder, after all. There were great
celebrations throughout Mungalarou that week – everyone got drunk
as ducks. Fireworks were set off, and people were singing and
dancing and playing music in the streets. For everyone took the
appearance of the Qilin as a sign that either Lanssa or the Raja was
held in high esteem by the Gods. 'Only for the greatest of rulers will
the Qilin show its face'."

"So the Raja's plan bit him on the backside?" Abdul asked,
grinning from ear to ear.

Granny smiled, nodded and sipped her tea. "Well put, child,
well put. It did indeed bite him on the backside. Lanssa's popularity
only redoubled after that, and it wasn't long before he held a position
of power second only to that of the Raja himself.

"Ofuul did not like that. Though we purport to be a democracy
here in Ishambria, the truth is that many positions are practically
hereditary. As long as there was no competition, it was a surety that
Ofuul's line would continue as Rajas after his retirement. With
competition, though, there was doubt … So he put off retirement. And
put it off and put it off until he was a doddering old man, senile as a
housecat, paranoid as a spy. Not a good combination. He saw enemies
everywhere, and people began to disappear left, right and centre. It
was whispered that he had them killed and their bodies dumped in the
ocean. He hated Lanssa most of all, though, for Lanssa was as hale as
a young man despite his dotage. With a spring in his step, he'd meet
the Raja every day to discuss laws and policies, practically bursting
with energy. Ofuul came to hate him for it, I think. While the Raja
deteriorated into a ruin of a man, Lanssa never seemed to age a day."

Granny sighed, blowing a great wreath of smoke. "And so the
day came when Ofuul sought Lanssa's death. Black-garbed assassins
would attack our house almost daily, and my father would throw them
back at first, but they were so persistent that he'd be forced to slay
them with his magic in the end. I lost count of how many. He had to
hire people at extravagant cost to test his food for poison; the testers
were almost guaranteed to die, but their families would be well
provided for. Fortunately, Ofuul was unable to coerce any Wizards
into assassinating Lanssa; though many were as jealous as the Raja,
they were all too afraid of Lanssa. In the end, Ofuul was forced to

look into darker methods of dealing death, methods long abandoned and buried in dark crypts.

"I don't know what vile pact he made with the Dark God, Gastar, but Ofuul somehow learned how to summon Demons from the pits of the Netherworld; learned how to summon them and bend them to his will. One day, he held a great banquet at his palace and invited all those of high social standing. My father was, of course, top of the list. In the middle of the banquet, however, a Demon burst through the window and attacked us. I remember it well ..." She puffed on her pipe with a faraway, haunted look in her eye. "Like black ink, it poured into the room, and then it stood, all squiggly and squirming. It was like a living liquid, like tar come to life. With long, gloopy, black arms it reached out and grabbed people, and where it grabbed them their skin sizzled and burned. Screams and smoke and the smell of burning flesh filled the room ..."

She blinked and remembered her audience was only a young boy. "Ahem. Anyway, Ofuul pretended to be as dismayed as the rest of us, but I knew even back then that he was faking. He knew it was coming; he was out of the room in a flash when it appeared, but he had made sure Lanssa had not been seated near an exit.

"Father threw mother and I towards the nearest door and said, 'Get out of here!' Then, he set to blasting the Demon with lightning and fire, wielding a different spell in each hand, his aura shining like flames. The Demon was unhurt by his spells, though; they passed right through its gooey body without damaging it at all, and it came for father then. It came straight for him, gloopy claws extended, liquid mouth gaping, teeth shining."

She shook her head, and for the first time Abdul got a sense of what she must have been like as a small child; frightened, vulnerable.

Her lip quivered as she continued and tears started to roll down her wrinkly old face, but she did not sob. "Mother tried to hide my face, but I saw it anyway ... it ate Lanssa with its big, gross mouth. Bit off his head and then ... You don't need to know the details."

Abdul let her cry in silence for a few minutes, his heart panging with sorrow and sympathy, and then he said quietly, "That's horrible." The words seemed so paltry, so inarticulate, so insufficient. "How did you escape, Granny?"

"Wine," she said, her eyes glazed, before she shook her head and her gaze snapped back to the present. "I broke free from my mother, snatched a goblet off a table and flung it at the Demon. I don't know what I was thinking; I suppose I just wanted to hurt it. Anyway, the goblet did not cause it any pain, but when the wine hit it, the Demon screamed like a banshee and its sinuous, watery body sizzled and smoked as if it were burning. For some reason, wine proved to be the creature's undoing. Wizards have speculated since that the foreign liquid interrupted its biological pathways, thus incapacitating the creature. Whatever the true reason, the Demon shrieked and was subdued. After that first goblet, everybody who had seen what I had done grabbed a goblet too, and we all poured wine on the Demon until it was dead. By the end, nothing was left of it but a black mark on the glossy pine floor."

Abdul was astonished and would have accused her of teasing him – his Granny liked a joke – if not for the tears streaming down her creased face.

"Wine?" he squeaked.

Granny nodded and puffed on her pipe. "Wine. That's why I always keep a dozen bottles around the house – at least."

Abdul jumped; a bird inside the house began squawking violently, obviously seeking attention.

Granny wiped away her tears, sipped her tea and looked indoors. "I'll just see what's got little Rampaj all riled up. Won't be a moment, child."

Abdul nodded and searched the agora with his gaze, letting his eyes drift over the array of birds awkwardly shifting from foot to foot. His eye caught on the hamsa, like a fish on a hook, and he found he could not look away. The bird's black eyes bored into him like drills, until he could feel them inside his head, spinning and spinning, glinting with that strange streak of blue.

Feeling dreamlike, he drawled, "I wish I didn't have to go home. I wish I was Lanssa Hartma."

The bird cawed loudly, startling him. Its eyes were still piercing him, spinning and glinting, glinting and spinning. He began to feel dizzy, and his vision blurred.

"Wha- what are you doing, bird?" he slurred his words, realising as he spoke that he had somehow walked over to the cage without noticing.

The bird cawed again, and he saw that the cage was open. Had he opened that? He wasn't sure. He could barely see straight, could barely stand for the dizziness.

"What's going on?" The words came out slow and heavy, like they had to move through molasses.

His eyelids were heavy as lead; every blink was an effort. Sleep seemed to be lurking behind him, ready to snatch him up at any moment. He managed to force his eyes open one last time and saw that the hamsa was out of its cage and that he had his hand wrapped around its bright yellow tail-feathers. The Wish-bird took off up into the sky and took him with it.

Darkness overtook him then, and he had the strangest dream.

*

When Granny returned to the courtyard and found it empty of both hamsa and grandson, she dropped her tea. The china cup shattered into a hundred little spearheads.

"Oh, bugger," she said.

*

One moment, Abdul felt positively buoyant like he was sailing on air or floating in water; the next, he felt crushed on all sides like he could not even find the room to breathe. One second, he felt stretched, ginormous; the next, he felt shrunken, withered, tiny. He felt dizzy, even though he felt still, as though he were the fulcrum and the world was spinning around him. Then, he felt dislocated, like the world had forgotten him entirely. He felt pressed up close to the ground, and then he was drifting into nothingness, away from everyone and everything he had ever known.

He opened bleary eyes and groaned. His head was throbbing, and the light from the outside world seemed only to make it worse. The wind howled and raged around him, buffeting him and chilling him to the bone. Odd, he thought; Granny's courtyard was usually tropical. His hand was wrapped tightly around something soft. He didn't feel anything under his feet. He took deep breaths while his stomach roiled and threatened to evacuate its contents. After a little while – time seemed non-existent to him in his state – he tried opening his eyes again. The pain was still there, but lessened somewhat. The wind rushed into his eyes and made them stream, and he shut them again.

Two thoughts struck him then like arrows in the back as he fully awoke and memories came flooding in. The first – was he flying? The second – had he just made a wish to a Wish-bird? Was he crazy?

He forced his eyes open, doing his best to ignore his gonging head. He saw clouds flashing past his vision for a moment, and then he was above them, looking down on a field of fluffy white. He looked up, his skull splitting as the unguarded sun glared at him, and saw his hand wrapped around the tail-feathers of the hamsa. He screeched in shock when he realised his predicament, high in the sky with nothing to stop him from plummeting to his death except the small bird, which did not even look large enough to be carrying him.

As though his cry was a signal, the hamsa dived and took Abdul with it. He shrieked as the wind rushed around him and the clouds engulfed him once more and then spat him out, this time rising above him once more as was natural. The Wish-bird kept dropping, with Abdul streaming out behind it like a banner, and the ground below grew closer and more defined with each passing second. Weeping, Abdul wailed for the bird to stop, but it paid him no mind. It dove unerringly, like an eagle that had spotted a rabbit, and the ground rose up to meet them with frightening speed.

At the last second before they smashed into the ground, the hamsa pulled up short, coming to a sudden stop. Abdul, windswept and numb, felt his heart pounding faster than the drumming hooves of a galloping horse. He was shaking all over as he risked a look down and saw that his feet were dangling about a foot above the ground. He forced his hand to uncurl from around the bird's tail-feathers – it was stiff with tension and fright – and dropped to the floor. His legs buckled as soon as he landed, and he ended up on his rump, sprawled and crying like a babe.

Hovering, the hamsa cawed and then spoke, its voice as harsh as its croak, "Well, we're here. Get up, fool. You can't be Lanssa if you're sat down there."

"B-be Lanssa?" Abdul sobbed, wiping his eyes. "I don't understand."

"Well, that was your wish, wasn't it? To be Lanssa Hartma?"

Abdul gawped. "I didn't think – !"

"You didn't think what?" sneered the bird. "That it would work? Well, it did. So get up. Your wish has come true."

"Where are we?" asked Abdul, getting to his feet, brushing himself off and glancing around at the sumptuous gardens in which they had landed, which fronted a handsome, old, white stone palace complete with turrets and spires and domes.

"We are at the home of Ofuul Umari-Kishnan, Raja of Ishambria, in summer of the year 201 AC."

"201?" Abdul gasped and almost choked on his own spit. When he could talk again, he hissed, "But the year was 256 AC just a minute ago in Granny's garden!"

The bird nodded and – though beaks cannot smile – Abdul thought the hamsa was smirking at him. "It was," it said, "a minute ago. Now it is not."

Abdul almost did not dare give voice to his thoughts. "We have ... gone back in time?" he whispered, round-eyed.

"There may be one more shock awaiting you," the bird said, seeming to be hiding a chuckle in its voice. "Perhaps you should look down at yourself before you go inside."

Abdul did so and almost fell over again trying to get away from himself. He was garbed in long, black velvet robes over brocades – far more expensive gear than he had thought he would ever be wearing. He thought even his moccasins might have cost half his father's annual wages. Not only that, but he was big – bigger than he had been. He appeared to have the body of a full grown man. He touched his face; it felt unfamiliar and bristly. He had a beard – he was sure that was new. He touched his head; a man's turban enwrapped him.

"What has happened to me?" he rasped, realising that even his voice was not his own anymore. It was deeper and raspier.

He was not sure, but he thought the hamsa rolled its eyes. "I told you. You are Lanssa now. That was your wish."

"Whose staff is that?" he asked, seeing a staff on the ground.

"Yours, of course," came the Wish-bird's patronising reply.

Abdul picked up the staff and felt a tingle run through him from his fingers as they touched it. He was in no mood to enjoy the sensation, however.

"And what am I to do now?" he demanded, feeling helpless anger rise and tears threaten again. His hands balled into fists. "You have put me in the body of an old man fifty years in the past! I don't know what I'm doing here!"

"Why, you be Lanssa, of course. Come on. The Raja will be waiting."

The bird flapped its wings and glided off towards the palace.

Abdul sighed and followed after, not knowing what else to do.

"Won't people wonder why you're in the palace?" he asked when it became clear that the Wish-bird was not going to stop outside.

"Oh, don't worry," said the bird nonchalantly, "nobody but you can see me."

Shaking his head and muttering to himself that magic was a farce of which he wanted no further part, Abdul shuffled into the palace in the midst of a great crowd of equally regally-garbed, elderly folk. He was stopped at the grand double doors.

"Lanssa Hartma," said a stooped man so old he looked as though he must have witnessed the Witches' rise. His jowls hung slack off his face, and his eyes seemed to be bugging out of their sockets thanks to his sagging cheeks. He was radiant in his raiment, though; he wore a golden silk turban and robe, a patterned crimson doublet, golden trousers and black moccasins. "So good of you to join us. I am so pleased." The look in his beady eyes said that he was anything but pleased to see Lanssa.

Abdul regarded him for a moment, wondering where he had seen the man before. The memory hit him like a punch in the face; he had seen pictures of this man in more than one place, for this man was infamous throughout Ishambria.

"Greetings, Raja Ofuul Umari-Kishnan," Abdul said stiffly.

He exchanged tense pleasantries with the man for a moment and then stomped into the palace, following the river of aristocrats to the dining hall – a grand, vaulted room with a magnificent mahogany table capable of seating eighty people as its centrepiece. The walls were speckled with portraits of old Rajas and frescoes depicting past wars and momentous moments in Ishambrian history, such as the liberation of the country from the rule of the dreaded Witches of Convent.

Shown to a seat distant from any doors, Abdul was fuming as he sat down. "This is the night, isn't it?" he whispered to the Wish-bird, which was hovering next to him. He could feel the wind from its flapping wings on his cheek. "This is the night that old gelding kills my grandfather, isn't it? This is the night he kills *me!*" He gulped and then ground his teeth together, his jaw muscles flexing. "I know why you brought me here now. I know what I have to do."

"I don't know what you're talking about," said the hamsa loftily. "Look out now – here comes your family, *Lanssa*."

"My family? What?"

He turned and almost toppled as his legs were pressed together and engulfed in a hug by a ball of pink fabric. As he gently prised the ball off him, he saw that it was in fact a young girl swaddled in pink brocades. Her chubby face looked vaguely familiar, and Abdul started when he realized that without the chubbiness that comes with childhood this child would be the spitting image of his Granny. It must be Lanssa's daughter, he thought – so it *was* Granny. His head hurt thinking about it. The face was recognizable, but the long auburn locks and smooth, freckled skin were a surprise.

"Hello, Daddy!" she piped.

"Are you well, dear?" asked a husky, feminine voice. "You look like you've seen a ghost."

Abdul looked up to behold a handsome old woman smiling down at him affectionately. She reminded him of Granny too a little, but had a far softer mien. Where Granny was akin to a nail in the foot, this woman seemed more like a feather stroking gently. He knew instinctively who she must be – his great-grandmother, Lanssa's wife, Iribel.

"Iribel," he said quickly, "you have to get out of here!"

He was not quick enough, though. The doors slammed shut and the Raja began to speak, drowning out his words.

"Honoured guests," began Ofuul, raising his arms and sweeping the room with his gaze. In a room full of healthy-looking people, he was like a gargoyle. "Thank you for coming. Please be seated. Today we are gathered to …"

As he droned on, Abdul and Iribel were shown to their chairs by the servants. Abdul did not object, seeing the swords belted at the waists of the guards by the doors. He did not want to cause a fuss or give Ofuul any excuse to demote him. He guessed a public snub would be enough to boil the Raja's blood. He decided simply to wait. He knew what was coming; he would be ready.

Dinner passed slowly with Abdul watching the windows the entire time, waiting for one to burst. He kept his staff within easy reaching distance at all times and poked his food around his plate, barely eating a bite. He sipped his wine once, then narrowed his eyes at the goblet and left it full, taking only water after that. Iribel and others around the table tried to engage him in polite conversation, but he was taciturn, turning them all away with monosyllabic answers or grunts.

"What's wrong?" Iribel asked him in a low voice eventually. "You're acting very strange tonight."

Abdul sighed and was just considering how to answer when a window shattered inwards with a cacophonic crashing noise, shards of glass pinging all over the pine floor. Everybody screamed and leapt to their feet, and Abdul watched in unadulterated horror as a thick, foul substance like black ink poured in through the open window, slopping easily over the jagged edges of what remained of the window pane. The viscous substance pooled on the floor for a moment, and then it began to rise. Once it was six feet tall and vaguely man-shaped, it stopped, its ghastly juices flowing up, down and across, all around its whole body. It did not drip; it swirled. It had no features; only a black waterfall for a face.

It roared somehow in a mangled fashion and reached out with supernaturally long gelatinous arms to scoop up two people, one in each arm. Both began to shriek at once, and all around could both hear and see their skin burning and blistering. The lavish dining hall at once became a cage everyone needed to escape. People screamed and fled for their lives, knocking over plates and bowls and glasses and ornaments and throwing one another out of the way. They careened at the doors, and the few guards there wisely stepped aside to let them past; the aristocrats were in such a state Abdul would not have been surprised to see them maul the guards to get away.

As people began to flood out of the room and out of the palace, Abdul prepared to face off against the Demon. He pushed Iribel and the small girl – his Granny – away, towards the door, planting himself between them and the fiend from the Nether. The Demon had not particularly noticed him yet, was busy eating other folks within closer reach, but to his dismay he noticed his arms rising against his will so that his palms were pointed at the fiend. Then, from his own lips but without any volition, he heard Lanssa's voice incanting ancient, eldritch litanies. Fire and lightning bloomed in his hands, and he cast them reflexively, unwillingly, at the Demon, watching in mute terror as the deadly elements fizzled out on contact with the nightmare from the Netherworld, not seeming to affect it in the slightest.

The Demon noticed him then, and it came for him. He heard the hamsa squawk, and finally he seemed to regain control of his alien body. He lurched toward the table and seized his full goblet of wine.

Spilling some, he cast the goblet at where the Demon's face should have been. Expecting to see the fiend melting, he was mortified when it was once more unaffected and came on faster than ever.

"Gods have mercy!" he moaned.

The fiend opened a huge, viscous mouth, and Abdul saw teeth glinting just before he dove under the table. He heard the jaws snap shut behind him and the growl of discontent. Pushing aside the tablecloth and emerging on the other side of the table, Abdul grabbed the closest goblet. Sniffing it first, he then tossed it at the Demon. The goblet struck and the liquid inside spattered on the fiend, but there was no noticeable effect. It was not ale that Granny had thrown either, he deduced, wishing she'd payed more attention to what had been in the goblet.

The Demon shot out a liquefied, black arm to encircle him, and Abdul had to duck and skid out of its path. He caught hold of another goblet, sniffed it, grimaced and cast it at the nightmare. The Demon didn't even seem to notice. Not spirits either, then.

The Demon leapt over the table to get at him, but Abdul ducked under it and came out on the opposite side from the creature once again. He reached out for another goblet, but the Demon had been waiting for him to do so this time. It shot out an arm at the same time as he did, wrapping its malefic black tentacle around his outstretched limb. Abdul shrilled as his skin started to blister and burn, and he thought death was upon him. He could not barely see through the tears, but he did catch sight of a little pink ball flying past him towards the Demon.

Blinking away the tears, he cried out in anguish, "No, Granny! No! Come back!"

Only once the words were out did he realise how ridiculous they must seem to an onlooker; an old man calling a young child 'Granny'. It did not matter, though; they were both about to die regardless. He thought of something else then; if Granny died, Abdul would never be born. He wondered whether he had caused himself to cease to exist and almost laughed out loud at the tragic irony of the thought.

Just before she too was enwrapped by a sinister black tentacle, little Granny seized a goblet off the table and threw it at the Demon. It was a good shot. The liquid sprayed over the Demon's face area, and it let out a keening wail of agony at the contact. Thick, acrid smoke billowed off its frame, and its viscous form seemed to melt and start dripping and pooling on the floor. It let go of Abdul's arm, and he gasped a sigh of relief.

"Throw more goblets!" he shouted to no one in particular, taking up one himself and hurling it at the gloopy fiend. The second goblet made the fiend scream. "It was mead!" Abdul realised aloud, sniffing the dregs. "It was mead in the goblet! Everybody throw mead on the Demon!"

With Iribel and little Granny and a few other aristocrats who had also been trapped in the corner, Abdul soon shrank and melted the screeching Demon. Like Granny had said, all that was left of it by the end was a smoking stain on the floor.

Catching his breath and clutching his injured arm, Abdul was surprised when Ofuul Umari-Kishnan burst back into the room, red with rage beneath his dark complexion, flanked by four armed guards. Abdul had assumed he would have been long gone.

"This is not the way it should have gone, Lanssa," Ofuul hissed. "You should be dead!"

"Oh, I should, should I?" Abdul growled, feeling rage uncoil like a serpent in his belly. "So you admit then that this was *your* doing! *You* summoned that Demon! *You* tried to kill me!"

"I admit it," sneered Ofuul, "but only because there won't be anyone left alive to witness it! *Impraza linvinga'ouro!*"

He threw out both hands in tandem and shot from his splayed palms a humming, wavering beam of crackling yellow energy, which smote down a man in blue silk in a puff of smoke and then swept quickly across the room to mow down the remnants of the gathering, leaving only Abdul, Iribel and little Granny. Abdul could smell the charred corpses of the recently deceased from where he stood protectively in front of Lanssa's wife and child. He could see some of them; they were charred and smoking. He gulped. It seemed Ofuul knew how to do more than just summon Demons. He wondered how the Raja could cast magic without a staff imbued with *Kun-Yao-Lin;* then he wondered how he knew what *Kun-Yao-Lin* were.

"And now, Lanssa," rasped the Raja, turning on his long-time enemy, "it is just you and I. As it should be. Time for you to die, my old nemesis. I wish I could promise to spare your wife and child … but they have seen too much."

"I'll kill you before I let you touch a hair on their heads!"

Abdul spat back, brandishing his staff with his hale arm.

Then, the war of Wizards began. The air was soon electrified, screaming and making every hair in the room stand on end. Booming incantations abounded, and spells sizzled and roared, whooshing and whizzing back and forth across the hall. Fireballs, ice-beams, globules of superheated energy and streaks of lightning lit up the room with an otherworldly glow. The frescoes and portraits were soon burned off the walls, which were themselves in turn scorched and blackened and even frozen in places. Arcane winds howled throughout the hall, none of them emanating from the open window. The grand table was reduced to splinters when the ceiling beams collapsed on it, and the floor, maybe even the whole palace, shook with such fervour that there was not an ornament left standing and intact.

In the end, though, Abdul – who had no idea from whence the knowledge came to perform any of the spells – threw down Ofuul with a well-placed magic dagger, which he summoned from thin air and tossed through a beam of flames, using the Raja's own spell as camouflage. The dagger stuck Ofuul Umari-Kishnan between the eyes, and he fell over backwards, poleaxed, never to be heard from again. His guards fell over themselves running for their lives.

With all the commotion over and the room quiet and still, Abdul's knees buckled beneath him and he pitched over onto the floor, holding his burnt arm to his chest. At once, Iribel and little Granny crowded around him, asking if he was alright and offering their help, such as it was. Looking past them, though, he spotted the hamsa hovering close by.

The bird cawed harshly and said, "Grab my tail-feathers, Abdul. You've done what you came for. It's time to go home."

Smiling at the thought, his eyelids suddenly leaden, Abdul reached out and wrapped his fingers around the Wish-bird's tail-feathers. The bird took off, and Abdul let sleep carry him away.

Once again, he felt stretched and squashed, high in the clouds and deep in the dirt, spinning while still, as big as a mountain and as small as an ant, burning up on the inside and freezing stiff on the outside, trapped and at the same time drifting free.

Then, with a lurch and a groan, he was lying flat on a cold hard stone floor, lit by sunlight, striped by shadow.

The hamsa squawked and said, "Welcome back."

Feeling nauseous to the pit of his stomach, Abdul just moaned.

"What are you doing down there? And what are you moaning about?"

Abdul leapt to his feet in excitement; it was Granny who had spoken, and not young child Granny either but full grown, old, crotchety, wrinkly as a crumpled up piece of paper Granny. He loved her more than he ever had before in that moment and he hugged her tightly, his thundering headache forgotten. He was back in Granny's courtyard under the shade of the gnarly apple tree, surrounded by caged birds. He looked down at himself with a touch of trepidation and then smiled in relief; he was himself again, a beardless young boy once more.

"It's so good to see you, Granny!"

"I only went inside for more tea," she replied, utterly baffled. "I was only gone for a minute!"

"I know," said Abdul, sniffing, "but it's just ... good to see you. That's all. Oh, and the next time you tell the story about the Qilin and the Demon, be sure to say it was mead in the goblet. You never know when a detail like that might be important."

"Right," Granny drew out the word, obviously unconvinced, sure there was a plot afoot.

"What's got you so doubtful?" came a deep male voice from inside the house.

Abdul's head snapped around; he recognized that voice. He gawked as a tall, dark-skinned man, whose face bore a passing resemblance to Granny's, ducked under the lintel and emerged out into the agora. The man was all skin and bones draped in black velvet with thick, silver hair and a curly, grey beard.

"Oh, it's nothing, father. Abdul's just acting strange," replied Granny, off-hand.

"Father?" Abdul choked out the word.

The tall man frowned down at Abdul. "Yes, I'm her father. Don't you remember me, Abdul? I'm your great-grandfather, Lanssa. Lanssa Hartma."

"You didn't die ... that night with the Demon then?" gasped Abdul, his mind whirring around and around.

Lanssa scrunched up his face and regarded the boy appraisingly. "No, obviously not. Who told you about that night?"

"Oh, a little birdie told me."

Arvid, Aslaug and the Undead

The meadow was wet this time of year when the rains fell heavy and hard. The river nearby – known as Skalda's Tongue, for it originated high in the mountain range, Skalda's Teeth – had evidently overflown.

Arvid Erlandson did not mind, for the temperature hadn't turned yet and it was still comparatively warm, despite the season. The old man sloshed across the meadow, ankle-deep in water, humming to himself, absorbed in his own business. He had folded his burlap trousers up to his knees so that they wouldn't get soaked. He wore a woollen tunic and a brown muskrat-fur coat to combat the cold wind and a straw hat to keep the sun out of his eyes. He puffed on a little wooden pipe and blew out white baui smoke. He had come down to the meadow to find some herbs, both for his dinner and to soothe the old war wounds in his leg and shoulder. The wounds made his right leg stiff, and he couldn't lift his left arm above his head. He glanced up at the sky. A cloudbank had rolled in and he had lost sight of the sun, but from the level of light he estimated it was late morning nearing noon. He had time before lunch.

Ploughing a path through tall rushes and grasses, Arvid made his way toward the water chestnuts; the sedges with the edible corms. They would make a fine addition to his dinner, and the sedge leaves could be used for mulch to fertilise his own grown vegetables. Once he had plucked a few, he waded over toward the orchids he had spotted. His movement disturbed the nearby geese and ducks, who squawked indignantly at the intrusion and took haughty flight. A flock of seagulls overhead cawed that the poor birds were not welcome in the sky, either. Arvid had known gulls to eat baby ducks, so he was unsurprised by the hostility. It sometimes seemed like the whole world was at war.

He harvested the orchids and stuffed them in the leather pouch tied at his belt, knowing his wife would stick them in his dinner, too. She said they were good for his wounds, for battling infection and for healing.

It had been years since he had received the wounds at the feet of the Crawlers. The giant bugs' raptorial forelegs were vicious weapons; one such serrated, black leg had slashed his hip and leg when he was young, and another had pronged his shoulder, years later, and flung him yards through the air. He had dozens of other, smaller wounds from the Crawlers, too. He had, after all, spent the majority of his life at Northbane fortress, fighting the enormous insects. He had spent every winter of his prime in the pass at Jaata Murgen, keeping the bugs at bay, keeping them from invading the Highlands of Fjelburg, and he had succeeded. One of the few to survive until old age, he had not only succeeded but had retired; a rarity among Highlanders, who normally fought until they died.

At almost a hundred years of age, Arvid felt like he had earned his retirement. He had been glad to leave Northbane behind and move into the Golden Fir Woods between Jaata Murgen and Baldr's Safe, the capital. He had been glad to build his little lodge and settle down for the quiet life. He did not miss the fighting now, and yet he did not regret it either. He was sure that all the warfare, all the exercise, was the reason he was still alive now when so many of his friends lay dead in the dirt. Old he may have been, but he was still spry. His once-bulky frame was now stick-thin, and the skin that had once covered bulging muscles now hung slack. His pale face was as wrinkly as dry, cracked leather, and his snow-white hair was tied up in a topknot. His ivory beard was braided down to his chest. His eyes were the only part of him that retained the vigour of youth; green as fresh grass and unrelenting, they scoured the world rather than seeing it.

Now, as he looked around, his eyes widened in alarm. He saw people stumbling across the marshland in the distance. The amount of splashing around them suggested they were moving his way fast. Something about the way they moved – jerkily, stiffly, unnaturally – put Arvid on edge, made his teeth itch. He studied them as they came, and when they were close enough that he could see more detail, he gasped in shock.

There were fifty men and women half-staggering, half-running across the wet meadow, and all of them looked dead. Their hair was falling out, their skin was grey and flaky like a leper's, and their veins had swollen and shoved to the surface of the skin to stand out like a web of blood, like some foul substance was coursing through and distorting their arteries. Some carried weapons, and some did not. Some had gaping, festering wounds or limbs missing, and others did not. One was walking along with no head. All of their eyes glowed a supernatural blood-red. They appeared dead, and yet they were still walking, still coming for him.

"Skalda's icy tits!" Arvid cursed under his breath.

Like everyone else, he had heard legends of the undead; like everyone else, he had always assumed they were nonsense. Now, he was not so sure.

He turned away from the monstrous people while the closest of them was still fifty feet away and began to hurry north across the meadow, towards Skalda's Teeth. He made a beeline for the forest of golden firs at the base of the mountains; the forest where he had built his home. It was the only stand of golden firs in Fjelburg, so far as he knew, an anomaly growing beside the Tongue. The trees were unusually tall, too, stroking the sky with their feathery tops. He was no expert on such things, but his wife reckoned they must be hundreds of years old. She forbade him from cutting them down or harming them in any way. He was only to pick up fallen branches for firewood, she always said.

He shoved through the red-leaved bushes rimming the wood, the deciduous trees that had died and would come back to life next year. Then, he was among the firs, moving fast for his age at a steady lope. Despite his fitness, he was soon sweating, however; it was an uphill trek back to his home.

When he reached his home, a wooden lodge on a small plateau in a little clearing in the forest, he rushed through the door. His wife, Aslaug, was chopping leeks for lunch and looked up in surprise when the door banged open. Even at ninety odd years of age, she was still beautiful to him, with her morning-sky-blue eyes, her long, braided silver hair, and her round, pale, open face. She was short for a Highland woman, less than six feet tall, so the six-and-a-half-foot-tall Arvid always had to stoop to kiss her, but he did not mind. She had become plump in her old age, but it took nothing from her beauty in her husband's eyes.

"Aslaug," said Arvid without preamble; he and his wife were taciturn folk, "we have to leave *now*. The undead are coming for us."

"The undead?" she repeated in shock, her mouth hanging slack and revealing her cute buck teeth.

He nodded patiently. "Yes, the undead. I know it sounds crazy, but I know what I saw. They are out there in the meadow. They saw me and they followed me. We have to leave *now.*"

"Right then," said Aslaug, asking no further questions, "we'd best get ready then. We'll need clothes and blankets, food and water, weapons and tools and –"

She was interrupted by a bang on the wall, and they both fell silent.

"Get everything we need together quickly," Arvid said quietly. "I'll lock the front door and make sure the back way out is clear."

"The back way?"

"We don't want to go back the way I came, trust me. We'll just have to make it to that ford up among the ridges somehow, and go east from there and see if we can get to Baldr's Safe or some other town."

She nodded, her eyes wide, and hurried off to find sacks for travelling. Arvid lowered the bar into place on the front door and then set off for the back, moving quietly. He could see movement among the trees through the windows; jerky, lurching movements that sent chills running up and down his spine. It seemed like the house was already surrounded, somehow.

Passing through the kitchen, he added the largest two knives to his belt where his axe was already slung. Then, he slowly creaked open the back door an inch and peeked out.

"Surtr's fiery cock!" he hissed, invoking the God of Fire.

Again, there was movement among the golden firs, and then he saw one of the undead emerge from the treeline and shuffle towards the house. It had been a woman once, that much was clear, but her clothes were in tatters and her hair looked like dead reeds. Her veins stood out like brands on her grey skin, and her eyes were like little red lanterns. She wasn't moving as fast as the ones in the meadow he had seen, so he assumed she didn't know he was inside – not yet. She must have stumbled on the house by accident, by chance, he thought.

He watched through the crack in the door until Aslaug appeared behind him, carrying two hemp sacks full of clothes and rations. She handed one to Arvid, who took it and slung the strap over his shoulder. He saw that Aslaug was dressed for travel now, too, in a big grey wolf-fur coat.

He put his lips close to her ear and whispered, "The undead are out there already, don't ask me how. We should try sneaking past them. We don't want to be followed."

She nodded, her face set, and he stooped and kissed her on impulse. She smiled grimly and nodded again, knowing it might be their last. He led the way out of the door without further words. The sun had come out from behind the clouds, and the clearing was inconveniently well-lit.

They almost made it to the treeline without being seen. The tatter-clothed, reed-haired woman Arvid had seen had moved out of his line of sight, so they snuck out of the house and tiptoed across the leaf-strewn rock toward the golden firs some fifteen feet away. Their hearts thudded their ribs like hammers on anvils. Their palms were clammy where they held hands, and their mouths were dry. They could see three people wandering in and out of the trees on the right, and two on the left who appeared to be standing still. Luckily, none of them were looking at the house.

Padding carefully across the clearing, avoiding any dry twigs that might snap, Arvid and Aslaug began to think they were going to make it when they traversed a fallen branch without a sound. Then, disaster struck, and it struck hard like a sucker punch to the belly. The rag-wrapped, reed-haired woman moseyed back around the corner of the house and spotted them just before they reached the safety of the treeline, where they could have hidden.

The undead woman let out a loud moan so full of hunger it almost sounded like lust, and then she started after them. All of the other undead among the trees heard her moan, turned and saw the living two among them. They started going after Arvid and Aslaug as well. To top it all off, more undead appeared around the corner of the house and started giving chase, too.

Arvid and Aslaug looked around in fear and horror for a split second, and then Arvid was hauling his wife on, into the trees, cursing the God of Luck.

"El Vandu shits all over me yet again!"

The need for subtlety had abruptly evaporated like morning dew, and the need for speed had become paramount. Husband and wife ran into the woods and on up the mountainside.

The forest grew high up on the mountains, the golden firs being as hardy as any other conifer in the Highlands. So, the couple were able to use the trunks to pull themselves up the steep slopes while the stupider undead slipped and fell far more often. Arvid and Aslaug had therefore etched out a small lead over their pursuers by the time they reached the ford up in the mountains. The ford itself was more of a way over the river than a way through it; leaning peaks on either side provided the perfect start and finish for a leap to clear the burbling waters. It was not a short leap, however, nor an easy one, and any misstep would plunge the leaper into the roiling, frothing waters below, which gushed along fast up here.

To compound problems, even though they had outdistanced those pursuing them, there were undead waiting for them by the ford. A dozen corpses milled around aimlessly in sight of the two peaks, on the rocky ledges and among the trees, and many of them looked around and saw the couple when they came scrambling up the mountainside. The undead started chasing the old couple, their hollow, hungry moans alerting their oblivious fellows.

Arvid growled in annoyance, "They're everywhere! Where in the Gods' name did these freaks all come from?"

"It doesn't matter where they came from right now," said Aslaug, panting. "Let's just get to the ford!"

Arvid could see it was going to be a close race. He and his wife were approaching the peaks from the south, while the undead were converging on them from the slopes to the north and the woods to the east. Arvid and Aslaud tried to hurry, but age was a shackle, holding them back. The undead reached the peaks first and blocked the old couple's way, howling their hunger.

Arvid stopped and looked to his wife. "Is there anything you can do, Aslaug?"

She knew what he meant. She nodded. "It's been a long time, but I'll try. You might have to carry me afterwards, though; I'll be weak as a new-born calf. For now, keep them off my back."

He nodded and put his back to hers. Aslaug closed her eyes and started to murmur words in a tongue her husband did not recognise, waving her arms in strange patterns in the air all the while. The words made Arvid's hairs all stand on end and gave him goosebumps. He thought he could feel electricity in the air, like a storm was rolling in, but the sky was blue and speckled only lightly by white clouds.

"Surtur kambal!" she kept saying. *"Surtur kambal!"*

The undead from the woods to the east came the fastest, reaching the couple while Aslaug still stood, stroking and speaking to the air. Arvid put himself between his wife and the undead and tugged his axe from his belt. It was a war-axe, the very weapon he had used during his days at Northbane fighting against the Crawlers. It had a short haft, a bearded blade and a spike opposite. It felt snug in his palm, fitting like a glove even after all those years.

He tried talking to and shouting at a few of them, but the undead ignored him. Their only response was the moan they all shared; that empty, greedy noise that held no iota of intelligence or civilisation, only the basest of animal urges.

His practised swing clove the first undead's skull in twain with a single blow. Then, the axe got stuck and somehow the little man in leather with the split skull was not incapacitated. He continued to grab and claw at Arvid as though he hadn't even noticed the big blade lodged in his brain.

"What in Baldr's balls is going on?" Arvid raged, finally yanking free his axe and grimacing as cold, dark blood and brains spurted over him. He retched and spat; the gore smelled like old fish mouldering on a pile of dung. "What in the Gods' name are you monsters?"

He booted the man with the split skull back and watched him fall, before swinging at a second ambulant carcass, who seemed to be trying to bite him. Certainly, it came at him face-first anyway. This one was a man wearing mail and a dirty tabard in the fashion of the Fringers, those outside of the Highlands. Arvid caved in his ribs with a heavy blow, and though the man fell down, he immediately started trying to climb back up. He looked like an upturned turtle, stuck upside down in his armour with his sternum smashed.

Arvid leapt on him and hit him again and again, yelling and punctuating each word with a blow, "Why won't you die?"

He realised he had left Aslaug's side then and hurried back to her. She was shouting something different now.

"*Ilichithikiyai!* I was trying to make a fireball," she explained, "but I guess I can't remember the words or the cadences quite right after all this time. It didn't work, so I'm trying to freeze them now! *Ilichithikiyai!* That doesn't seem to be working, either!"

"Well, think of something," Arvid shouted, "and do it fast. We're surrounded!"

"I'm trying! I'm trying!"

Several cadavers were almost upon her from the north, and Arvid bulled into them and scattered them like a dog among pigeons. He lashed out left and right with his axe in a frenzy, letting blood on all sides. He could not seem to find an easy way to put the corpses down. No matter what he did, they kept coming. He beheaded them, clove open their brains, crushed their ribs, hearts and lungs, disembowelled them and even tried hitting them in the goolies just to see what would happen. Nothing took them down for long; no matter the wound, they rose back to their feet in seconds, wailing and coming once again.

Arvid soon started swinging low and taking the legs out from under the corpses, leaving them legless on the ground, where he could smash in their skulls with a well-placed boot. It seemed not only the quickest, but also the most efficient way. Even with no legs, the carcasses still writhed and howled on the ground and tried to pull themselves after him with their arms, but their threat was effectively ended.

Wreaking carnage among the undead with his axe, Arvid shouted over his shoulder, "Hurry, Aslaug! There are too many for me!"

"Hummuhushh! Hummuhushh! Damn it, I can't even remember how to blow a wind," Aslaug cried out.

Arvid had no breath or time to reply; all he could do was pray to the Gods that his wife remembered something soon. The undead were upon him, and he struck them back again and again, now wielding one of the kitchen knives in his left hand as well as the axe in his right. He was getting increasingly covered in foul, stinking gore, but he could not stop or else Aslaug would be defenceless. There was nowhere to run now that they had stopped; they were entirely surrounded, and the undead were closing in on all sides now. Arvid knew he could not cut through them all. Their only hope was for Aslaug to remember.

"Hurry, Aslaug!" Arvid said again when he found a second to breathe after crushing a naked, grey woman under heel.

A man whose face looked like it had been clawed off pounced on the old man then, and he grunted under the weight, using his axe haft to hold the carcass' snapping teeth away from him. He pushed the haft into the man's neck so hard he was sure it must be crushing his windpipe and choking him, but the corpse didn't seem to care. It pressed forward, wheezing and gnashing its jaws in Arvid's face. Using its own momentum against it, Arvid spun abruptly and threw the cadaver off him, sending it tumbling into its fellows to the south.

Then, another of the undead was reaching for him from the

east, a mountainous Highlander with an arm missing. Arvid cut off the man's other arm with a grimace of distaste and pushed him away. Without his arms to balance, the carcass toppled and was unlikely ever to rise again. Men and women, Fringers and Highlanders both, Arvid cut them all down one by one as they came for him and his wife.

He thought he might have cut down a few easterners, too, from the cut of their clothing, but it was hard to differentiate once all had become undead. It was strange to see foreigners in the Highlands, he reflected, especially so far north – if indeed they had been easterners. He wondered what they had been doing in Fjelburg, how they had become transformed. He wondered how they had all been transformed, come to that, but none were offering an explanation.

Arvid got his axe stuck in a skull again soon after that, and had to hold back a second corpse with his knife in its ribs. Neither corpse went down, however; both leaned on him, and the second with the knife in its ribs gnashed its teeth bare inches from his face. Staggering back, being slowly but surely overpowered, Arvid sent a quick glance north and south, hoping he could spin away from his current foes. There was no chance, however; the undead were closing in from both sides, and there was no room to spin now.

"It's now or never, Aslaug!" he managed to yell in a choked voice, feeling terror coil in his gut like a stirring snake. It was not fear for himself, however, but fear for his wife. "They're all over us!"

"*Pa'theon!* Okay, I'll try something else," Aslaug squeaked, also worried for her partner. "I think I remember this – Witch fire. *Ragia ellyriamv!*"

As soon as the final syllable slipped from her lips, she knew it had worked, finally. She felt the dormant power inside her awaken, stretch out and begin to prowl throughout her body; a tiger made of lightning strolling through her veins, pulsing in her blood, thrumming, thrumming throughout her so that she felt like she was made of energy, brimming over with it.

Warmth flowed through her body from her gut, up her torso, through her shoulder, down her arm and out of her outstretched hand. Vivid green fire roared out from her palm in great gouts that smothered and devoured the undead in front of her, wreathing them in flames and then melting them like ice sculptures on a hot day. Their skin blackened and charred and then oozed off their bones. Their blood sizzled audibly, and their eyeballs dripped out. They kept staggering forward for as long as they could, but then they collapsed into heaps of ash. Scores had come by then, and scores died under the Witch's flames as she swept her hand from left to right to encompass them all.

Arvid was agog; he had never seen such a display. He had known his wife was a Witch for some time now; she had confided to him after being forced to use her powers to save his life one day when he fell in the frozen Tongue, but he had never seen her use her abilities past that one time. Now, he saw her as she must have been in her prime, in her element. She was no longer a mere hermit in the woods, an old lady; now, she was a Witch, formidable and terrifying, a power to behold and fear.

It had been difficult to reconcile the knowledge that she was a Witch with their ongoing marriage; they had been on the rocks for a while, as they saying goes. She had sworn to him never to use her powers again, save in life or death situations, and he had relented and consented to stay with her. He didn't know if she was a Witch of Convent or not – she insisted there were other sorts of Witches out there, too – but he did know that there was scarcely a soul alive who had not heard of Convent, who did not hate the Witches for what they had done to humanity for all those centuries not so long ago.

The year was 313 AC, after all, 313 After Convent. People told time by how long it had been since the Witches' cruelty, and now he was married to one of them. He hadn't known whether to laugh or be sick at the thought. Slowly, though, he had gotten past it; he loved his wife, and he was convinced any evils – if there had ever been any – were in her past. Now, though, to see her hip-deep in power and hip-deep in corpses, he wondered again what she had once been all those years ago.

Regardless, in this instance, he was grateful for her magic. She had doubtless saved them both. With those to the north blazing like kindling, Arvid could finally spin away from his foes to the east – just in time before teeth sank into his flesh. So, pivoting, he tossed the two corpses leaning on him to the ground. His axe finally squelched free of the skull as he did so. As soon as it did, he turned his back on the grey-skinned monsters to the east, who were almost close enough to grab him, and launched himself instead at those coming up from the south.

The undead there had almost been upon Aslaug from behind, had in fact been reaching out their grubby fingers for her when Arvid tore into them like a rampaging Rock Troll. He bowled many of them over and flailed his axe and knife wildly to carve up those still standing, covering himself in cold, rank blood once more.

As he beheaded one with a savage swipe of his axe, he screamed, "Run, Aslaug! Cross the ford!"

He heard the roar of her green fire come to an end and then the receding pitter-patter of her feet as she ran across the uneven rocky floor. He smiled grimly at the sounds even as he hacked the reaching arm off another of the undead, a woman wearing an apron with a hole in her skull and evil in her eyes, a macabre parody of a mother or wife. Kicking and swatting at the corpses then, he began to back away himself. As soon as he had a little space, he turned and ran after his wife, slack-jawed at the sight that confronted him.

He was running over corpses, dozens of them, all blackened and half-turned to ash. Here and there, dismembered heads still licked raw lips and severed limbs still twitched. The rocky ground itself was blackened and looked like it might have melted and reset under the magical onslaught. Any plants or grasses that might have grown there had been annihilated. There were still carcasses coming from the wood to the east, but the north was clear for fifty yards; more than far enough for the couple to reach the ford. Beyond the fifty yards, beyond the blackened rock and the littered corpses, more of the undead were climbing down from the peaks. Arvid wondered what in the Gods' name they had been doing up there in the first place.

Aslaug was some twenty feet ahead of her husband when she twisted her ankle and fell on her face, crying out in pain and shock. Arvid was by her side in an instant, concern etched in the lines on his old face.

"Are you okay?" he asked.

She shook her head, tears welling. "No, I – I don't think I can walk, and I certainly can't make that jump! How stupid can I be?"

Arvid did not reply, but scooped her up into his arms as if she were a child. She had become slightly corpulent of late, however, so it was not as easy as he made it look. Staggering slightly under the weight, huffing and puffing, he set off at a walk toward the ford.

She railed at him and hit him on the chest, saying, "Just leave me behind, you buffoon! You can't cross the ford carrying me! You'll get us both killed, you madman! Put me down! Leave me behind, please! Save yourself, Arvid!"

"No," was all he said. "I can make it."

He took a wide approach to the ford so that he would have space for a run-up, veering dangerously close to the corpses to the east to get enough room. Once in position, he and Aslaug looked around. Once more, the undead were surrounding them on all sides, closing in fast, howling and snapping their jaws. They were within feet of him. There was no time left for error, hesitation or reconsideration. It was time to jump or die.

Hefting Aslaug higher in his arms, Arvid took off at a pelt – or as close to one as he could get while burdened. His feet hit the ground achingly hard, the jolts of impact running up through him and throwing off his stride. He gritted his teeth against the burn in his arms and legs and back and forced himself to move faster. He ran up the leaning peak that jutted out over the river and jumped.

Wind rushed through his hair, and he felt giddy with expectation as he sailed through the air. Time seemed to slow, and he wasn't sure if he felt light or heavy, wasn't sure if he was going to make it. He glanced down as he jumped and saw the white water rapids that would prove his doom if he fell. He found, in that instant, he didn't much care; they looked welcoming. His fate was in the hands of the Gods and there was nothing else he could do.

Then, they were across and Arvid was landing awkwardly on the sloping peak on the opposite side of the Tongue. He stumbled as he came down and pitched Aslaug out of his arms, but he didn't much care; they had made it!

He picked himself up first, Aslaug second, and then they turned together to look back across the river. On the other side, the undead were still coming after them. The corpses were not smart enough to study the terrain or jump, however, so they lumbered senselessly up the sloping rock after the duo and stepped off into the river, one by one, never taking their eyes off the old couple until the river swept them away.

With corpses still tumbling into the Tongue, Arvid and Aslaug turned away and headed east, the husband supporting his limping wife. Though there were a few golden firs on this side of the river, they diminished in number as the two strode and soon were all gone, along with the last reminder of the couple's home.

After more than a week of hurried but careful traipsing through the forests at the base of Skalda's Teeth, Arvid and Aslaug came within sight of the capital of Fjelburg, Baldr's Safe.

They first spotted it from afar from a low peak in the mountains, where they had climbed for a vantage point. Aslaug gasped at the sight, and Arvid paled and thought he might faint.

The mighty granite city had been carved into the mountains themselves, in a corner between ranges, so there was no entrance or exit to its rear. Its front was protected by a long, curving wall stretching for hundreds of yards between the two perpendicular mountain ranges. In front of that wall, a black army swarmed all across the land, small as ants in the distance but as numerous as the stars in the sky, as grains of sand on a beach.

Baldr's Safe was under siege, and Arvid suspected he knew who comprised the black army.

"The undead," he murmured, eyes round.

"It can't be them!" Aslaug protested weakly, her lower lip wobbling. "It just can't be!"

"Who else could it be? They have taken the whole country, Aslaug ... the whole country."

She shivered at his words, but could not deny them.

"What will we do now?" she asked eventually in a small voice. "Where will we go?"

"I don't know. Maybe it's not just Fjelburg ... Maybe they've taken over the whole world and Baldr's Safe is the last bastion. Regardless, it's clear we can't go there. And we can't go back. And we can't go south. I think we have to head north, Aslaug, into the mountains and try to survive there."

"Nobody survives there," she pointed out.

He sighed and took her hand. "I know. But at least we'll have each other, eh?"

Coming soon...
Chronicles of
Maradoum
Volume 2

If you enjoyed the book, a review on Amazon would go a long
way to showing your appreciation and would in turn be much
appreciated. Thanks for reading!

Follow my Facebook page: Ross Hughes,
Author
Or visit www.rosshughes.biz

Printed in Great
Britain
by Amazon

32143552R00111